THE PERFECT FIANCÉ

A totally gripping psychological thriller

T.J. BREARTON

Joffe Books, London
www.joffebooks.com

First published in Great Britain in 2024

Cover art by Nick Castle

ISBN: 978-1-83526-558-1

For the Buzzell family

PART ONE

The Affair

CHAPTER ONE

She caught them together at 6:52 in the morning, lying in bed like newlyweds. His arm thrown over her shoulder, his face buried in her mass of dark hair.

Colton, she said. But only in her mind. Her lips were pursed, quivering. Her whole body shook with an electric frisson. Fight or flight. It couldn't decide.

He stirred. Maybe he'd heard her come in, heard her breathing now, trying not to scream. Maybe it was his conscience. If he had one.

Colton rolled away from the woman. Gazing up at the ceiling, he pawed at his face and yawned. He seemed to realize his right arm was pinned beneath his sleeping companion and carefully worked it free. He didn't want to wake her. *What a nice guy.*

Julie was going to be sick. It welled up within her and she took a step backward, toward the door.

My bed. My house. For a moment, she thought it must be a dream.

But then he was sitting up, having heard the floorboards creak, probably, and he saw her. His eyes, she would later think, conveyed pure horror. As though Colton had, for a time, truly believed he was invincible, only to now see death staring him in the face.

"Shit," he said.

Yes, shit. *He doesn't even have the decency to say something original. Next will come the excuses.*

Instead, Colton swung his legs out of the bed. He was wearing black boxer briefs, she saw, the ones that said *Eyushijah* on the waistband. She'd bought them for him online. They made the bulge of his penis look big. Not that he needed that. They were comfy underwear, that was why she'd bought them, and oh my god she really was going to be sick—

"Don't get up." Her voice was steadier than expected. There was some pride in that, though not much.

He stayed sitting as the woman beside him stirred, made a little moaning sound. Like she was all tuckered out from a night of wild sex, expecting to wake up and snuggle her man beside her. What were their plans? Coffee? Breakfast in bed? Another sweaty romp, this time with morning breath?

The sickness rose up again.

"What are you doing here?" Colton said. He swallowed a couple of times like this wasn't going down smoothly.

"Who is she?"

He didn't answer, just held her gaze. He looked so stupid to her in that moment. She'd never been one to judge a person's style, but suddenly his trendy mustache appeared ridiculous. The way his dark hair curled around his ears seemed babyish and immature instead of sexily cute. He was a man-boy. Maybe even just a boy.

Dizzy with sadness, sick with the betrayal, Julie still noticed the way her fiancé now stared at the woman with incredulity, as if he couldn't believe she was there. Did he even *know* her name?

"She's, ah . . ." he stammered. "Her name is Monique."

There it came. The sickness Julie had been trying to suppress was coming out. *Monique.* For God's sake — Monique. It sounded made up. Julie rushed to the trash can and retched. Not much in her — just coffee and a donut from the road,

4

and that was three hours ago. And anyway, she'd expected to be arriving home at breakfast. To eat it together.

He was coming toward her.

"Get back!" She wiped her chin and regained her feet. Colton froze, looking shocked — had he never heard her yell like this before? Maybe not. Maybe they didn't even really know each other. Maybe they hadn't been truly tested yet.

This is NOT a test . . .

This is a dealbreaker.

Still, she remained in the room. Stood waiting as he slowly sat back down on the bed. While Julie was emptying her guts, the woman had sat up. She faced the wall as if ashamed, or non-confrontational.

"Colton," the woman said in a low voice, "what is happening? What is she doing here?"

"I don't know. She just showed up."

"I'm his fiancée," Julie said, tasting bile.

"Great," Monique said with sarcasm. The way she was facing away, shoulders hunched, she might've been poking at her phone. Summoning an Uber? Or maybe just hiding her face?

Dear God, did they know each other? Had they met before?

Julie could barely bring herself to look at the woman, let alone ask: *Where did you meet him? How long have you been sleeping with him?*

Not that she blamed her. This Monique person clearly had no idea who Julie was. She'd only just found out she was a home-wrecker.

Julie and Colton had only been in this house for a month. None of their pictures together had been put up on the walls yet. There should have been one framed photo of the two of them rock climbing last year, but it wasn't on the dresser.

He'd hidden it away.

She could see his mind working, trying to find a way out of this. "I have no idea who she is," he said to Monique.

Julie's heart dropped into some deeper, darker place. *Wait — what?* This was his strategy? Double down on his betrayal? Pretend he didn't even know her?

"I've never seen this woman before in my life," Colton said, avoiding Julie's intense gaze.

Her thoughts were scrambling now, the best things to say eluding her. Later, she would go over everything in this moment she might've done differently, things she might've said, questions she might have asked. But for now, it was what it was. "Why are you saying that? You . . . pig."

There it was. Let the anger come. As a therapist, she knew that anger was just another misdirected emotion. It was a protector, a shield. Really, she was grief-stricken, heart-broken; sadder than she'd felt in years. She felt violated. But the anger was suddenly in charge.

She glared at Colton but spoke to the woman lying in her bed at last, saying the words slowly and emphatically: "My name is Julie Spreniker. Colton and I have been engaged for four months. Our wedding is planned for June 10th, this summer. We bought this house together about five weeks ago, and we moved in just three days after we closed the deal." If she could have stabbed him with her vision, she would have. "It's in *my* name, because Colton has no credit. You can check the mortgage statement.

"But what are you *doing* here?" Monique asked. She'd turned her head to peek at Julie, just one glassy eye looking through thick tendrils of wild morning hair.

"Surprising him. My conference ended a day early because of the storm that's coming. I didn't tell him. I got in the car and left Buffalo at three this morning."

Talking about such mundane, familiar things was calming. She felt more in control now, though still utterly blown away that Colton would lie like this. Like he thought this was the way to play it.

Unless maybe he was trying to save face with Monique. This whole ruse — *I don't know her* — suggested this was more than a one-night stand. This was a woman he had a real relationship with.

"How long have you two been sleeping together?" Julie asked, and the words almost brought back the vomit.

"Ah God," Monique said, as if to herself. "Shit. This is all fucked up."

"Yeah. It *is* fucked up," Julie said. Monique had pulled the bed sheet up to cover herself, but it had slipped a bit off her left side, exposing the edge of a breast. Julie felt fixated by the dark semi-circle of nipple, unable to turn away. But having worked with people who'd gone through trauma — Big T and little t — she knew how during extreme events, the mind would block some things out while focusing on random details.

She shifted focus back to Colton. "It's fucked up, because I'm going to be his wife. Or, I was."

Time to go, an inner voice cautioned. *Nothing good can come out of being here any longer.*

No, certainly not. Colton admitting who she was didn't matter now. The direction of her life had just changed irreversibly; it would take time to accept that fact. But remaining here was impossible.

She walked towards the open door, weak in the knees, but then stopped. Staring into the hallway, to the stairs going down to the main floor, it hit her: *this was her house.* Why would she leave?

"Get out," she said, turning back around. "Both of you, get out, please."

Neither of them moved. Colton looked dazed with shock. Like he couldn't believe she was calling his bluff. Playing hardball was never her thing — but these were the simple facts: this was her home and he was the cheating a-hole.

"Maybe we should just go," Colton said to Monique.

Pathetic.

"What?" Monique asked. "What are you talking about? Go where?"

The more she talked, the more Julie thought she recognized her. Almost like someone from the movies or TV. But what sense did that make? Was Colton sleeping with a famous actress?

"I just mean," Colton said, in a kind of let's-be-reasonable whisper, "she might be . . . you know. Dangerous."

"I'm not going anywhere," said Monique. "And neither are you. You hear what I'm saying?"

Interesting. The woman was claiming territory. She'd bought Colton's insistence that he didn't know who Julie was.

"You can put your clothes on, and then go," said Julie.

Colton finally connected with Julie. The shame in his eyes should have satisfied her, but it didn't.

"Go on," she said to Monique, feeling steady on her feet again. "Put your clothes on. I won't watch."

Monique waited for Colton to do something. When he didn't, she threw the sheet back and started searching the floor for her clothes.

Julie watched, breaking her promise — Monique had a damn-near perfect body. Smooth and tanned skin, long legs, ribs showing a little bit, supple butt like a young mare. Colton was slower. His body was good, too; he went to the gym three days a week and had hard abs, broad shoulders, a flat stomach. He was self-conscious about his "chicken legs" — perhaps why he wore several tattoos there, including a snake coiling around his right thigh. He toed into his jeans and shimmied them up, leaving the belt unbuckled. As he stretched on his black T-shirt, Monique stepped into her black cocktail dress and pulled it up around her, snapping the straps over her shoulders.

Looks like a nice night out, Julie thought ruefully. On the other hand, she was wearing running pants and a hooded sweatshirt that said *Herkimer Brewing*. Clothes to drive home in. To return to your life. To surprise your man in bed, make a little breakfast.

"We'll just go outside and we'll figure it out," Colton said again. He was back to sitting on the bed, pulling on his colorful socks. Julie saw his dark-brown Doc Martens, one near the bed, the other in a corner. They'd been ripping their clothes off and diving into bed together.

"You're an idiot," Monique said to him.

He stared down as he pulled on his shoes. To Julie, he seemed utterly bewildered. He had no idea what to do next.

It didn't matter. Monique was already heading for the door, all hair and shoulders. Julie stepped back and let her pass, showing her back as she squeezed through, smelling like sleep and shampoo and last night's wine.

"Monique!" Colton called. But she was already going down the stairs. Julie walked onto the landing that overlooked the entryway below. The townhouse had an open, two-story room in front, stairs just beside the front door. She watched as Monique crossed the oriental area rug. The woman made as if to grab the front door and fling it open, head outside. But she stopped abruptly. Julie took a couple of steps to get a better angle.

A figure darkened the doorway. Someone else was here, standing just outside.

Who the heck would be here at this hour, just barely 7 a.m.?

Julie drew a breath, prepared to call down — "be right there!" — as the door swung open. A man stepped in, his baseball cap pulled low and covering half of his face.

Her words fizzled in her throat. Monique tried to run, but the man grabbed her, and his hand closed over her mouth.

CHAPTER TWO

Monique struggled against the man, kicking wildly as he carried her deeper into the townhouse, disappearing beneath the balcony. Julie, frozen with shock, watched as a second man stepped up to the door and entered, also wearing a hat.

He looked up at the second floor, his eyes trapping her there.

Oh god. Oh god oh god oh god—

He started up the stairs, taking them two at a time.

Her paralysis broken, Julie retreated into the bedroom and shut the door, locked it. "Call 911," she said to Colton. *"Call 911!"*

She dug into her pocket for her own phone. Footsteps pounded toward the bedroom. She looked for something to barricade the door. The dresser? She ran and threw her shoulder into it, managing to move it a scant couple of inches. Not enough time. The door shook as the man out there rammed into it.

"Open up! I know you're in there!"

She fumbled for her phone, but the damn case around it always made it stick in her pocket. "Call 911," she repeated to Colton, seeing his own phone in his hand. He looked dumbstruck, confused, but started keying the numbers.

The man outside the room collided with the door again. It was a substantially made door, not one of those plastic, hollow-cores from Lowes, but he had already splintered the wood around the lock. "I'm coming in whether you like it or not. Or you can just come out of there — I'm not going to hurt you. We just need to talk."

Yeah. Right.

Julie hurried to the window: double hung, closed and locked. The storm window was in place. Her hands shaking, she rotated the lock above the first window frame, then grabbed the upper edge and pushed the frame up. The storm window was harder. She was shaking so badly her fingers didn't want to fit in the little grooves to get the locking tabs back.

"Hello," Colton said, breathless. "This is 1143 Waverly Place, Herkimer — there are, ah, multiple intruders in my house. Please come right away."

The man outside rammed the door a third time, the subsequent *crack* sounding wider, deeper. Julie risked a glance back and saw brown wood beneath the white paint around the door jamb. One more impact, and he would be in the room.

Her fingers slipped, but then she found purchase on the tabs, squeezing them out of the way at the same time she slid the storm window up. But she lost her finger-grip and the pane locked into the next setting, creating a gap too narrow to slip through. She fumbled for the tabs again.

"There is a man outside my bedroom trying to break in right n—" Colton was saying when the door flew open. Julie had to look: the man was in the room. The ball cap on his head said *O'Neill* on it. He reached for Colton.

Colton dropped the phone and rushed him, slamming into the stranger like a linebacker, pushing him back through the door. The man caught the door frame, stopping the momentum, as Julie squeezed the tabs in again and slid the window up, keeping pressure this time, until it was all the way up. "Help!" she screamed down.

It had snowed quite a bit before she'd left, but that was three days ago. Some early March warmth had melted most of it away, and what was left wasn't going to break a fall from a second-story window. A jump would hurt.

Colton kept trying to drive "O'Neill" out of the room, but the man brought fists down on Colton's back and Colton went to the floor.

O'Neill then glanced up, locking eyes with Julie. He wore sweatpants and a zip-up hoodie. Comfortable clothes for lounging, walking your dog, breaking and entering.

Stepping over Colton, he moved toward her, but Colton caught him around the leg.

From downstairs, barely audible: "What's going on up there?"

"I got it," O'Neill shouted. "They're both freaking out — I'll handle it."

Who were they? What were they doing here? Maybe this was the wrong house. What had the first man done with Monique? What was he doing to her, down there, now?

"Please," Julie said. "We don't have anything."

But O'Neill didn't hear; he was trying to break free of Colton's grip on his leg. He punched Colton in the head, then tried to kick him, but because his other leg was caught, he fell over with a crash.

Colton scrambled to his feet and lunged at Julie, toward the window. "Go," he said, grabbing her. "Go." His face was red from exertion. The same panic she'd seen in his eyes when she'd shown up in the doorway was back. He was terrified for them, desperate to get away.

O'Neill pulled a gun. "All right," he said, sitting up, aiming. "I've about fucking had it."

Seeing the gun, Julie made her choice. She got one leg out the window, then the other. O'Neill was getting to his feet, and as he did, he racked the slide on his pistol.

"They're going out the back window!" he yelled.

Her knees scraping against the side of the house, Julie pushed herself out until she was just hanging on by her fingers. Then she dropped.

The fall was longer than she expected. The shock of landing seemed to crunch her spine and crack her teeth together. Pain shot up both legs, something went *sproing* in her right knee. She rolled through the snow until she was on her hands and knees looking up, just as Colton came through.

He didn't do as well but sort of fell sideways out the window. She wanted to wait for him, but the man up there had a gun. So she ran, intuiting that the front of the house was unsafe — there might be more men there, or the one downstairs could come outside searching — and opened the back gate to the narrow road behind. Only then, the seven-foot-high wooden fence between her and the house, did she risk looking back for Colton.

He was hurt, lips pulled back in a pained grimace, holding his left shoulder. The man appeared in the window. He aimed at Colton, then withdrew the weapon, looking around, perhaps considering witnesses. Or maybe realizing these were the wrong people, that something got messed up.

But Monique. Monique was still inside.

Colton lurched toward her, snow caked on one side of his face, blood blooming through. He continued to grit his teeth while holding his left arm to his chest.

"Go," he said to her again. "Go, go . . ."

But where? Her car was out front, not back here. Maybe it didn't matter. All they needed was some distance. The alleyway ran between rows of townhouses, high fences with locked gates obscuring the homes.

Colton stepped through the gate and she slammed it behind them. Together, they hobbled down the alleyway and she tried the next gate. No good. They moved on, Colton breathing hard, grunting with the effort. Every gate was locked.

Ahead was Waverly, their street, which curved around through the neighborhood. *Just get to the street and keep going. Scream for help.*

A siren rose in the distance. *Thank God.* In minutes, police would arrive. Even now, the sound would surely slow O'Neill, knowing capture was close.

A noise from behind her: her gate banged open. O'Neill stood there in the alley, gun at his side, staring at them. She doubted he'd jumped from the window but thought he had gone downstairs and out the back door.

He started walking, then running, and the gun came up.

Oh God, why not just let them go? It had all been such a blur so far, and with the hats covering half of their faces she didn't even think she'd be able to recognize either man in a lineup.

Julie kept going, pulling Colton along, the street just twenty yards away now. Ten. Five. She heard an engine: a vehicle coming around the bend. "Hey!" she yelled in anticipation. "Hey! Hey — help!"

The vehicle passed the mouth of the alley, the blur of a generic cargo van, something for making deliveries or checking TV cables.

"*Wait!*" she screamed.

A screech of brakes. The van had stopped! Whoever was driving had seen them, maybe heard.

"No," Colton said.

The one word unknotted her thoughts. As the van reversed into view, and she saw the driver looking at her, she understood.

They were trapped. The man with the gun was behind them, the van now in front.

Julie stood frozen in place. Like the proverbial deer in headlights. Her eyes were fixed on the van idling in front of her, the side access doors swinging open. The sound of the man in the alley came from behind them, his pants swooshing as he jogged over. Colton said something, but she didn't register it right away.

It wasn't until the man grabbed her, forcing her into the van, that she realized what Colton had said.

"I'm sorry."

CHAPTER THREE

They'd met online. Through Facebook accounts they hardly ever used. Somehow, at some point, they'd friended each other. It was one of those six degrees of separation: Julie had grown up in Saranac Lake and Colton had gone to college at nearby Paul Smith's, where a former high school boyfriend of Julie's was also attending. A decade later, they were all linked on social media.

Colton claimed Julie had friend-requested him, but to her recollection, it had been the other way around. After several weeks spent occasionally commenting on one another's photos — he was big into rock climbing, she liked to travel — they'd directly messaged each other.

Colton: *Hey, so, do you know Mason Ridgell?*

Julie: *I do. Why?*

Colton: *He mentioned you. Said you were his first girlfriend.*

Julie: *We were pretty young. Ninth grade. He broke up with me the next summer.*

Colton: *Yeah, he's a dick.*

It'd made her laugh.

And a couple of weeks and many messages later, he'd asked her out on a date.

He sat beside her now, his face contorted in pain, the melting snow turning the blood runny and bright red. He had a split lip from the fight with the man in the bedroom. A welt formed on his upper cheek, bruising bloomed around his eye. And his arm, from the way he was holding it, was in bad shape. Rotator cuff, maybe. Or a straight break.

Each time the van took a corner, or slowed, or sped up, he winced and gnashed his teeth. It didn't help that there was nothing to hold onto. The back of the van was empty, no seats, no handles to grasp, everything lined with clear plastic. Julie was only able to keep traction by planting her palms and widening her legs.

Plywood partitioned the back from the front. A rough rectangular cut, fastened with hinges, made a crude door. In the door, another rough cut for a small window fitted with hardware cloth. It all looked homemade, a DIY death mobile.

Colton hadn't said anything since they'd been forced into the van. The other man — his hat was blank — had grabbed her and pulled her into the vehicle. She'd screamed and fought, but he'd been too powerful. He'd pinned her down and gone through her pockets, taken her phone while O'Neill forced Colton into the van at gunpoint. Then Blank Hat had slipped through the plywood door, pulling it shut behind him. The sound of metal slamming up front suggested O'Neill had gotten in the passenger side.

But she didn't know any of this for sure; there could still be someone back at her house. Or more. There could be teams. She didn't know what had happened to Monique, or whether any of her neighbors had seen what had happened to them.

They'd been in the vehicle now for, what? Two minutes? Five? At one point she thought she could hear the sirens still going, but they'd swiftly faded. Did police even use sirens when responding to an intruder call? Was there some protocol to approach silently? Her interactions with police were relegated to welfare checks and pick-up orders — people with mental health disorders who might be a danger to themselves or others.

Oh, Mom, she thought. The late Arlene Spreniker wasn't on her mind quite as much these days, but Julie reached out for her now, for some of her comfort, wisdom.

The van hummed along. She thought maybe the driver was going to draw attention, speeding and driving erratically, but she realized it was just the vacuity of the space — she felt every bump in the road. The plastic crackled as they lurched and slid around with the movements, like some kind of torturous theme park ride.

"Why did you say 'I'm sorry?'"

Her own words — the sound of her voice — surprised her. She surely should be screaming, panicked, curled in a ball. But something had taken over that reminded her, in some fundamental way, of her mother's death. That walk up the stairs to her mother's bedroom near the end. You weren't the same person in moments like that.

In an oblique way, that lack of control was freeing.

Colton held his arm and gritted his teeth and didn't answer. Legs splayed out in front of him, he was like a kid who'd fallen off his bike, broken his arm, waiting for adult rescue.

"Where do you think they're taking us?" Julie asked.

He only stared at the plywood partition. Julie looked there, too. To the small cut in the door, four inches by four inches, fitted with that tight hardware cloth. Like something you'd use to cage an animal. She hadn't heard anything from up there, not even the radio.

"Why aren't you talking to me?" she demanded.

The van took a hard curve and Colton listed toward her. She put a hand on him to help keep him upright.

"Ah, God," he said, eyes squeezed shut. "Hurts."

"Let me see."

"I know what it is. It's out of the socket. When I landed, it . . . I felt it."

"Maybe we can put it back in."

"I can't even lift it."

"Let me help you."

"Not with everything moving like this."

Another minute passed. Shock ruined critical thinking, but one thought came through: Colton had called emergency services. Police were going to notice the van. Not only that—

His phone! It felt like a jolt of electricity. Hers had been taken, but she didn't recall the same happening to him.

"Where's your phone? Colton? Colton, do you have your phone?"

His expression killed her hopes. "It's in the bedroom."

"Ahh . . ."

"I dropped it when he came in. I just . . ."

She shook her head, telling herself it was okay.

It was brave, what Colton had done. Honestly, she didn't know he'd had it in him. Not that she needed a man to be a fighter; she didn't need any violence in her life. But Colton had defended her. Defended himself, anyway. And he'd done a halfway decent job — the guy had still come after them, but Colton's actions had bought them time to escape.

Maybe he too had experienced another part of himself taking over. Something bigger, machinating things.

The road was a steady whine beneath them, no more sudden turns.

Highway, she thought. *Interstate.*

She realized Colton was crying. She felt herself pull away, angry again. How fucking selfish could he be?

"What's the matter with you?" Julie let the fury course through her, and voiced the question she couldn't before. "Why were you with her?"

His voice was a whisper. "It's a long story."

But she kept thinking about it. How the men coming in hadn't hesitated. Blank Hat had come in, grabbed Monique. O'Neill had gone right up to the second floor. No indecision. The men had been expecting people there. Colton, at least. Maybe Monique?

"Do you know who these men are?"

18

Colton failed to answer.

"Colton, who are these people? Why did you say, 'I'm sorry?'"

"Because I am," Colton said. "I'm sorry for all of it. I'm sorry you're here, I'm sorry that this is happening to you."

"What do you mean? *What is happening?*"

He faced the plywood again, as if thinking about the men up front. She watched his Adam's apple rise and fall with a swallow. "You seem like a nice person," he said.

A *nice person?*

"But obviously you have some . . . you know." And he made a gesture at his head, stirring the air next to his ear. *Some issues.*

"What are you talking about?"

He faced her. And he spoke clearly and directly for the first time since they'd been taken into the van.

"Lady, I really don't have a fucking clue who you are."

CHAPTER FOUR

This again. Back at the house, acting like she was a stranger had made some sense — if you thought of him as complete belly-crawling scum, anyway. To protect his relationship with Monique, he'd acted like Julie was just some crazy woman who'd gained access to the house, a head case with a fantasy about a fiancé and a home that weren't hers. Maybe they'd forgotten to lock the front door . . .

Had they?

She couldn't remember whether she'd keyed in. It was one of the minor details that the wave of trauma (big T) swept from her mind, never to be remembered.

But now? What was the point in Colton carrying out the charade? Unless, of course, he was trying to protect *her*, and had been all along.

It could be that these men were here because of Colton. Something he'd gotten involved in.

Drugs?

She ruled that out. He was pretty puritanical about that stuff. He stayed fit for rock climbing.

Gambling?

There was a casino not far away, on Mohawk land, but she didn't even think he knew how to play poker.

It could've been Monique. She had spoken with a slight accent. Boston, maybe? Were these her roughneck brothers, using Julie's house to stash stolen goods?

If Colton had been trying to protect her from these people by feigning not knowing her, she should go with it? Start acting a bit deranged? Would they let her go?

But before she could go any further down this line of thinking, the van jerked violently.

She braced herself and tried to help Colton from going flying as the vehicle jostled over seemingly rugged terrain. When it finally stopped, her heart rate picked up again. While the van was navigating over ruts and potholes, she'd been able to keep her more terrifying thoughts at bay, focus on Colton, think about his injuries and her own — her once-torn ACL flaring up now from her jump.

All of that vanished as footsteps approached the vehicle. The side doors flew open and a man stood there, silhouetted against the daylight behind him.

She hadn't come up with a plan. Nothing. She'd spent the drive — how long had it been? Half an hour? — thinking only about how she'd been dumped into this mess, not how to get out of it. Now, she scrambled to get as far away from the open door as possible. "Colton!" she yelled through fresh tears. She desperately wanted to penetrate his earlier denial of who she was. "Colton, help!"

"Go ahead, scream," said the man at the open door. "No one can hear us. I'll wait."

Of the many things flying through her mind: it was O'Neill, but without his hat. Second: though she recognized his voice, he didn't sound Bostonian, like Monique had. He didn't have any accent, really. If anything, there might've been a hint of "upstate" in his tone. Like he'd say "to*mo*rrow" instead of "tamarrow." Just like she would.

Where were they? Forty minutes outside of Herkimer was not far. She knew the terrain. West was Syracuse, an hour away. East was Saratoga Springs, about the same. In between, small villages dotted the low-lying hills. Same with going south.

But north took you closer to the Adirondack Park. To wild forests, protected land. Ferris Lake, Shaker Mountain, Black River. Places unspoiled by civilization. Full of thick, primeval forest.

She kept looking at Colton, but Colton wasn't looking at her; he was clocking O'Neill. Whatever was going on with him — the pain of his injuries, feigning not knowing her — he wasn't going to do anything to help her. And she shouldn't be relying on him, anyway.

"All finished?" O'Neill asked. "You want to get out of there, or what?"

"No," Julie said, shaking her head.

"No? Okay . . . You don't need to go to the bathroom or anything?" His face was becoming clearer as her eyes adjusted to the light.

Don't look at him.

But that was impossible.

"Please let me go."

"Ah, you don't want that. Not now."

"It's okay, it's okay . . ." The panic was rising up again, the chance at escape causing all her nerves to fire at once. "I'll be all right. You can just let me go. Please."

"I don't think it's a good idea. You'd get lost." But he leaned back and looked around like he was actually considering it. "I mean, I guess you could follow the road. It's not much, just a couple of wheel ruts, but you could follow it along . . . Yeah." He looked into the van again. "It's the cold, though. I think it would get to you. So, why don't you come inside? We'll get a nice fire going and you can warm up."

"Please. Sir. I think maybe you . . . I think . . ." Her mouth was suddenly not working. *Keep it together.* "Maybe you think I'm someone else? My name is Julie Spreniker and I'm a therapist for the county. I don't know why I'm here. I think maybe it's a mistake."

His eyes shifted to Colton. "And how about you, bro? You think it's a mistake, too?"

"She just showed up," Colton said. His tone flat, he sounded defeated. "Acting like she knew me, like she knew us. But I don't know who she is. I've never seen her before."

O'Neill was distracted when someone spoke out of view. He started to respond, but Julie was on her feet, rushing forward, squeezing past him. He grabbed at her as she went, catching her arm, but she yanked it free.

She ran, seeking the tire tracks, following them, no thinking other than that, just going. She couldn't help Colton by staying here, trapped alongside him. She needed to get help. She would send help for Colton, and then everything would be okay.

The morning was overcast, the light grainy and without shadows. The tire tracks in the snow were subtle, but there. Her sneakers were soon filled with snow, her leg knotted with pain. It felt like someone had injected her knee with thick fluid.

The man was behind her, breathing hard. Julie was terrified he'd shoot her. Maybe he wouldn't have done it back in town, but this really *was* the middle of nowhere. The pines and birch were slender and sparse, but the lower fir trees blocked visibility. She saw no houses, no buildings of any kind. It was true: this was pure wilderness, somewhere north.

How long had the van bumped its way in? Ten minutes? Given how rough the terrain was, that might mean a mile or less. She could run that.

But her mind objected.

No, I can't *run.*

Not on this leg.

The pain lanced up with each lunging step. And O'Neill was taller, stronger, faster, catching her all too easily. He grabbed her hood and yanked her back, halting her, causing her to fall. Landing on top of her, he flipped her over beneath his straddling legs. She screamed and writhed, fully panicked. She tried to hit him, but he pinned her arms. She wanted to kick him, but his weight crushed her.

After struggling for a few more seconds, the tears mixing with snot and saliva and now nearly choking her, she sputtered and coughed and opened her scrunched-up eyes. Looking up at his face, she saw him fully at last.

"I know you," Julie said.

CHAPTER FIVE

"I know you," Julie said again.

He was breathing hard, but it was slowing. He stood up and then reached for her. "Come on. Get up."

Maybe she shouldn't have taken his hand. But he helped her regain her feet.

"I didn't think you would actually run," he said.

It took her another moment to steady herself, her heart beating so hard she worried she might have a heart attack. But she was thirty-three. In good shape. Ate mostly vegetables. Oh God, why was this happening?

"I've seen you before," she said when she'd gotten her wind back. She stayed bent over, hands on her knees, staring at the ground. "You're Colton's friend?"

"I wouldn't exactly call us friends. Saw me where?"

But she couldn't quite recall. At the restaurant where Colton bartended? Maybe on a climbing trip?

They know each other — that's the important part.

Her mind ran away with the possibilities: This was some kind of beef. Payback. Or, they wanted something from him.

"Why are you doing this?"

He didn't answer. "Come on. Let's go up to the cabin. We'll talk to Michael."

Presumably, he meant the other man; Blank Hat. Now Julie raised her eyes to the van in the distance. She'd made it a good fifty yards, but she could see the vehicle just around a slight bend in the road. She could also see the edge of a cabin beyond it, the rest of it hidden by trees. The doors of the van hung wide open. Colton was a shape in the gloom. He hadn't run. Hadn't even tried.

"Will you at least tell me your name?"

"Keith," said the man beside her. "Come on."

Walking in the snow, with these sneakers, and this bad leg — it was almost as impossible as running. She grew frustrated. But she realized something, with a sudden shift in mood: The revelation that Colton knew these men had changed things, taken the sharpest edge off of the terror. Nobody that *knew* Colton was going to kill her. Or rape her? Right? This had something to do with Colton and *them*, some bad shit he'd gotten into.

Don't be so sure. People do worse things to those they know.

She knew that was true. The things she'd seen — the abuse her clients suffered — when not self-inflicted, almost always came from someone close. Someone trusted, someone they knew.

Colton is a bartender. He comes into contact with all types of people, both local and from out of town. You obviously don't know the half of it.

Not only that, but they both worked a lot, with Colton gone two nights a week. It meant many hours not seeing each other. Texting, sure, but still apart.

Living almost separate lives, it felt like, at times . . .

Was Keith from the restaurant? The idea had just come to her, swam up from the depths of her subconscious like the icosahedron in a Magic 8 Ball, but it felt right.

He didn't work there, she didn't think, but she'd seen him there on one of her rare visits.

Sitting at the other end of the bar, maybe. Had he made eye contact with her, then left?

They reached the van, and Keith leaned into the open door. "All right, man, get out."

Colton moaned as he moved, bent over, to the edge of the van. Keith waited, not helping, as he stepped down to the ground with a grimace. Blood had dried on his face from his split eyebrow and lip, and the swelling of the cheek on that side had worsened.

Keith didn't seem as beat up as Julie had first thought, maybe a little scrape along his jaw. He folded the doors shut. "All right, up to the cabin."

She was stiffening up in the cold, warm adrenaline fading.

As they walked, Keith said behind them, "Fucked up pretty bad, huh?"

"It's out of the socket," Colton said.

"I was talking to *her*. Your knee — that from jumping out the window?"

Don't answer. Don't talk to him.

"It's an old injury," Julie said. "I messed up my knee in high school."

"Ouch. Oh, yeah — Saranac Lake, right?"

This time she stayed silent, and he didn't press. Ahead of her were stairs. A deck jutted from the second story of the log cabin. The building nested against a steep hill, deck covered with a foot or more of snow. "Keep going to the front door," Keith instructed. The main entrance was past the steps. Now Keith took the lead and opened the door, then motioned for them to go in.

"I don't want to." Julie stared at Colton, willing him to look back. "Colton, what is going on? You know him, right? From the bar?"

Colton looked at Keith instead of her. "Listen, man — she just showed up. I don't know who she is, but she just came in the door talking about 'it was her house,' shit like that."

Keith laughed, then asked, "You think that's gonna stop this?"

Colton didn't answer.

"I don't see the point, bro. She's gonna know everything anyway." Keith's eyes had seemed dark before, but that was the light behind them — out here, they shone bright blue.

His dark hair was matted from the hat he'd worn, two days' stubble covering his hard jawline, a gap between his front teeth.

"You look cold," he said to her. "You don't want to stay out here. Come on inside."

"I'd rather stay."

"No, you wouldn't. Listen, if you run, I'll catch you again. And Michael's got the keys to the van, so you can't take it anywhere. We're miles and miles from the nearest town. So just come on in. Let's get you all squared away, okay?"

He was so calm. And "squared away" — typically a military saying. Colton had called 911, yet this guy was telling her his name, showing her his face, as if he was afraid of nothing.

Don't cry. Just don't do it.

But it was too late. "Please just let me go. Whatever this is, it doesn't have anything to do with me." Suddenly, it came to her: "Like he said, I don't know him. I realize that now. I'm just confused. I have a delusional personality disorder, and I know I should be sticking with my meds, but my boyfriend kicked me out and I guess I just . . . I got confused."

Keith watched her for a moment, his eyes lively with amusement. "That's pretty good. A little expositional, but not bad on the fly." He reached for her. "Come on, you're shivering."

I promise I'm not going to hurt you.

It was all she wanted to hear. Just something that indicated, even if it was bullshit: *You're safe. This doesn't have anything to do with you, or hurting you. You were just there. You weren't part of the plan.*

But he didn't. And whether she was part of "the plan" or not didn't matter now. She was here. She'd seen his face, knew his name.

This can't be happening. Things like this just don't happen . . .

Maybe her disbelief meant answers. It was such a crazy situation that there had to be some explanation. It would all be some big mistake. Even Colton's infidelity. There was a reset button here somewhere, a cosmic do-over switch that could be thrown, that *would* be thrown, and she'd go home, life would go back to the way it was, back to the way it was supposed to be.

Any minute now.

But nothing happened. Julie shook her head. She stepped back. Eyes blurring with tears, she said, "No. I'm not going in. Now let me go."

The good humor drained from Keith's face. He reached for her again, and this time he wasn't gentle. Colton said, "Hey, hey — don't—" but Keith had a hold of her by the shoulders and shoved her through the door.

She grabbed the door frame and resisted and screamed for help. He chopped one of her arms with his own, hard enough to almost break it, and made her release her grip. With another push, he sent her sprawling into the cabin, where the other man — Michael — knelt by the wood stove.

CHAPTER SIX

The fire Michael was building started to catch. He brushed off his hands as he stood. He wore dark outdoorsy pants, a red checked flannel jacket, waterproof boots. The blank hat was gone.

Colton stepped into the cabin next, then Keith, who shut the door.

Julie could see her breath in the air but already felt the warmth emitted by the stove. The front was still open; the orange flames licked and the kindling snapped.

Michael took a few steps to where Julie had sprawled to the floor.

"It's all right," Keith said to him. "She's all right. She didn't get hurt. She's just being difficult, and I've been very patient."

Michael looked down at Julie for a moment longer, staring at her so intently she felt heat rise in her face. Almost like he knew her. The intensity gave way to a certain bemusement.

Like you're not supposed to be here.

Like this is all some big mistake — tell him!

Keith tried to help Julie up, but she jerked away. Slowly, on her own, she stood. Michael continued to stare, but now he seemed to be checking her over. He looked her up and down, then stepped close enough that she could smell him, a bit of sweat, a bit of a musky cologne, and took her chin gently in hand. "Wow," he said. He turned her face right and left.

"I told you she's fine," Keith said.

"Okay." Satisfied, Michael returned to the wood stove and closed its thick metal door.

Not knowing what that was about, Julie took a quick look around. The cabin was one big room, including an upstairs loft with a dormer that led to the deck. In the back, a set of bunkbeds, two couches, a small enclosure for a bathroom. To her right was the kitchen and dining area; to her left, the wood stove and a couple of chairs. Old-fashioned snowshoes hung on the walls beside ancient-looking cross-country skis. Jeremiah Johnson could have lived here. All that was missing was the bearskin rug.

Michael walked back toward her. He looked more city than country, she thought — even his woodsy clothes seemed tailored, high-quality, at least. His dark hair was cut into a fade, his beard trimmed to his jaw line. So far he'd only said those two words, otherwise just staring with wide-set eyes.

She wasn't sure if he'd been in exactly these clothes, but Michael had been the driver of the van, and also the one who'd grabbed Monique. Of that she was certain.

"Where's the woman who was in my house?" Julie asked.

His gaze ticked past Julie. Keith, looming behind her, then moved off to the kitchen area. He started the gas stove, then ran some water into a kettle. "I'm having some coffee. Anyone else want coffee?"

"I'm fine," Michael said, then returned his attention to her. She noticed a bump on the bridge of his nose, like a wrongly healed break. "Why don't you sit down, okay? Right here by the fire." Now that he was talking, his voice was easy and smooth.

Not budging, Julie could hear Colton behind her, the kind of labored breathing he did when he was in pain. He really did have an issue with his shoulder.

"Come on," Michael said. "Sit down. The fire will get going here, and we can dry your stuff out. I've even got some clothes, I think, that will fit you."

Both Michael and Keith seemed to have the same idea: mock hospitality. As if it ruled out psychopathy.

But Julie decided to sit. Any more resistance wasn't going to help — no point throwing a tantrum. Better to cooperate for now and see where things were going. She took the seat closest to the stove; a wooden chair with butt and back cushions upholstered in some type of Native American print. At least they weren't tying her up. But then, where would she go? They'd already demonstrated the futility of that.

Finally taking his eyes off her, Michael then squinted at Colton, as if he couldn't be trusted. "All right, so, you've torn your shoulder or something?"

Keith watched from the kitchen. The water was in the kettle and coming to a boil, and he stood leaning against the sink, his face hard to read.

"It's the rotator cuff," Colton said. Julie really could hear the pain in his voice.

"Probably needs to be put back in?"

"I'm fine. It's okay."

"Well, we can't have you squirming and in pain this whole time." Michael closed the distance. "Come on, ease the arm down." Then he took a hold of it, gently, and started to raise it. "How's that?"

"Ahh," Colton said. He gritted his teeth. "Ahh . . ."

"Any higher? How's that? Can you raise it any higher?"

"That's it! That's as high as it can go!"

"Aww, come on. Let's see."

Julie felt the fear collecting in her gut. *Oh God, oh don't . . . .* She grabbed the handles of the chair, ready to jump up and stop what she saw coming.

Michael pushed Colton's arm higher, and Colton screamed in pain and started to fall back. Keith launched off the kitchen sink and came running over, catching Colton from behind. Michael still had a hold of his arm.

32

"Stop it!" Julie yelled. But with the men surrounding Colton there was nothing she could do.

Michael jerked on his arm. "How about that?" Colton's screams were drowning him out. "I think you're supposed to yank on them," Michael shouted to Keith.

Keith bobbled his head, like it might be true or not.

Michael yanked hard, and Colton's reddened face went slack as all his weight fell against Michael.

Who stepped back, letting him drop to the floor in a heap.

The shaking started in Julie's chest and spread to her limbs. Seeing Colton on the floor like that, unmoving, was too much.

"All right," Keith said, reaching down for him.

"No, don't wake him," Michael said. "Then he'll be screaming. The whole point was to keep him from pissing and moaning about it."

Keith took a breath. "We're gonna have to do something. Do you know how to put a shoulder back in?"

"He'll be fine," Michael said. "Let him sleep it off." Despite the flip words, the menace came off him in waves; he wanted to inflict pain on Colton.

Maybe this was more than business.

Keith trapped Julie with a look. "Has this happened before?"

While her body shook, her mind stayed frozen. She forced a nod, unable to speak. *Yes. His shoulder has gone out before.*

"So you know how to . . . put it back in the socket or whatever?"

She nodded again.

Michael studied Colton some more. "He's breathing?"

Keith leaned closer. "Yeah, he's breathing."

"I didn't think he would actually pass out."

"Did you think he was *faking*?"

Michael glared. "He's been lying about so many other things, so . . ."

Julie finally cut through the tense moment. "What do you want?" Somehow, if she knew their motivation, if she could connect with them on some human level, it would all end. Keith was familiar, and knew Colton, but Michael was still a stranger.

But instead of answering, Michael grabbed a thick black puffer coat. "I'm going to take a break. Otherwise, I'm going to kill him right now."

The ice-cold matter-of-factness in his tone scared her more than anything.

He slammed the door behind him. She looked at Keith now.

"The woman from this morning?" Keith phrased it like a question. "Yeah, so . . . she's with Michael."

"She's with Michael?" The words didn't add up in her tortured mind.

"Yeah. Monique is his wife."

CHAPTER SEVEN

It hit her like a ton of bricks. *Of course.*

It wasn't just Julie who was scorned. Michael had been cheated on, too.

And he was simmering with rage, wanting to kill Colton.

The information mollified her some. Brought things down to earth a little bit. Michael was an angry husband. This she could relate to.

She wondered where Monique was now. Despite the circumstances, she'd been worried about the woman's well-being since Michael had grabbed her. But she didn't ask. The fact that Michael was her husband was enough for now. Julie preferred to think that Monique was somewhere safe, back at her own home.

She didn't want to find out that Michael had done something with her instead.

Another question nagged her: why the theatrics? Why show up violent and angry, and risk someone calling 911, exactly like Colton had done?

Maybe the answer to that: they hadn't expected Julie to be there. It was Julie's disruption that caused Monique to leave the bedroom and go downstairs, right when the men were arriving. If she hadn't been there, they likely would have been the ones to walk into the bedroom and find Colton and Monique in bed together. That made sense. They'd wanted to scare them both.

Michael, perhaps suspecting she was cheating, had followed Monique to the townhouse and entered to confirm it.

But then it escalated. The men had abducted Colton and Julie in broad daylight, and with a gun. Well, that'd scared Colton, all right. But why take Julie, too? And wasn't it all a bit extreme?

She didn't see the gun now. She didn't know where Keith had put it — maybe it was in a concealed holster. She now found herself wondering if it was even loaded. Or even real.

Probably that was wishful thinking. *Sure, it's just a prop. Wouldn't it be pretty to think so.*

Keith was watching her, standing there in his athletic warm-up clothes, drinking instant coffee. He seemed to know his way around the place. "So you're engaged to this guy, huh?"

"For four months."

He glanced up in thought to work out the date, his lips moving a little. "Meaning, he proposed, what? Halloween?"

"A little earlier. We took a drive up to Saranac Lake, Lake Placid, to see the changing leaves. We hiked Owl's Head Mountain and he proposed."

He studied her hands, folded in her lap. "Got a ring?"

"I took it off for traveling. It's a little big on me, and I worry about losing it. It's in my bag back at the house."

"I don't see a ring on *him*."

"Men don't usually wear engagement rings."

"Oh, is that right? Huh. I wouldn't know." And he took a sip of his coffee.

Keith wore rings, though. Two of them. A turquoise one on his right ring finger and an opal on his pinky; she saw them clearly as he tipped the mug back.

Julie felt bad for Colton, left lying like a discarded rag doll. He groaned then, eyes opening. He grunted as the pain registered in his brain.

"Hey, look who's up," Keith said, setting the coffee aside.

Colton's eyes got wide as he scrambled away from Keith, pushing with his heels. He slid on his butt, holding his arm, all the way back to the wall.

Keith looked amused. Julie thought that for a minute back there, in Michael's presence Keith had been worried for Colton; now he was grinning and enjoying himself. "Hey, man, we just had to know if you were crying wolf. Let me help you. So, if she puts it back in, will that be it? Or will you need something else? There's painkillers in the medicine cabinet in the bathroom."

"I need ice." Colton's voice was hoarse, thin.

"Hmm. Ice. Not sure about ice." He went to Colton, who pressed himself into the wall, nowhere left to go. Keith asked, "So how do we put it back in?"

"Do you have a sling?"

"Yeah. Right in my back fucking pocket." He sighed. "I'll see if I can find something to use," he said, and went rummaging around in the kitchen.

When Michael returned, his face reddened from the cold, he hung his jacket, saying, "Still alive, huh?"

"Yeah," Keith said, coming up with a large cloth napkin. "We're going to fix his arm."

* * *

Colton seemed terrified, but he talked them through it. He had no choice. His arm wouldn't function like this, and the pain was surely excruciating. First, they had to get him standing. Then he instructed Keith — not Michael — to grab the wrist of his injured arm.

"Easy! Please, please be easy," Colton begged. "It's dislocated, and we're going to pop it. Okay? We need to guide the ball of my arm bone back into my shoulder socket. But it hurts, man. It hurts. Is there anything to drink?"

Keith told Michael where to look, and Michael came back with a bottle of whiskey. Colton took a long swig, grimacing at the heat.

"All right," he said. "But let me be the one to pull . . ."

Julie could hardly watch. Shoulder dislocation was nothing to trifle with; she'd had her own first-hand experience. Putting the shoulder back in on its own could make things worse. It was called a closed reduction, and it really required a medical professional to prevent damage to the muscle, cartilage, tendons, even the blood vessels.

Colton jerked his shoulder back, instantly howling with pain. He swooned like he might pass out again but stayed on his feet. After they eased him into the other chair by the wood stove, no one talked for a while. Michael added some more kindling to the fire, then a larger piece of wood. Whatever he'd done out there had seemed to calm him down.

Cheated on, she thought. *Both of us.*

She could hardly look at Colton, simultaneously furious and sorry that he lived with such need for validation, so narcissistic he would throw away the life they had together just to sleep with someone else.

Or maybe it had developed into something more than that? Did Michael seethe with anger over a one-night stand, or did he know something she didn't?

Keith had found painkillers and shook two out for Colton, who took them with some whiskey. Keith then took the bottle away. He went over and sat at the kitchen island, where he watched them.

Finished fiddling with the wood stove, Michael stood, walked slowly toward Keith. His thick-soled boots that thudded over the plank floors were Mammut brand. Not cheap.

"Now what," Michael said. He glanced at his watch. "I got another hour to kill. What do you want to do?"

He was talking to Keith, but he stared at Julie when he said it. He walked to her and stopped so his pelvis was right next to her face. "Maybe it's time for a little payback? What do you think, Colton? Fair's fair? Eye for an eye? Pussy for a pussy?"

Julie felt the shakes return. Michael being a cuckold didn't make things any better; it made things worse. He had a reason to not only hurt Colton, but her, too. Like this.

He crouched beside her, breathing on her neck and in her ear. "Colton tells us you're a random stalker. Just somebody in the wrong place at the wrong time. What do you think about that? Can you prove it's not true?"

"Please leave her alone," Colton muttered, and Julie winced, expecting it to trigger Michael into a rage.

Instead, he was calm. "She doesn't look random to me. She looks like a very specific woman with a very specific purpose."

She wanted to crawl away. Michael was like some animal, a predator enjoying her in his trap.

He finally moved away from her, stepping in between the chairs — she in one, Colton in the other. "Come on, Colton. Tell me about it. Convince me of your story."

"No," Colton said. "Forget it. Like you said, it's pointless."

"Hey, you started it. Now you need to finish it. Fucking tell me, or I'm gonna get upset."

At last, Colton answered. "She comes into the bar sometimes. The restaurant where I work."

In spite of herself, it hurt Julie to hear him talk like this. "Go on."

"It's been happening for a couple of months. The first time was just after Christmas. She said her name was Julie. She usually nurses one drink — a gin and tonic. Sometimes she'll have two."

Michael had walked back to the kitchen island and leaned against it.

Colton continued, "She's always alone. She kind of stares at me — I'll catch her staring and she pretends to be looking at her phone."

"And she just happened to know where you live?"

"The most I ever talked to her was one night and I told her where I lived. It was just part of the conversation. I didn't think anything of it. But I could tell there was something a little off about her."

Julie felt a chill. He seemed to lie so easily. Who was this person? Who had she been sharing her life with?

"And so," Michael asked, "this morning?"

"And then, this morning, out of nowhere, she's standing at the foot of my bed, acting like she's my wife."

"Fiancée," Julie said, just a whisper.

"Fiancée," Michael whispered back, smiling. "And what do you say, random stalker lady? What's your story?"

She thought about what to say. Like she had in the van, she considered whether it made sense to play along. But how could it help her? Michael, the way he looked at her, seemed to know who she was. They both did.

But then, that could be just her own delusion at work.

Oh, give me a break.

No, she didn't believe it. Not really. It was just one of those things. Someone says something enough times, you start to wonder. You give a little ground, and before you know it, you're a full-blown conspiracy theorist.

She wouldn't give in. "I've been with him for five years. We just got engaged."

"And what were you doing there at seven o'clock this morning — what was the suitcase by the bedroom door all about?"

"I've been at a conference. It ended early, in anticipation of the storm."

Michael looked out a window. "Hmm. I've been checking the weather app on my phone. There's nothing going on."

She shrugged. "They were worried it was going to hit today. This afternoon. Over there, first. Buffalo is west of us. Weather goes west to east."

"Oh, it does, does it?"

His mockery made her feel foolish, having explained something that was common knowledge.

"How'd you get in?" he asked. "You have a key?"

"Of course I do. But I didn't need it; the door was unlocked."

Michael's gaze shifted to Colton, who said, "I had a little too much to drink last night. I guess I forgot to lock it."

"Uh-huh." Back to Julie. "Did you tell him you were coming home early?"

"No. I wanted to surprise him."

Michael's eyebrows climbed up and his mouth dropped open. He let out a huge guffaw, then clapped his hands once, loud. "A surprise! I guess that backfired, huh? A surprise . . . That's hilarious."

Julie watched Keith while all of this was going on, who was quiet, just listening. She noticed his rings again — how there was more to the turquoise one than she'd first thought. It had writing around it.

Michael was moving closer to Colton. "Left the place unlocked. Got yourself all drunked-up last night, left the door wide open. And then this morning, boom, guess who's looking in at you from the foot of your bed?"

Colton stared up at Michael a moment, then turned his head and looked at her at last. A stranger all the way through. Nothing recognizable in his eyes, no five years together, none of the minutiae of memories, none of the intimacy.

The words from his mouth pierced her in their cold betrayal.

"This is a woman with mental health problems. She showed up at the wrong place at the wrong time. I don't know what else to say."

CHAPTER EIGHT

"Can I use the bathroom, please?"

Julie's question broke a silence that followed Colton's comment about her being a mentally unwell stalker. She needed to pee, that much was true. But more than that, she just needed to get away.

Michael and Keith conferred with a glance, and then Keith said, "Here, okay, follow me."

At the back of the cabin, a wooden door led to a small enclosure. "You ever used a composting toilet?"

"Yes," she lied. She was worried, perhaps irrationally, if she said *No,* he wouldn't let her use it. She was also distracted, looking closer at his ring.

"Okay," he said, dubious. "You know, so . . . There's no flush."

She was grateful for the latch on the door, the kind of lever that fell into a catch. Inside the small room was a wooden box with a plastic seat fitted into the opening. It smelled like pine, and she lifted the lid and sat, her mind buzzing with everything just said. That she was some weirdo obsessed with her local bartender, and not Colton's wife-to-be. Not even living in that house.

The thought that he could say such things with so much conviction made her stomach tight. He really seemed like he believed it. She wondered how much Keith and Michael were buying it.

Keith and Michael. Those might not even be their names. She didn't know a thing about them. Only what she'd seen of them so far.

Michael had expensive tastes and he was angry. Keith seemed more willing to compromise. They were both dispassionate about her, but maybe hated Colton. They knew what they were doing.

The van. Generic, white — a kidnapper's van like something from a mob movie. Toss in the victim, kill them, wrap the body in the plastic lining. These guys were serious. Murder seemed perfectly in the realm of possibility. Maybe it was only to scare Colton, but she wasn't ready to think about the possibility it wasn't.

She thought about Keith's ring, instead. It bore two engravings:

This We'll Defend circled the center stone.

And between that and the band: *United States Army.*

Even if Keith seemed more affable, he was a trained killer.

She reached for the flush but remembered there was none. Water came out of the sink; a mere trickle. She used a sheaf of paper towels to dry off as she looked out the small window.

Out there, the hillside rose up, plentiful with trees. On the edge of her vision, though, another building. She leaned up close to the glass to see it better. Just a shack, really, and smaller than this one. Some kind of outbuilding.

Looking at it made her queasy.

Pushing the door open, she fully expected to encounter Keith on the other side of it, waiting for her. But he was back with Colton, sitting in the chair where Julie had been.

Michael, on the other hand, was gone again.

* * *

43

Colton held a makeshift icepack against his shoulder — a crude chunk of ice Keith had pulled from a trunk freezer wrapped in a dirty dish towel. He avoided her gaze — this was now the norm — but Keith looked over as she approached.

"How's that knee?"

"It's okay."

"We got some ice for Colton's shoulder. Let me get you some."

Keith entered the kitchen area, and Julie sat down in his place.

As Keith rummaged around to get another towel and the ice, she bent closer to Colton. There was very little ambient noise, just the muffled crackle of the fire in the wood stove, an occasional gust of wind outside.

"What do you want me to do?" she breathed.

He didn't answer. Either he hadn't heard her, or he was worried he'd be pushing it by also talking. Still, she found herself yearning for a response. Anything. Maybe: *Just go with it.* Meaning, *go along with what I'm doing.* Even *I don't know* would be something. A connection.

She so badly wanted to believe that Colton was trying to protect her, even if his efforts had initially confused her. If he was, she could understand his reasoning for treating her this way — mostly, anyway — but it was so lonely. Despite his cheating, despite how much that hurt, how betrayed and undervalued she felt, she still felt connected to him.

They'd been together for five years. They'd started living together the day after he proposed, in her little one-bedroom apartment, where he'd been sleeping most nights anyway. Not quite three months later, they were moving into the townhouse. Buying furniture. Picking out the new rug for the entryway.

They were best friends. At least, she'd thought so.

And maybe that was part of the problem? They'd had plenty of steamy nights in the beginning, days they couldn't wait to get home to rip each other's clothes off. But had it cooled down too soon? Had they settled too quickly into

44

domesticity, not enough nights out partying, not enough inventive love-making?

And then there was the townhouse. Buying it had been her idea. Had he felt pressured? From the beginning, Colton had worried about his credit, or lack thereof. "They're not going to lend me any money for a mortgage," he'd told her. Culinary school had set him back — he was still in debt tens of thousands of dollars. She had college loans, too, but not as steep, and assured him that she could cover it. "We're going to be married, baby. My money is your money. It doesn't matter."

Maybe it *had* mattered to Colton. He'd always said he was bartending instead of cooking to avoid the stress of kitchen life. "All those guys are dysfunctional," he'd once told her. "Stressed out, alcoholic messes." But she knew the money was good in bartending. Chefs could do all right, but on busy Friday and Saturday nights he was pulling in three, four, even five hundred dollars a shift behind the bar.

Enough to save up to open his own bistro, a dream he kept close to the vest. "I don't want to just cook ribeyes and dressed-up burgers all day," he'd said, one night out to dinner. "It's fancy pub food."

He was a true talent. His food melted in her mouth, whether a simple grilled cheese sandwich or a more elaborate duck breast with apricot chutney. She worshipped his Italian roulade — a mouth-watering stuffed and baked steak, or his slow-cooker sauerbraten.

Had she not been supportive enough of his dream to open his own place? Had putting the townhouse all in her name been a mistake? How could he build credit for a business when he didn't own anything? "You should buy a car," she'd told him, "and make the payments."

But he never had. He still drove that old Toyota truck he'd owned since they'd met. The one parked on Waverly Street right now, just down the way from her own Honda Fit.

The police were on their way when she and Colton were kidnapped. She'd heard the sirens. Were they going through their vehicles right now, looking for clues as to who they were? Someone on the street must have seen what had happened. Vans don't careen round corners like that without raising suspicion. People don't get snatched out of their driveways without someone seeing it. The police must have a description of their assailants. A plate number. She wondered how close they were to finding them.

Or maybe nobody had seen anything, and the cops were without leads.

Monique, though. If she'd been left behind, surely she'd be providing information.

Of course, she could also be trying to protect her husband, keep him out of trouble.

Keith returned with another jagged chunk of ice wrapped clumsily in a towel and handed it to her. "Here you go. Put that on your knee."

"Thank you."

She glimpsed his ring again, thinking about the Army, what he might've seen and done. But before she could say anything, the door opened and Michael came back in, blowing on his hands.

Snow clung to his legs up to his knees, as if he'd been off the beaten path. But he didn't have any more firewood with him, or anything else. He could have been trying to get a cell signal — she doubted the coverage was very good out here.

After giving everyone a quick look, he said, "All right, I'm hungry. Keith? Where'd you put the supplies?"

"Some of the stuff is in the trunk freezer, and here's the rest in the cupboards . . ."

The two men walked off to the kitchen-side of the cabin, talking and rummaging around. Colton cleared his throat as if to get her attention.

She faced him, hopeful. He checked the men again.

"You . . . need . . . to get out of here."

Yeah, no shit. Of course she needed to get out here — they both did. Or did he mean just her?

But she turned away from the look in Colton's eyes, not liking the fear she saw there.

46

The knowing.

You need to get out of here.

She looked over at Michael and Keith in the kitchen. "Do you have my phone?"

They glanced at each other. Michael mumbled something she didn't catch, but Keith dug in his pocket. Then he walked over her, dropped her phone in her lap.

"Knock yourself out," he said.

CHAPTER NINE

It was her phone, all right, still covered in the light blue Otter skin that often got it stuck in her pocket.

The device was on, 74 percent battery left. Plenty of life, because it'd been plugged in for most of her ride home.

Setting it in her lap, she looked at Keith and Michael, but they'd gone back to preparing food, neither man watching her.

Was this some sort of test to see what she'd do?

But, of course, it said *No Service*.

911 often went through, though — or she could send an SOS. Did it make sense to do that? Why were they just letting her have the phone back? She glanced at Colton again, afraid that terrible hopelessness remained in his eyes. But he wasn't looking at her.

Shit. What to do?

It was after nine, according to her phone. Two hours since she'd gotten home and this nightmare began. No one had texted her, apparently, since then. Either that, or nothing was coming through.

She scrolled through her messages to her friend Annette. Their last text was from two days ago; Annette had asked about the conference. Julie had responded with a gif of a sleeping cat falling off a windowsill.

Her thumbs were poised to send Annette a text now. But what? She glanced at Keith, his back to her. Surely he'd check to see what she would do. This *had* to be a test.

To be safe, she sent an exploratory message only. A simple, *Hey, you out there?*

She watched then as the little green bar started across the top of the screen, got about halfway, and stopped. Staring, she willed it to complete the journey, *text sent.* But it didn't. Instead, a red exclamation point.

Unable to send.

Keith came back, a wooden spoon in one hand, a napkin in the other. "All set?"

She held onto the phone only a moment longer, then placed it back into the napkin he held out. He wrapped it up and stuck it back into his pocket.

"Yeah, service out here is terrible," he said, flatly. "You have to go up on the hill to get anything at all." And then he walked back into the kitchen.

* * *

Morning passed into late morning. Without her phone, Julie couldn't be sure of the exact time — the only clock in the cabin, on the wall near the sink, had stopped at 4:10 — but it had to be nearing noon.

Keith made spaghetti and asked Colton what he thought of it. Colton's suggestion, his voice deadpan: when using sauce from a can, heat a little butter with some garlic in a skillet first, and then add the sauce. "It'll give it a little extra flavor."

He no longer had the ice for his arm — it had melted, soaking his black T-shirt and puddling on the floor, as had hers. The towels sat in a pile beside her chair. Neither of their hosts had offered to refresh the ice, nor had Colton asked. He'd taken painkillers a couple of hours earlier, but they seemed to be wearing off.

It was clear the men were waiting for something.

49

But, waiting for what?

After eating, everyone sat around the fire, picking their teeth and staring into the wood stove like it was any another day. Just passing the time.

Julie passed it, too, examining her surroundings. Three deer busts hung overhead, one on each wall except in the kitchen, where the cupboards took up space. Crass hunting-camp humor filled out the rest: *Welcome to Camp Quitcherbitchin* read one metal sign, depicting two mugs coming together in a "cheers" gesture. *If you're not a happy camper, take a hike.* On the wall near the wood stove hung a few novelty items: license plates, bumper stickers and those little personalized wooden signs. She'd been reading one over and over.

> *If any little word of ours can make one life the brighter,*
> *If any little song of ours can make one heart the lighter,*
> *God help us speak that little word and take our bit of singing*
> *And drop it in some lonely vale and set the echoes ringing.*

She kept coming back to it. It was so incongruous with the rest of the décor — if you could call it that.

"We'll be right back," Keith said. He and Michael had walked up the open stairs and were exiting to the deck. He shut the door behind them.

"Please tell me everything," Julie said to Colton, after a few seconds. "I can't take it anymore. You have to tell me what's going on."

"I don't *know* what's going on."

"You don't know? Or you don't want to? You said I need to get out of here. But so do you. Right?"

"You should quiet down." He was speaking low again, so as not to be overheard. "I didn't mean anything. I think the whiskey went to my head."

"Don't lie to me. Fine, I'll go ask them myself."

"Julie, stop!" He sat straighter in his chair.

She stared at him but lowered herself back down. "So, are you gonna talk to me?"

"I just meant, maybe you can run."

"I tried that and it didn't work out so well. My knee is in terrible shape. I can barely walk. And it's freezing outside."

"Take the van."

The words sent a bolt of terrified excitement up her spine. "Who has the keys? Michael?"

"Yeah."

"How would I get them?"

Colton started to respond but gnashed his teeth against a wave of pain.

"Colton," she said, switching subjects, "you need a doctor."

"I'll be okay."

His color looked bad to her. Colton had Italian in him — his father's great-grandparents had been expatriates from Trieste living in Egypt. But that Mediterranean complexion had paled.

"You're sweating. I know you're in pain."

"Why are you worried about me?" There was that sharpness again in his voice. "Huh? I'm the cheating asshole. I'm the one who got us into this, and you're looking at me with those big sorrowful eyes. I can't take it."

"I'm going to find something for you, some more meds. I'll make a sling. Those bunk beds, right there, those pillowcases." She started to get up a second time.

"*Please*," Colton begged. "Sit back down. If you get me something like that, they're obviously going to notice. And then you'll have to explain it."

"They don't want you to have a sling?"

"You don't know anything about these people."

"That's what I've been *asking* you. What could they possibly want with me? I've never met them, I don't know who they are . . ."

But the memory of Keith, seeing him at Herkimer Brewing, slid back into her thoughts.

Colton shifted in his seat, gingerly this time, wincing as he repositioned his arm a little. He had it resting on the arm of the chair.

"You didn't do anything to them," Colton said.

Okay. That was something, anyway. "And have you been lying about our relationship, and who I am, in order to try and protect me?"

A brief hesitation. "Yes. I didn't know what else to do . . ."

"So, you admit we're engaged."

"Yes."

"We live together."

"Yes."

"And you're cheating on me."

"I . . . yes."

They were silent a bit with the weight of that. She gazed toward the side deck. The men were still out there. One of their voices raised, though she couldn't hear what they were saying.

"They're arguing a lot."

"Well, things have changed," he said.

"What do you mean? Changed from what?"

"I just mean, you came home early," he said. "They didn't, ah . . . I don't think they expected us to jump out the window, either."

"Do you think he would've shot us?" Julie went back to the early morning, the panic and terror of escaping her house, a man with a gun coming after her.

Colton didn't answer.

"How do I . . ." she started, and the new line of thought stirred emotion. She suddenly had to choke back tears. *How do I get the keys from Michael?* was going to be the question.

Colton seemed to intuit this. Keeping his eyes on the deck door, he said, "I'll think of something. I'll get you the keys, distract them, and you run."

She hated that it gave her some relief to hear that, even if she'd be leaving him behind.

"Listen to me: I'm going to get something for you to make into a sling."

"No — don't."

52

"I'll be right back." And she got up from the chair and headed toward the rear of the cabin, despite his low, almost growling protests behind her.

She walked into the back, where the arrangement of the bunk beds formed a kind of room-within-a-room. Hunting jackets and boots littered a corner. No porn mags in view, but, on the wall, kitschy 1950s illustrations of naked women serving drinks and cooking in a kitchen.

"Julie," Colton whispered harshly. "Please get back here."

She focused on the beds, removing a pillowcase from one of the pillows. Thinking better of it, she decided to take the whole sheet. It was in rough shape, the floral pattern long faded, the edges tattered. As she gathered it up, she noticed the framed photo on the bedside table.

Picking it up, covered in dust, she blew on it. Usually, in a place like this, you had at least one picture of the camp owner and his buddies presiding over a fresh kill, all orange jackets and red flannel hats, men grinning ear-to-ear from the adrenaline. This was exactly one of those pictures. And in it, a man stood next to a teenaged boy who was gripping a large buck by its antlers.

Julie's breath caught.

She couldn't be a hundred percent sure, but the boy looked like Keith. She peered closely to study the man beside him, his hand on his shoulder.

The sheet dropped from her hands to the floor, forgotten.

She knew him. In fact, she'd met him several times over the past five years. A big man with a handlebar mustache and blue eyes wrapped in crow's feet. Like some kind of ex-biker. He'd been distant, barely speaking to her.

While he was younger here, fewer wrinkles and less gray in the mustache, there was no doubt who he was. The man beside young Keith was Colton's father, Dale Rossi.

PART TWO

Brothers and Sisters

CHAPTER TEN

Ray Costa was thumbing his phone.

"What'd you get?"

"4.5."

"Is that good?"

"It says the average American has a carbon footprint of 5."

"So that's good."

"Not really."

"What does the number mean?"

"It means if everyone lived like me, then it would take four and a half earths to sustain us."

"Oh, come on," Danice said. "We don't live a very extravagant lifestyle."

"It doesn't matter, I guess. Maybe we don't think we do, but according to this, we do."

"Let me see." She came closer, reaching for the phone. "Can I take it? I want to see what I get."

He handed it to her.

As Danice started poking away, Ray sipped his coffee and looked out the window. The police were still out there, several cars in the street, marked and unmarked. They'd been there going on two hours.

Danice, still using the phone, asked, "Anything happening?"

"No. Just more of them."

"More?"

She went to the window and looked out as another patrol car pulled up. "All right, I gotta go see what's going on." Handing him back his phone, she shrugged into her jacket. When she opened the door, a uniformed police officer was coming up the walk.

"Hello," Danice said.

Ray, hearing her, got up from the chair and moved beside her.

"Ma'am," the officer said. "I'm Trooper Taylor. Do you have a minute for me to ask you a few questions? Your husband, too."

CHAPTER ELEVEN

Walking back to her seat by the wood stove, Julie felt Colton watching her carefully. He waited until she sat down to ask: "What happened? Change your mind?"

Avoiding his eyes, she nodded. "You were right. They'll get upset and it won't be worth it."

She could sense his suspicion. He hadn't always been the most perceptive of her moods, but he seemed to know something was up, now.

Of course he does. He's been lying to you this whole time.

"Are you in love with her?" The question burst out of her before she had a chance to even preview it in her mind. If the lies were growing, it was the one truth she needed most.

"You really don't want to hear the answer to that," Colton said.

"Yes, I do."

He sighed. "There *is* no good answer. When someone asks that question, it's a trap. If you say 'yes,' it's hurtful, because you love someone else. If you say 'no,' it's hurtful because it means you risked the relationship just to have sex."

She noticed the philosophical way he talked, keeping distanced, making it hypothetical.

She tried a different tack. "How long have you been with her? Where did you meet?"

"Shh," he said, looking stricken.

The door opened and the men re-entered the cabin, the air heavy with purpose.

"It's time," Michael said, and he went to the wall by the front door, pulled down a backpack. He took it to the back of the cabin, out of view.

"I think I'm going to be sick," Colton said.

"Go ahead," Keith said, and Colton rose unsteadily to his feet. Clutching his arm, he shuffled to the bathroom in a hurry and closed the door with a slam.

Keith, as if nothing was going on, took an apple off the wood block and started cutting it with a small paring knife. After a moment, he offered her some.

She wasn't hungry, but something told her to say yes. *Take every opportunity you get. Every chance to connect.*

He brought her an apple slice. She took it, finding it interesting that he cut up his apple instead of just biting in. Returning to the stool, he watched her a moment, his eyes so bright blue they seemed to emanate light from across the room. Eyes just like his father's, perhaps.

"All right." Michael emerged from the back, grabbed the thick parka from the hooks beside the door, put it on and slung the pack over his left shoulder. He then took his phone out, seemed to check something and stuck it away. He walked out the door without another word.

Julie listened as the sound of crunching snow faded away.

"Where is he going?"

"Not too far. Just meeting somebody."

"Who?"

Keith sliced more apple but didn't answer.

"Is he coming back?"

"Oh, yeah."

"Will you tell me what's going on?"

He studied her a moment as if considering it, then crossed the room to sit in the chair beside her. She braced herself, ready to hear about all the lies, the secret life Colton had she'd never known about. How she'd spent five years with a man who hadn't even confided in her he had a brother — if that was, in fact, what Keith was.

But Keith said, "You know about ancient civilizations?"

"What?"

"Prehistory, we're talking about."

"Not really."

"Well, I'll tell you something. And this is totally true. Every so often, on this planet, everything gets wiped. Just, *boom*, reset, wiped out completely. Giant meteor that took out the dinosaurs. Or massive floods, submerging everything underwater. The poles switching, changing magnetic values, continents drifting apart — did you know there have been multiple super-continents? It's not just Pangaea; there were a whole bunch more. Forming and un-forming and reforming. For millions of years."

It was all so out of the blue, it took her a moment to catch up. "I think . . . Yes, I've heard that."

"Ice ages come and go. You know how the American Indians first get here? They crossed over from Mongolia when the ice was up. Walked right over in their woolly mammoth clothes."

She waited, listening.

"So, everything is always rearranging, but we think it's never really happened since modern humans got here. And it hasn't, really. Things have been stable. And then we realized it's for a reason."

She raised her eyebrows, inviting him to continue.

"People think pyramids are just in Egypt," Keith said. "But that's not true. They're all over. There's over three hundred in Central America. They're in Japan, they're in Polynesia. They're everywhere."

It plucked a nerve in the back of her mind — she'd just been thinking about Egypt. In respect to Colton's heritage, anyway.

"Pyramids," Keith said, "are gravitational lenses. They work off the moon and create constant erupting volcanoes — pressure releases, basically, for Mother Earth. It's why we've had such relative stability over the past hundreds of thousands of years. And now, we know who built them. The Elohim — a super-intelligent prehistory civilization, possibly not even from Earth. And we have proof. Michael found it."

He stopped talking and stared at her, his expression stoic and earnest.

Julie's mouth hung open a little, waiting for some kind of response to form in her brain.

But then Keith cracked a smile and threw his head back laughing. He playfully tapped her shoulder a couple of times. "I'm just fucking with you. I'm *totally* just fucking with you. Oh man, your face . . ." He got up and returned to the kitchen, picked up his apple and, taking another bite, leaned on the wood block and looked at her, still chuckling, then calmed down.

If Keith wore a mustache like Colton, they'd look all the more alike. In that moment, his features, his expression, their connection to each other was no longer a question.

"You're Colton's brother," Julie said.

Keith just watched her for a moment, his mouth resetting to a grim line. She wasn't sure what was going to come next — denial? Something else? But he only took a breath, his blue eyes gone ice cold again. "Yeah," he said. "I am."

CHAPTER TWELVE

Colton made his way back to the chairs by the wood stove, still pale and sweaty.

"Everything come out all right?" It was a flip remark, but Keith was no longer jovial. If he ever really had been.

Colton sat without answering, leaning his head back and closing his eyes. The shoulder pain seemed worse.

Julie had been racking her brain, trying to come up with a reason he would have kept something like this from her, something so major. She could only conclude that he wished Keith wasn't his brother.

Still, it was a long time to keep something like that a secret.

"I just asked Keith a question," she said. "I asked him if you two were brothers."

Colton looked at her, not speaking. When he did finally say something, it was partly defensive. "We have the same father. We didn't grow up together."

"Why didn't you ever tell me?"

He shook his head. "'Brothers' should be a choice."

So it was as she thought — he didn't want Keith in his life.

The legs of a kitchen barstool scraped across the wooden floor as Keith dragged it closer. He took the last bite of his apple and threw the core away in an open trash bin nearby, where it landed with a thunk. "Colton and I haven't had the closest of relationships."

"Do me a favor and just stop talking," Colton snapped. "I mean, just . . . stop . . . talking."

Keith patted the air in Colton's direction. *Be silent.* "Colton is older than me. Four years my big brother. Our dad, he's an old-fashioned sort of guy. Works with his hands, likes to hunt — and Papa was a rolling stone. You know what I mean? 'All that he left us was alone.' I bet he's got more kids out there we don't even know about. We probably got brothers and sisters we never even met."

It lined up with what little she knew about Dale Rossi — that he'd never been married, that Colton had been born out of wedlock, along with his two sisters, and Dale skedaddled shortly thereafter. But he'd never spoken of a brother, half-sibling or not, and neither had Dale.

"How about you, Julie? Any sibs?"

It wasn't that Keith was never jovial, no. He was either silent and brooding, cold and menacing, or given to this sarcastic kind of mock jocularity. She had clients like this.

"How about me?" she asked. "Yes, I have a brother. Younger."

"Just a brother? No sister?"

He made the question sound odd. She wondered why he kept glancing at Colton. "Nope, just a brother."

Keith seemed to accept it. "How about your parents? Still together?"

"My mother died."

"Oh no. What happened?"

"It was a long time ago. Almost ten years ago, when I was in college." Keith seemed open to conversation, even if it was via this falsely polite and hospitable version of himself. If she wanted to know more, she'd better go along with it. "My mother had breast cancer when I was a teenager, and we thought she beat it. But it came back."

Keith shook his head. "What about your old man?"

"Lives in Colorado near my brother."

"So you're kind of on your own out here."

"I have lots of friends in the area." She felt defensive suddenly. "College friends — I went to Russell Sage. Colleagues. Lots of people I know through the clinic. People probably looking for me right now."

Maybe that message to Annette eventually got through . . .

"Wow." Keith was nodding. He crossed his legs, feigning a kind of curiosity. "Russell Sage — that's the women's college?"

"I got my master's there in Community Psychology."

"That sounds impressive."

"How about you, though? I want to know why you and him aren't close."

Colton was shaking his head again; he didn't like this. Keith studied his half-brother a moment before answering. For just a second, he seemed genuinely thoughtful about it. "I mean, my dad and Colton's mom split before I was born. Colton stayed with his mom. You ever met her?"

"Yes. She's in Florida."

"Well, she raised him up — that's why he's such a softy. When our father split with my mother, I stayed with him. My mother wasn't, ah . . . the court said she wasn't a 'suitable placement' for me. I saw her here and there for a while, but she sort of faded out of the picture."

"Did you and Colton ever see each other? Did your dad ever get you together?"

"No, Colton's mom didn't want him having anything to do with our dad. If you met her, you know what I mean. She's a controlling bitch."

He paused, as if for Julie to confirm or deny it. If anything, Julie would have classified Colton's mother, Ann-Marie, as nervy. Not a formal term, of course. But Ann-Marie Jacobs was that — she could be sweet, and she seemed to genuinely like Julie, but she wasn't exactly reliable. Over the last five years, they'd met half a dozen times, with at least that many plans to meet broken or rearranged. Ann-Marie had never remarried, but she had a guy who sometimes lived with her. The whole thing seemed to make Colton uncomfortable, and they'd generally avoided talking about it.

The way Julie had seen it: they were two people with imperfect pasts forging a new life together. Seeking to break that intergenerational trauma that plagued so many.

And how has that worked out for you?

"I mean, there were times," Keith was saying. "I remember once — Cole, maybe you remember this — we went to visit Dad's brother Glen over by Watertown. Glen is a real farmer type and had this big old barn with the hay bales in it, and we used to make forts out of the hay bales. Colton, though, he was allergic to hay. You know, hay fever, but like, for real. So he'd be sneezing and wheezing and coughing. We buried him in there once, me and the cousins. We built this fort up and then we put the bales across the top, trapped him right in there and climbed down from the loft." Keith started laughing at the memory, and eventually laughed so hard his face was red. "He couldn't get out, but you could hear him, you could hear this muffled . . . this muffled sneezing in there . . ." Keith could barely finish, bent over with laughter, the first raw and real emotion he'd had all day.

"Did you eventually help him out?"

Keith wiped his eyes with the back of his hand as he sat up. "Nah, he worked his way out, eventually. Just like he dealt with his arm here this morning. It was good for him. Toughened him up."

"What did he say to you about it afterward? Was he upset with you?"

Keith blinked at her, perhaps sensing a trap. "He didn't say anything. He was probably too embarrassed. God . . . those muffled sneezes . . . I can still hear them . . ." He howled with laughter again.

Julie waited until he calmed down. "Did he ever tell anyone, though? Like tell a grown-up? Tell your dad?"

Confusion in Keith's eyes, maybe even a little irritability crossed his gaze. "What's he gonna tell? We were just messing around." He watched Colton a moment. "Nah, I guess he never told anyone. He was a pussy, but not *that* much of a pussy, I guess."

"Would you have gotten him out if you'd really thought he was stuck in there?"

Too much, Julie thought, regretting it right away. *Too much too soon.* But she was thinking how Keith had been when Colton had passed out. How he'd gotten in between his brother and Michael.

Keith gave her a look like his amusement with her was fading. "I didn't need to get him out," he said eventually. "He was fine."

A heavy silence followed.

It was Colton who broke it. "Can I get some more ice?"

"No," Keith said. "Fucking deal with it." And he hopped off the barstool and suddenly went outside.

Julie heard what she thought was the flick of a lighter, a Zippo snapping shut.

And for some reason, her gaze was drawn back to that simple poem on the wall.

And drop it in some lonely vale and set the echoes ringing.

CHAPTER THIRTEEN

"What are you doing?" Colton asked. "Are you *psychoanalyzing* him?"

She didn't answer the question but had one of her own. "Why are we here, Colton? Why is your *brother* involved? Look at me."

"It's really better that you don't know anything."

"Why? Why do you keep saying that?"

"It'll just be easier. For you."

"Bullshit," she spat, losing her cool at last. "I don't believe that. I don't think you're protecting me. I think you did something you regret. Is that right?"

"It's complicated."

"Michael stares at me like he knows me. Like I'm something . . . under a microscope. He grabbed Monique when they came into the house. You didn't see — I watched how violent he was with her. He put his hand over her mouth." She took a stabilizing breath. "Did he do something to her? Colton? Did he hurt her, and that's why they're freaking out?"

If Colton had been pale, he was now a shade paler. "Ah, Jesus . . ."

"That's it, isn't it? This whole thing — to scare you, to get back at you for cheating — and Michael hurt his own

wife in the process. Oh my God. That's why there's so much
. . . did he kill her?"

"No."

"How do you know? Where is she? And what does any
of it have to do with your brother?" Julie wasn't going to let
up now. She was getting answers if she had to tear them out.
"Did he introduce you to Monique, or something? Talk to
me!"

"It just happened, okay?" Colton was forceful, finally
losing control.

"What? What 'just happened?' You mean meeting her?
Or this morning?" She leaned forward in her chair the way
she might with a client, sensing a breakthrough. "*How* did it
happen?"

He sighed. "Keith came by the restaurant a couple of
times . . . It was just after you and I got engaged. You were
leaving one night as he was coming in and you saw him. He
said he wanted to know how I was doing. I didn't think he
had an agenda."

She knew it. She *knew* she'd seen him somewhere. "How
long had it been since you two had seen each other?"

"Years. He reached out after the magazine, left me a
voicemail, but I never responded."

The magazine. He meant *Climbing Magazine*. Colton had
done an ascent in Patagonia, a big trip with other climbers.
Julie had been there, too — but as a spectator, a girlfriend;
not a climber. The magazine people showed up and took a
million photos, wrote a big article.

Colton said, "He found me on Instagram, sent me a
DM. I didn't even respond to him. And then, later on, he
came by the brewery."

"How did you meet *her*?"

"It was actually through Keith. She saw me in *Climbing*,
too, wanted to meet me, he said. Keith told her we were
related but . . . "

"She found out you had a brother when even *I* didn't
know?"

But Colton seemed distracted, mumbling, "It was all that fucking article."

"Well, if she knew about Keith, did she know you were engaged? Did she say she was married?"

He gave her a hard look. "No. She never told me she was married. Not at first."

"Not at first."

"Michael's a serious guy, Julie. He's not someone to mess around with."

"I'm not. What are you saying?"

She thought about the way he'd pulled on Colton's arm, studied him when Colton had passed out, like a psycho killer wondering how long it would take his latest victim to bleed out. *Five minutes? Or six? Maybe I'll set my watch . . .*

"I just . . ." Colton was saying. "I should've never agreed to see her. I know that. Oh God, I should've never agreed . . ." He bent his head forward, apparently unable to continue.

"So did she know about me?"

"Yes," he said, sniffling. "Oh yes. She knew about you."

"What does that mean? And she didn't care?"

He didn't answer.

"God, Colton . . ." Julie felt that sickness in her gut again.

She let out a heavy breath. "At least we got the call out to 911. I mean, if the van, or anything, can be traced to Michael . . . Maybe it's good that he has a record. And he's friends with Keith, and Keith is your half-brother, that's a solid connection. The police might even think to look here. Because it's your dad's cabin, right?"

Colton made no response.

"They broke in the bedroom door. We left the back window open. It's got to look bad to the police. They'll find us. Colton? Why are you looking at me like that? Colton . . . ? Why aren't you answering me?"

He wouldn't talk, and turned away.

"Colton!"

When he finally faced her again, his wet eyes were red.

"Tell me you called 911," she said. "I heard you. And there were sirens . . ."

But his tears keep coming. Silently, his eyes wetter by the second, staring at her, now his lower lip quivering, too.

Oh no . . .

"You didn't call 911?" Her own voice came from far away.

His mouth opened, saliva stretching between his lips. The tears mingled with mucous leaking from his nose into his stupid, stupid mustache.

Slowly, he shook his head.

"No. I never called 911."

CHAPTER FOURTEEN

"But I heard the sirens," Julie said. "They were coming."

Maybe Colton was lying *now*. Part of some idea he had about protecting her, like he'd been pretending not to know her.

Though if memory served, the sirens *had* gone silent fairly quickly. She also remembered questioning whether police would raise sirens like that if they were responding to a home-invasion call. Maybe? Perhaps more importantly, if she was completely honest with herself, the noise had sounded like a different kind of emergency response. There was a distinct pitch to an ambulance, different from local or state police.

No . . . it makes no sense.

"You fought with him," she said, meaning Keith. A real fight, too. So why fake a call to the authorities, but at the same time try to stop the intruders? Colton had even jumped out of a second-story window after her, dislocating his shoulder in the process.

Her head was spinning with the incongruities.

He'd stopped crying but sat stooped over like he might be sick again. He mumbled something inaudible.

"What? What, honey? What?"

Despite her anger, this was still her partner of five years and the tenderness was automatic. She didn't have all the answers yet. Colton seemed to be in as much a predicament as she was in, even if he'd played a role.

"I tried to stop it," he said.

"I know you did. So why didn't you call?"

But it hit her: he was protecting Keith. Maybe protecting himself, too. Not wanting the police involved.

It no longer seemed to be about a jealous husband. Though Michael *did* seem to hate Colton, and want to hurt him, this was about more than a cuckold's revenge, or teaching Colton a lesson.

Because why would Keith be involved? And why abduct her, too? This was kidnapping, for God's sake, a federal crime. The FBI got involved with things like this.

Colton had to be involved in something big.

He straightened in the chair and looked up at the ceiling, saying, "Ah, God."

He looked at her, and his eyes were hard and glittery, his mouth a grim line, and for a moment she thought he was resolving to tell her. But footsteps crunched toward the door, and a key hit the lock, and the door swung open. Keith came striding in, only glancing at them as he moved toward the kitchen. He ran water from the tap into a brightly colored plastic cup with cartoon characters on it and drank.

He looked at his watch.

The clock on the wall still read 4:10, but Julie thought it might be about one in the afternoon. "What time is it?"

"What do you care?"

He was still upset about earlier, it seemed. About the way she'd probed into his childhood with Colton. The bullying and the hay bales.

"I'm sorry if I made you uncomfortable before," she said. It came out genuine, and it was — no matter the person, everyone had started somewhere in life, everyone had experiences beyond their control when they were young. Bringing attention back to those old memories, reprocessing them and healing, was tricky work. She'd been indelicate with Keith.

He shrugged. "Whatever. I'm a big boy. I can handle it." After a moment, he set down the plastic cup. He walked to Colton and knelt down in front of him. "Have you been *crying*, big bro?"

Colton sniffed noisily but maintained eye contact. "Fire's going out."

Keith shrugged, but he went over and stoked it with a few fresh pieces of wood, some smoke escaping, and with it the scent of burning pine.

This could be my life, Julie thought. And maybe in some alternate universe, it was. Maybe in some other universe, she was sitting here at this cabin with her fiancé and his brother because they were spending a weekend together. Colton's father was not estranged from him, but a jolly older man who liked to hunt and fish and had this lovely cabin in the Southern Adirondacks, to which Colton and Julie sometimes snuck away. This time, they'd invited Keith, Colton's baby brother by four years. Maybe Keith's girlfriend, too. A double-date, a wilderness cabin weekend, like you see in the movies.

Keith walked back toward the center of the room. He definitely bore a likeness to Colton, especially in the nose and mouth. They shared a Mediterranean complexion, but the hair was different — where Colton's was wavy-curly, Keith's was pin-straight. And Keith had blue eyes, where Colton's were brown. You couldn't really see the resemblance by picking out any one feature: it was an overall thing, a kind of essence.

Keith looked between them. "So."

They waited.

"I'm sure you two did a lot of talking while I was out there. I heard you."

Once again, Colton seemed to search the floor for answers.

"Cole? The time is coming, buddy. You know it is. When Michael gets back, it's all going to have to come out."

Colton calculated it silently.

Keith shifted his attention to Julie. He'd changed clothes into jeans and thick logging boots, a dark-blue ski parka dirty around the wrists, patched on one sleeve by a square of duct tape. He pulled the barstool around the wood block in the kitchen and sat down. "I guess the storm is going to be pretty bad. We didn't really give it enough credit. But can you blame us? Weather people love to stir the pot."

The thought of blizzards and storms took her back to childhood, playing board games by candlelight during long blackouts.

The thought of her mother suddenly seized her, emotion swelling, and Julie held a breath, careful not to let it become a sob.

Arlene had gotten sick when Julie and her brother were still kids, but she'd beaten it. Julie had vivid memories of that — she'd been fourteen when her mother had shaved her head, gone through radiation, and into remission. The hair had come back, the weight had come back, and for seven more years, they'd all believed it was over.

"So, you came back early because of the storm," Keith was saying. "What was the thing you were doing out there?"

"I was attending a conference for mental health therapists. About social media and its impact on teenagers."

"They sent everyone home early, or you just decided to book it out of there?"

"There was a keynote speaker for the final day, and she was flying in from . . . I don't remember. But she was worried about the flight home, so she wanted to cancel. And the organizers just decided to let the whole last day go."

"And so everyone left?"

"Some people did. Some people wanted to wait it out, but I got going."

"So you get home early, and — big surprise — there's your man in bed with another woman. That must've been like a gut-punch."

It had been. And the way he phrased it now caused her to relive some of that pain again, in an instant. But his callousness felt a little forced. She saw humanity in Keith; she got the sense he was playing a part. Like Colton.

"It definitely hurt," she told Keith. "It still hurts. I never expected this from Colton — I planned to spend my life with him."

"And now? Not planning to spend your life with him anymore? Have you passed a point of no return?"

She faced her fiancé, who managed to look at her this time. A mix of things there. Guilt, shame, pride. Remorse.

"I don't know."

Keith clapped his hands once, loud, making her jump. "You hear that, Cole? You still got a chance, man. This is an amazing woman."

"Stop it," Colton said.

"Stop it? Stop what? I'm being a nice guy. And this situation, man, when she finds out . . ."

Colton looked back at the floor.

"So," Keith said, "you're there in the room, you've caught them in bed . . . what did you think of Monique?"

"What did I think of her?"

"Yeah."

"I don't know what you mean."

"I mean, this is the part I don't understand. When I got up there, she was already out of the room. But I mean . . . what? You never got a good look at her?"

The way he asked it sharpened Julie's attention. She saw Keith look at Colton, the two of them exchanging some wordless message. They clearly knew something about Monique she didn't.

"Her back was turned. She had the blanket pulled up around her, her hair was in her face."

"Yeah, she's got a lot of hair. Okay . . . that makes sense — her back was turned."

Julie wasn't sure what he meant. She thought back to the morning, the woman sitting on the edge of the bed, mostly facing away from her. Her model-esque body, her thick dark hair. It was a little longer than Julie's, but about the same color. Except for these observations, Julie hadn't been focused on her appearance. There had been way too much else going on.

"I saw her," Julie said. "I saw a woman in my bed who was not me. A woman who . . . didn't expect me." She thought to say more but stopped herself. There was nothing more worth saying. And it seemed like Keith was getting some kind of perverse thrill out of this. Even if some of his hard edges felt false, one thing seemed real — he really did like to torture Colton. Julie wondered if he hated him even more than Michael did.

"So, what are you thinking at that point?" he asked. "'You dirty skank?' Did you want to jump on her, rip her eyes out?"

"I didn't know her. I didn't blame her."

"Ah, well, that's big of you. Yeah, I guess in the heat of everything, you're not exactly able to take everything in. I've had times I didn't see shit, didn't understand. You got people everywhere, shit's blowing up, you don't know your ass from your elbow." He fell silent after that, set both feet down, then rose off the bar stool. After checking his watch again, he glanced at the door.

"When do you expect Michael back?" Julie changed the subject.

"Soon."

"Listen, Keith, I'm sure Michael is upset about what Monique and Colton did."

"I don't think he ever liked that part of it, no."

"He hurt Colton so bad he passed out."

Keith tilted his head. "True."

Still hoping there was something kind in him, someone that cared for his brother, she asked, "What would it take for you to let us go, right now, before he gets back?"

"Oh, I don't know." Keith studied Colton when he said it. "A lot."

She resettled herself. She was close now. She could feel it. "Colton didn't call 911."

"No. Colton wasn't supposed to call 911, that's true."

"Because he cares about you."

Keith shrugged it off. "He wasn't supposed to fight me, either."

Supposed to.

"What happened," Keith continued, "is that your man here got cold feet. Couldn't handle the pucker factor."

"I asked you not to do this," Colton interjected.

"Oh yeah? You asked me? You think you got some power over me? You think you're in charge here?"

"They're going to be here any minute," Colton said. "She's going to find out anyway."

"My point exactly. And when she does, she's gonna know you made a deal."

Julie's confidence began to drain, rapidly. "Colton? You made a *deal*? What does that mean?"

He stared away from her. "You weren't supposed to come home," he said, as if somehow this whole thing was her fault. "It wasn't supposed to happen until later. That was the deal."

"What deal*?*" It felt like the room was starting to tilt. "Colton, oh my God, what deal*?*"

He took a breath that settled his shoulders, deflated his chest. This was everything, the truth he'd been withholding all along. She knew it.

"The deal for them to take you."

CHAPTER FIFTEEN

State Police Investigator Louis Stamper smiled at the older couple. Though they hadn't been the ones to call 911, the Costas had the best view of the Spreniker place, across the street from them. They'd seen a van pull hastily away from the curb and rocket up the street.

"It was moving," Ray Costa said. "The driver was in a hurry. I thought it was . . . I didn't know what to think. Guy just needed to get somewhere. But then the police started showing up over there, and I figured it had something to do with it."

Costa, sixty-five, had been checking the skies for signs of inclement weather when the van took off. He didn't get a license plate, nor could he give a description of the driver. But Danice Costa, Ray's wife, said there'd been some break-ins in the area not long ago. "That's the first thing I thought," Ray Costa then said. "He wasn't acting like a delivery driver — he was acting like a getaway driver."

Stamper considered it all and chatted with them for a while longer, but Trooper Taylor had already taken their statements, so at about 10:15 a.m., Stamper stepped back outside into the gray morning.

"Big storm coming," he said to Taylor.

"Yeah. The usual March thing, I guess. Lake effect."

The cops walked down to the street, Stamper eyeing the Spreniker place. It looked like the ones to either side of it. The whole street was part of a recent development, the units were narrow but deep. On the back side was a small fenced-in yard, with an alley cutting between this street and the next, a place for accessing the backyards, leaving out trash bins, all of that.

Angela Daubin, at 1138 Waverly, across the street and two doors down, had made the 911 call. At seven o'clock that morning, she'd been standing just outside her door, giving her little Cavapoo dog a pee break. She'd actually seen the white van pull up and two men get out. Then she'd gone back inside. "But something told me to look again," she'd said. "Instinct."

Daubin was thirty-three, and a nurse. She lived with her husband and worked the night shift at St. Vincent's Hospital, nearby. She had wavy, short hair and a round face, lots of freckles. A paisley floral pattern decorated her nursing scrubs. She didn't know Julie Spreniker personally but had seen her a few times. "Seems nice. Drives one of those little grocery-getter cars. Dresses like she's, you know, a school teacher or something. I don't know what she does. Anyway, I went inside but kept the door cracked and watched. When I saw them standing on the stoop, there, talking, I don't know, it's like they were coming up with a plan. Then one of them pulled the gun."

She'd described the weapon as a "basic pistol," the men as average height, Caucasian. And the hats they were wearing — "just standard baseball hats. No teams or anything that I noticed."

"How did they get in?" Stamper asked. "Did they have a key? Someone let them in?"

"They just went right in. They seemed surprised, actually. One guy, he turned the knob, and they kind of looked at each other. By this point, the only reason I didn't call yet is because I just didn't know, it could be a joke, or something.

Maybe they were spoofing somebody. Even the gun . . . Stuff like this happens, even in nice neighborhoods. I just thought, *This is some kind of prank*. But like I said, just for half a second. And then I heard the scream for help."

Daubin, too, had reported all of this to a uniformed cop before Stamper had gotten there.

"You heard the scream of a woman that sounded like she was just inside, you said. Maybe close to the front door, or . . . ?"

"No, I don't think so — I think it came from deeper in the house." Her eyes were wide but pink from fatigue. She'd come home from her shift and hadn't been able to get in bed yet.

"And that's when you called 911."

"That's exactly right."

"But you kept watching."

"I did. I stood at the window as I called. I gave my address, and the neighbor's address, and I told them I'd seen two men going inside, thought one had a gun, and I'd heard a scream."

Daubin had also been unable to see a license plate.

"I thought about going out there to get a look, but I didn't know when they'd be coming back. If they might see me . . ."

"No, you did the right thing."

"Anyway, the one guy came out the front again and got back in the van."

"Just one guy," Stamper had confirmed.

"Yeah, just the one guy. Average height. Short dark hair. Beard, I think. Maybe just a goatee, like I told the trooper. That's all I could see. Otherwise, he was a blur. And he took off."

"Which way?"

She pointed. "Up the street. Right there. Went flying around the corner and out of sight."

"And no one else came out the front of the house?"

"No."

"How long did you keep watch out the window?"

"I mean, I've pretty much been watching, off and on, since seven o'clock this morning."

Stamper had talked with Daubin for another few minutes, but she was clearly tired and he told her she should get some sleep — he'd be in touch if he needed anything else. And then he had followed up with the Costas, who confirmed the time and the white cargo van racing away up the street.

Stamper crossed that street now with Trooper Taylor, headed back for Spreniker's place. Taylor had put out a BOLO on the van and so far they'd gotten several hits: two delivery vans, public transportation for some special needs folks and an efficiency-minded family man.

He stopped and looked up the steps — a dozen of them — to the front door of Spreniker's grayish-blue townhouse. The narrow unit had three floors; you walked into the second floor off the street. He'd already been in there — definitely signs of a struggle. Bedroom door busted in, dirty shoe prints everywhere, drops of blood. It was enough to consider it a crime scene, to get the Forensic Identification Unit in there to start collection and processing, get Kay Howells looking at the blood.

He carried on around the block, tracing the route the van might've taken after the one man left the house. *And right in broad daylight? Running in and out of this place on a crowded suburban street?* The guy was either reckless and stupid, or maybe showy and stupid. *Who does that? Who rolls up to a place at seven in the morning? And to do what? Burgle it?*

Spreniker wasn't supposed to be there, that was one thing. Stamper had called her work, talked to her supervisor, and the mild-mannered therapist had been in Buffalo for a conference that had ended a day early. Her vehicle had been identified out on the street — a Honda Fit. The drive from Buffalo took a little over three hours. So, as long as she'd left by about 3:30 a.m. and didn't make any stops, she would have been home before the men entered the premises.

But Colton Rossi, the boyfriend, had also been there. At least, his phone had been found on the bedroom floor.

Altogether, it made the whole thing seem like an abduction. The variable was just whether it was supposed to be only Rossi, or Spreniker, too. In that case, the abductors' actions weren't showy so much as they were hasty, even improvisational.

"So, okay, the van comes around the street corner here . . ." He said it as much to himself as to Taylor, who had joined him. They walked along until they reached the mouth of the alley behind the townhouses. He went until he was at the Spreniker backyard where the gate was unlocked and ajar, crime-scene tape crossing in front.

". . . Just one guy in it — the other guy is still inside, maybe? Fighting with them in the bedroom? Does he flush the two of them — Spreniker and her fiancé, Rossi — out the window?"

"It was open, yeah," Taylor reminded him. "The neighbor never saw them come out the front, and they're not showing up anywhere else."

Stamper bent under the tape and walked into the yard, careful to stay to the side. "Let's just go right against the fence here, like that — step in my tracks . . . Okay." He could see the space just below the window. A few flakes had fallen in the last hour or so, but the evidence was there, the snow disheveled in this spot. It looked like maybe three different sets of prints leading away toward the open back-gate.

"Yep. I bet they do a high jump from the bedroom window. The ground slopes up to here, the bottom floor of the house goes into the ground, like a basement, so instead of a third-story window, it's really second-story back here, but that's still a good jump." He looked for blood but didn't see any. "Of course, they could've maybe made it downstairs and come out this way, too." He pointed at the door over to one side of the back of the house, but as he said it, he only saw one set of footprints that seemed fresh coming from the door. He tracked these into the yard, where they blended in with other tracks, clumps of snow, bits of branches and other tree-leavings, just a general mess of things.

"Go back to the gate and out into the alley again, what's the distance to the end of the alley, the street?"

Taylor did as he was told. "Twenty yards."

"Maybe the guy in the van, he comes around, he's waiting there, while the second guy pushes them to him. Spreniker and the boyfriend. They get bundled into the van, and away they go."

Stamper stood there a minute, his breath rising, as he pondered it.

Colton Rossi.

The name rang a distant bell. Stamper's colleague, Lindsay Cuthbert, was working up a full background on both Rossi and Spreniker, going through DMV, birth certificates, credit history. She'd tell him if the name Rossi turned up anything else.

"A robbery doesn't end in an abduction, though, usually," Stamper said.

"No, not usually," Taylor agreed.

"This started as something else. Some kind of plan that got bungled up. Because she came home early, maybe?"

"Maybe."

Well, theories were only that. It was time to get to work on the evidence, on more witnesses. While the troopers continued with door-to-doors, Stamper would talk to people Spreniker and Rossi knew.

Rossi worked at Herkimer Brewing, apparently. Pay stubs were found in the kitchen. Maybe he'd start there.

CHAPTER SIXTEEN

"The Hadza tribe," Keith said. "Ever heard of them?"

Julie shook her head; she hadn't. Nor was she in the mood for any more of Keith's games.

You weren't supposed to come home, Colton had just said.

It wasn't supposed to happen until later.

That was the deal.

"African tribe," Keith said. "They hunt baboons, talk to birds. They can run at top speed for hours, stop and dig a hole and take a few handfuls of brown water — that's all they need. *Hooah.*"

He acted excited, almost giddy, using military slang like he was back on deployment.

"Ripped with muscles, back muscles, ab muscles — there is *zero* obesity. Zero depression or anxiety or addiction or anything like that at all. They don't know what a supermarket *is.* Do you know what's wrong with the world, why civilization is ending?"

Julie made an enquiring noise. She felt on the verge of giving up. Of just caving inward, turning to mush, crying until the end of this horrible day. Whatever it was all about.

"Utter dependency on the system," Keith was saying. "Complete and total helplessness. Take the system away, and society collapses. People will just *die*. I've been on foot patrols in the Panjwai district, and let me tell you, those people over there, they know what's happening. They know Americans and Europeans and the Chinese are the only ones who can do anything about it, about the coming collapse, but they're the ones most helpless to stop it. Because dependent consumers are just too damn profitable. Got to keep the system working."

"Keith . . ." Julie said. "Please."

He looked at her with disappointment. "Oh. Come on. There's nothing I can do about the situation you're in. It's already done. But listen to what I'm saying."

"I hear what you're saying," she said quickly. "I do. I think the whole world is in a bad way, Keith. And that we have much bigger problems than what's going on right here in this room."

He stopped talking for a moment, like she'd given him something to think about it.

"I also know that you could just let us go, Keith."

"Did you ever read the Book of Revelation?"

"Michael is gone. You could just let us go before he gets back."

"It's not what people think it is. It's not about people going up into heaven."

"Keith, if Michael left, he's going to get caught." She straightened up a little, some strength returning. "That van? Racing around in broad daylight? Grabbing us and throwing us in the back? There are cops looking for us right now."

Keith glanced at Colton, who was just sitting there, not saying anything.

Julie went on, "Colton might not have made the 911 call, but I heard sirens. I know my neighbors — they're nosy. Somebody saw something. And somebody called."

She let this sink in, but Keith only shrugged. "Doesn't matter," he said. "It's already all happening — there's no stopping it."

"But what is the *point*?" she asked, keeping calm as best she could. "What is the objective?"

She used that word on purpose, and saw she had his attention, even if he wasn't going to answer.

"I don't have any money. Keith . . . Colton tried to stop you. He didn't call 911 because he doesn't want you to go to prison — you're his brother. Whatever you did, whatever plan you and he made, it's not too late. But if you stay here, if you keep us here right now, you will go. People get caught now, for everything. I work with police all the time, and forensic specialists . . . Trust me. Nobody gets away with anything these days. If you're lucky, you get a Netflix special."

He smiled.

"But really, if you let us go, they'll go easier on you."

"You'll put in a good word for me?"

She sighed, squeezed her eyes shut a moment. "Someone saw. I know my neighborhood. There's a retired couple that live across the street. There's a nurse who works at St. Vincent's. My neighbor in back drives for UPS and—"

Keith held up his hand. "All right. Enough."

Things were quiet for a while, and she looked at the broken clock. It had to be actually getting close to 4:10 now. The light was changing outside; a few snowflakes were drifting down.

That was the deal.

The deal for them to take you.

She realized she'd been avoiding that part. Sitting here for the past ten minutes or so, she hadn't quite taken the full measure of that statement, didn't know if she could really wrap her mind around it.

And while it was the most revealing piece of Colton's confession, it was also the most horrifying.

Take *her*? Why?

Keith added some wood to the fire. He stood looking at his phone a moment, but with no service at the cabin, he couldn't be looking at much. Then he sat on the bar stool again and studied her.

"First of all, Michael used another vehicle just now. He didn't take the van. Second of all, this whole thing would already be over if you hadn't showed up early. And your man there, Mr. Coltrane, he's the one thinking with his dick. So don't look at me like I'm the bad guy."

"I understand. But Keith . . . I just don't have anything. And if it's about sex—"

He gave her a hard look. "It's not about sex. Not for me. Maybe for him."

"Keith," Colton said suddenly. "Come on."

"What? She was supposed to seduce you, yeah, but you two weren't supposed to develop a fucking *thing*, man. What did she tell you? She was going to leave him? After it was all over, she was going to leave him for you? I mean — how fucked up are you?"

Keith stared at Colton. So did Julie. She didn't like what she saw, either. Colton looked determined, his jaw set, rage emanating through his wet eyes. "You don't know anything about it."

"I don't? Sure I do. You're a preening, self-obsessed dickbag, Colton. When they came to me with the idea, I said, *absolutely it will work.* Because I knew you were shallow as fuck. And I knew you couldn't resist this one. Too kinky, man. Too far out."

Colton squeezed his eyes shut as he slowly shook his head. He looked like he wanted to be anywhere else. That he wished fervently to undo all that had been done.

"Just talk to me," Julie said to him, her voice soft. "We can figure this out. What's Keith talking about, exactly? What did they offer you? Did they blackmail you?"

"Do you believe in God? Or fate?" Keith asked her. "What do you believe in?"

"Keith . . ."

"No, I'm saying . . . I'm telling you what you want to know. Because this whole thing — you showing up early, busting in on them, but not really getting a good look at her — that seems almost like some kind of fate to me."

She didn't know how to respond at first. Mostly because she was still trying to make sense of Colton's emotions, why he seemed so deeply ashamed, beyond having cheated.

Her traumatized brain fed her bits and pieces of that morning.

You never really got a good look at her.

Hadn't she? A good body, that wild volume of hair.

Her face. You never got a real direct look at her face.

No, maybe that was true, she hadn't. But so what? Would she have recognized her?

There was something familiar — you felt it.

"I mean, think of all the things that had to come together," Keith interrupted her thoughts. "You two had to meet. It was on Facebook, right?" He meant her and Colton.

"We had friends in common," Julie stipulated. "And he reached out to me. He knew someone I dated in high school."

"Sounds like destiny. And then, weren't you a big deal or something? Some kind of athlete?"

Julie didn't answer.

"I figured your athletic backgrounds, or whatever, that's how you hit it off. And are you older than him?"

"Yes, I'm almost two years older than Colton is."

The big baby.

Keith nodded like this made all the sense in the world. "So you're like — what? Thirty-two? Thirty-three?"

"Thirty-three."

"And Monique is right there, almost the same age, thirty-two. I mean, the odds are just . . . That this all came together like it did. And then here we are, and you still don't know. You still can't see it. That's why I asked if you believed in fate."

"Keith," she said. One last try. *Go for it.* "You can stop all of this, right now. Nothing is worth hurting us, and I think you know it. So, please, for the last time — before Michael gets here, I'm begging you to think it through. Really think it through. You can help your brother. You can help me. Whatever you think about fate — it isn't this. You can change it all, right now."

His expression darkened. "You don't know shit about me, or what I need. You don't even know about your own boyfriend, or who he is."

"Shut up," Colton said.

Keith ignored it, focusing on Julie. "Plus, I'm telling you, there's something bigger than us at work here. It's not unthinkable that she found you, but it's pretty high odds. So there's that kind of divine purpose I'm talking about. We don't want to fuck with that."

"That she found *me*?" Julie wondered. Wasn't this all about her finding Colton?

"You can feel good, maybe, that you're a part of this bigger picture," Keith said. "And listen — as far as your neighbors seeing us or whatever . . . The plan may have changed, but everything happened just the way it needed to. You're now missing, Julie, and they're never going to find you. Not in this life, anyway."

Colton yelled and rushed his brother, crashing into him, knocking him back against the wood block, the two of them spilling onto the floor. Colton screamed, his face red, and he hit Keith in the mouth and in the nose, again and again.

CHAPTER SEVENTEEN

The Herkimer Brewing Company had just opened the doors for lunch. The restaurant was spacious, the dim lighting hipster-cool. Large glass windows viewed a central room with large steel containers for brewing beer, Stamper figured. He wasn't much of a connoisseur. Back in his drinking days, it was Molson Canadian or Amstel. Budweiser worked, too. Whatever was cold and at hand.

The manager was Warren Flandreau, a big man, dressed in jeans and a T-shirt advertising his business, his wide face peppered with beard stubble. Stamper had the faintest concern, back of his mind, that Flandreau might break his bones during the handshake.

"Yeah, Colton has been here over five years," Flandreau said. "He's one of my best. Hired to run the kitchen. But he ended up training his sous chef to basically take over, and he moved out to the front-of-house."

"Does that happen often?"

"In this business? Not really. You want to sit down? Can I get you anything?"

Stamper had taken the seat at the bar with every intention to move back to Flandreau's office eventually, if he had one, or at least somewhere private. But first he wanted to get a look around.

"No, I'm good," he told Flandreau, but the big man moved around behind the bar anyway, as if he might serve Stamper a drink.

Stamper counted two waitresses so far, moving about briskly, but not yet in the weeds of a full lunch rush. Only three tables had people. The patrons didn't seem to pay him any mind, but the waitstaff did. Like they could tell something was up. *Who's that talking to Warren?*

He noted their lack of uniforms — one in jeans, the other black slacks. Stamper himself was style-conscious, always had been. If there was a stereotypical plainclothes-cop look, he tried going the other way, getting away with what he could — jeans, a dark-blue button-down shirt, black suit jacket beneath his ski parka. He kept his hair short but didn't go in for the buzz-cuts and fade, letting it get shaggy around his ears and back of his neck a bit. He looked better with a beard, but a beard was pushing it.

"Wow, so five years," he said to Flandreau. "You must know him a little bit?"

"Oh absolutely. I know Colton. He's a good kid."

"When was the last time you saw him?"

"Last night. His shift. He does the weekend nights — he's got the prime spots — but he does two weekdays, too. Tuesday and Wednesday. You being here, him not, I'm getting the feeling I'm going to have to call Mo."

"Mo?"

"Maureen. She's our other bartender."

"What time does his shift start?"

Flandreau looked at his watch. "Starts now. The waitstaff gets here at ten and sets up and we open at eleven, Tuesday through Saturday. Closed Sunday and Monday." He said it like he'd said it a thousand times, which he undoubtedly had.

Stamper noticed the younger waitress glancing over at him again as she walked away from her table. And then again, as she pushed into the kitchen.

"So what's going on?" Flandreau asked.

"Well, I guess you better call Maureen," Stamper said. "We're not sure where Mr. Rossi is at the moment. He lives over on Waverly with his fiancée?"

"Yeah, yeah." Flandreau's eyes were wide, his eyebrows climbing onto his forehead.

"Well, there was a disturbance, a neighbor called 911, and a unit responded about five minutes later, found that no one was home."

"What do you think happened?"

"We don't know. That's the thing." Which was true. And even if he had a theory, he wouldn't share it with Warren Flandreau. The less you said, the better.

"Maybe you have an office? Somewhere we can talk more privately?"

"Uh, sure," Flandreau said. He seemed a bit shocked by the whole thing. "Right this way."

* * *

It was downstairs, the back corner of a basement filled with dry storage — bottled beers and soda tanks, massive bags of pretzels and chips. Flandreau sat at a desk, seeming to fill half the small office with his shoulders alone.

They talked for a little while about how he and Colton had met — "a routine interview." How he was a reliable employee and a good bartender, "but a great chef," Flandreau said. "We really hated to lose him from the kitchen, but he was just miserable back there. He's much better public-facing. I think he likes it, he likes to be out there, interacting. He's a people person."

There'd been nothing out of the ordinary over the past few days or weeks. Business as usual. And Rossi had no personal troubles he was aware of.

They moved on to talking about Julie Spreniker, but Flandreau had even less to say. "She hardly ever comes in. It's not like she hangs out."

92

Stamper thought about that a little, about a man working in a place that was very social, probably with lots of attractive women coming and going, and a fiancée who just kept away. He'd worked in restaurants when trying to be an actor, and they could be full of drama. Managers sleeping with waitresses, chefs sleeping with waitresses. But that certainly wasn't everywhere.

* * *

He caught up with Brianna, one of the servers, on his way out, just for a couple of quick questions. Her name seemed more suited to the times than Maureen.

"Yeah, Colton is great," she said. "He's my favorite bartender to work with. Mo is okay, I mean — she's cool. But Colton is fun. We always have fun . . ." The young waitress acted like she was going to say more but went quiet.

"He seem like everything was good in his life?" Stamper asked.

"Oh yeah, sure. Colton's a happy guy, I guess. Seems to have everything he wants."

She seemed a little disappointed about that.

"You ever meet his fiancée?"

"Yeah, I did, once. I was here after the shift, hanging out, just having one before I went home. And she came in — they were going somewhere, I think. Taking some trip. And he introduced her to me."

"When was that? You remember?"

"About a year ago, maybe."

"Okay. Thanks."

She was giving him a funny look. "Do I know you from somewhere?"

He thought about how to respond. "You ever get pulled over for speeding? I was on road patrol before I made investigator."

She grinned, coy. "No. It wasn't that. I mean, yeah, I've been pulled over. But that's not where I know you from."

93

He took a breath, held it. "Maybe you saw me in a commercial?"

"Like, a TV commercial?"

He let it out. "Yeah, truck commercial. For a GMC truck. It was national. It was the beginning and the end of my acting career."

"That's it!" She got excited, but it faded quickly — something darker seemed to cross her mind.

He waited, hoping she might come out with whatever it was.

"Okay, well, I ah . . ." She started to leave.

"Hey." Stamper handed her his card. "Call if you think of anything else, okay?" He gave her a look, friendly but serious.

"Yeah, okay." And she hurried away.

CHAPTER EIGHTEEN

The noise of an engine stirred Julie out of a tortured daze. She sat up straighter, nerves tightening.

Colton was there beside her, slumped in his chair, hands tied behind him now, dislocated shoulder be damned. If he was in pain, he wasn't showing it. He wasn't showing much of anything since attacking Keith; it was as if he'd gone into some kind of survival trance.

The engine came closer, then shut off. Doors opened and closed.

Julie heard voices.

Keith met her gaze, absently tonguing at his split and swelling upper lip. Then he watched the door.

Her heart thumped as she started to sweat. This was it. Or at least, it felt like it. Keith had continually kicked the can down the road, never giving her direct answers.

Do you believe in God?

Or fate?

But he'd let a few things slip.

It's not unthinkable that she found you, but it's pretty high odds . . .

Footsteps coming toward the main cabin. Murmuring from outside the door.

Keith glanced at Julie one more time, a crooked smile on his face. The smile disappeared when his gaze flicked to Colton. But Colton was still gone, acting unaware that any of it was happening.

The door opened and Michael came in, his face blank and inscrutable, snow in his hair and eyelashes.

And behind him, a woman. At first, hidden by his broad shoulders.

"Welcome back," Keith said. He stepped aside so the two arrivals could come in, Michael pulling the woman behind him by the arm.

She wore the same black cocktail dress Julie had watched her shimmy into that morning in the bedroom, but now she had a bag covering her head.

Michael led her to the stool where Keith had been perched for most of the afternoon, where he sat her down. Monique's hands were tied behind her. At least she'd been given boots — Sorrel-brand galoshes — and a maroon-colored windbreaker. But she was shivering, and she moaned like she might be gagged but trying to speak.

"Shut up," Michael said to her. And he turned his eyes on Colton. "So? How are we doing?" He walked closer to Colton and frowned at him. Then he slapped his hands together in front of Colton's face, making Julie jump. Colton jumped, too — he was cognizant after all. He blinked a few times and looked up at Michael with glassy eyes.

"What happened here?" Michael asked. "Got yourself all tied up?"

"He attacked me," Keith explained.

"Hey," Michael said, snapping his fingers like a doctor trying to revive a patient. "Hey, you see what I brought? I brought you a present. There she is." And he gestured to Monique, sitting awkwardly on the bar stool. Julie could hear her breaths, see the sack sucking in and out. Could smell her, too — an aroma that brought back the morning, the odors of sleep and lust and shampoo all mixing together. This woman Julie had briefly hated, not for who she was but what she represented.

Michael seemed to give up on Colton and focused on Julie instead. As he gave her a long look, she saw that thing in his eyes she'd noticed earlier that morning, turning her face one way and the other, saying "Wow," like he couldn't quite believe what he was seeing.

"All right," Monique said. "It's getting hot in here."

Her voice surprised Julie. She wasn't gagged after all. Even more surprising — her words carried authority.

What is going on . . .

Maybe it *did* all go back to Michael getting revenge, punishing Colton. Maybe it was some kinky sex thing, and Monique and Michael had already made up. Maybe this was some kind of role-playing, now.

"It's just so fucking amazing," Michael said, staring at Julie. That thing in his eyes — that disbelief — still there. "I can't help myself."

"Well? I can't breathe in this thing, so . . . ."

Julie saw the sudden anger in Michael's face, and he stalked over to her. "You're the one that asked for this." He reached like he was about to pull the bag off her head, but she reared back, away from him. "Hold on — just a second. Describe it to me first."

"Describe it?"

"What does she look like?"

He seemed perplexed for a moment, like he didn't understand the question. Julie was having a hard time following, too. She noticed Colton had come around, though, and was watching the event unfold with a kind of morbid curiosity.

"She looks . . . like she has no idea."

"Damn," Monique said sarcastically, from inside the burlap sack. "That's descriptive."

"She looks like she's expecting you to be a victim. Okay? The poor wife of an abusive husband. A jealous husband who wants to punish his slut wife. Who wants to—"

"All right. Jesus. I just wanted to enjoy the moment."

"Yeah, but none of it's helping our timeline," Michael said, glancing at his watch. "I gotta get going. This has taken way too long."

"I had errands to run. And I couldn't use the GPS. Christ — I just wanted to have a little fun. This one fun, unexpected thing. All right, fine — do it."

Julie, barely understanding any of what they were talking about, nevertheless felt a new and growing fear. Keith moved a little closer, wanting to see everything clearly. Colton had at last emerged from his fugue state, now rapt with attention.

Something was going on here that she hadn't seen coming. The key to this whole thing.

Monique wanted this? But why? Because she'd trapped Colton? Why had Michael been gawking at Julie all morning like some kind of specimen on display?

It was all going to be answered when the bag came off the woman's head. Julie just didn't know how.

And then Michael grabbed a handful of the burlap and pulled.

The bag came off, up and away. Monique took a deep breath of air and wiggle her nose like she'd been about to sneeze. She pushed hair out of her face, blinking. That wild volume of hair, pulled into strands by the burlap sack, like she was just waking up even now.

And then she finally turned to Julie, looked her right in the eyes.

Julie stared back, uncomprehending.

It was like looking in a mirror. The woman sitting across from Julie was her identical twin.

CHAPTER NINETEEN

Stamper finished his sandwich, then stared out the windshield a minute as he picked his teeth. The mental health clinic was a squat, gray building in the snow. The snow fell around it, in big fluffy flakes. The governor had already declared a state of emergency. It was going to be a doozy, they said.

Stamper tucked his notebook into his inner breast pocket and went in.

Julie Spreniker's supervisor was a tall, slender woman decorated with a scarf and earrings that reminded him of something Greco-Roman. She showed him to Spreniker's office, understated but well-appointed with landscape paintings and a large potted ficus tree in the corner.

Spreniker saw between eight and twelve clients a day, the supervisor said.

"Anything unusual lately?" Stamper asked.

"How do you mean?"

"I know you can't comment on any of her clients. I mean, how has Ms. Spreniker seemed?"

"Good. She's been fine. Obviously, she hasn't been here this week — the conference in Buffalo was Monday, Tuesday, and supposed to be today."

"And tonight and tomorrow are supposed to be pretty bad with this storm."

"The county will likely close tomorrow," she confirmed. "I'm actually going to be sending some people home early tonight."

He checked his watch. 2:15. "So, even though the conference ended early, did you expect Ms. Spreniker at work today?"

"No. I did try to call her, though, just to check in."

"What time was that?"

She glanced up at the ceiling. "Ah, right about nine, I think. Just after group soup."

He guessed that meant *group supervision*.

She moved to the desk and touched the back of the swivel chair there, gave it a thoughtful twist. If she was going to say something else, she decided against it, instead offering Stamper a pleasant smile.

He picked it up: "And what happened when you tried to call Ms. Spreniker?"

"Nothing. It went straight to voicemail."

It's what had happened when he'd called, too. Could just be the phone was powered down. It could also mean damaged, or out of range. He'd endeavored to have it pinged and was waiting to hear back, along with the court order to go through Rossi's phone, the one found at the scene.

"And her fiancé — have you met him?"

"A few times, yes."

"Any thoughts on him?"

The supervisor narrowed her eyes a bit. She had elegant cheekbones, a wide mouth. Stamper got the idea that she could be a tough boss when needed.

"Julie seems happy," she said finally.

He nodded and smiled politely. "And no issues lately, nothing in her personal life, you said. Just humming right along."

"Just humming right along," she agreed.

"You mind if I look around a little bit?"

"Be my guest. I'll need to stay here in the room, though."

"Of course."

He poked around Spreniker's desk and found everything was tidy, with the usual items: a jar of pens and pencils, a stapler, a Scotch tape dispenser. She kept a photo of herself and Colton standing in front of a steep rocky mountain, red straps girdling them, shiny carabiners hanging copiously. He picked up the framed image. "She's into rock climbing?"

"Ah, no, I wouldn't say so. She's gone on a couple of trips."

He looked around a little bit more — Spreniker's filing cabinet was off-limits unless he had a court order — and the supervisor accompanied him on the way out.

In the car, snow falling more thickly now, he went through Colton Rossi's Instagram on his own phone. He'd run roughshod through it earlier but now scrolled with different eyes. Lots of pictures of the dude on rocks, hanging off of rocks and summiting rocks with his hands triumphantly in the air.

To "send" meant to "ascend," basically, to successfully reach the top of a climb. A belayer at the base of the rock managed the rope that helped the climber in case of a fall or slip. Colton did lots of free soloing, though, without ropes.

Julie Spreniker made some of the photos. Stamper had to go back quite a ways — two years — to find the image framed on her desk. She hadn't gone climbing since then, it seemed, but she'd been with him since, on the ground watching. One of the images had garnered lots of attention: *Chiaro di Luna*, Patagonia, six months ago, Colton on the summit, grinning ear-to-ear in a green jacket and reflective shades. The caption read: *Made CLIMBING MAGAZINE!*

Most recently, though, his Instagram featured a short series of images at the bar where he worked. The Hammer IPA was a new beer from Herkimer Brewing, and there'd been a big celebration around that about a week prior. Since then, a few selfies, and one picture of a pile of ropes and clips and belts — rock climbing gear — with a caption about an upcoming climb that included a "big wall" he couldn't wait to reveal.

Stamper put the phone away, thinking about the splintered bedroom door and the open bedroom window. The tracks leading away through the snow. He had a footprint tech there now, hopefully getting some good shoe sizes before the snow buried everything deep. What had happened to this local therapist and her rock-climbing, bartending boyfriend? They seemed like normal, everyday people.

But then, wasn't that always just the way?

* * *

Back at the townhouse, the crime-scene people were wrapping up and didn't have much to tell him other than what he already knew, although there was one thing that was interesting.

"There's vomit in the bedroom trash can," one of the techs said.

Stamper looked up from the large oriental rug in the entryway toward the bedrooms. "Vomit? Like — recent?"

The tech was standing on the balcony. "Looks like. It's going to the lab."

"Is it, like, all in the trash can, or what?"

"Yeah. Seems to be a direct hit."

That was kind of interesting. People tossed their cookies because they were sick, physically or emotionally. But to make the trash can, to score a two-pointer like that? It suggested some control. That maybe it had occurred before the break-in.

Moving carefully through the house, he retraced the sequence of events: A woman across the street sees two men enter the home, one with a gun (she thinks), hears a cry for help, and calls 911. 911 polls the call, and a state trooper is closest, responds. Trooper Taylor finds the front door not only unlocked, but ajar, and shouts into the house — *Anyone home?* With the door open and exigent circumstances dictating, Taylor enters the residence, eventually makes his way upstairs where he discovers the broken bedroom door, the open window, icy cold air blowing in. Taylor calls his sergeant and BCI — Louis Stamper then makes the trip from Oneida HQ to Herkimer and has a look.

He'd covered a lot of ground since then, but it had only been about eight hours, and a full background picture was still forming. Who owned the home? Who paid the bills? What was the overall financial situation? You always had to look at that.

Colton Rossi didn't have anything big on his record — a DWAI from when he was nineteen, a couple of speeding tickets since then. But the name, Rossi, still rang familiar.

What are we talking about, here? Exactly what kind of crime was it? Why escalate from a B&E to assault and kidnapping if you didn't have to? Because nothing stood out as a reason why that would happen. If they'd wanted to kill them? Okay, just do them right there. But to chase them out of the window and scoop them into a van, if that's what happened?

Julie Spreniker and her fiancé had been kidnapped on purpose; that much seemed settled. But why at 7 a.m.? And for what reason? Sure, he had a little notoriety as a rock climber, but that didn't matter, did it?

Then why did Stamper think it did?

He left the house for now, into the swirling snowflakes, tucking into his ski parka. What he needed was to get back to the barracks, see about their phones, what they were saying to people.

People loved to talk. Most of them wanted to tell you everything about them, even their crimes.

CHAPTER TWENTY

"What were you thinking?" Monique asked Colton. "Like, really, did you lose your mind?"

"He was doing it in the van," Keith said.

"He was doing it in the van?"

"Saying he didn't know her."

"What happened to his arm?" Monique seemed to notice how he was holding it, protecting it. "From jumping out the window?"

Julie was trying to follow the conversation, a challenge because it was like watching herself talk.

Moving closer, Monique crouched down. Taking hold of Colton's knees, she looked up into his face. "So you had a change of heart, huh? You love her after all. You wanted to save her."

"Leave him alone," Julie said.

Monique made a disgusted face at her. "And you — you come into the bedroom, you stand there, seeing your man in bed with another woman. And you didn't even notice what I looked like."

"Your back was turned," Julie said. "You were hiding from me."

It had all been a blur — she could hardly remember details. The next thing that was really clear was trying to get the window open. Contemplating the jump. Everything since then was crisp, but the interim, the bedroom, the discovery: more feelings than visuals.

"Well, yeah, I didn't want a big scene. We weren't ready for you yet — you weren't supposed to be home until tonight."

One moment did surface: Monique sitting on the edge of the bed, doing something with her phone. Had she given the signal to Michael and Keith? That contradicted what she was saying, though, about Julie coming home early and not being ready.

Ready for what?

You don't want to know.

No, maybe she didn't. Maybe she didn't want to.

But, of course, she had to.

* * *

"We think twins are this wildly unusual thing," Monique said a few minutes later. "This freak of nature. Something that happens just once in a while." She added, "Or with fertility drugs."

She'd gotten out of the cocktail dress and pulled on clothes Julie recognized as her own. A full-zip Marmot fleece and a pair of khaki cargo pants. Even the boots were hers — one of her best pairs for winter. The effect made Monique look even more like her. It was really doing her head in.

"It's actually pretty common, though. I read that something like one in eight pregnancies actually starts as a twin thing, but one embryo absorbs the other. Is that fucking crazy or what? One in eight people, like, ate their twin in the womb."

It was a rhetorical question, but it seemed like Monique was awaiting a response.

She stood, and walked to the window, and looked out — Michael had just left. His departure seemed like a key part of an unfolding plan. Julie found herself wondering if Monique was checking to see that he was gone.

"I don't have a twin," Julie said at last. She sounded solid, even if she suddenly felt insubstantial; a ghost.

Monique turned from the window and smiled. "Then who do you think you're looking at?"

Julie examined her properly for the first time. It was hard to be sure, but Monique looked a little taller, a little skinnier. Their faces were certainly strikingly similar. Julie had a small cleft at the end of her nose. She had always despised it, but on Monique it looked good, even sexy.

In fact, the woman's whole demeanor seemed to exude a kind of sex appeal Julie had never known herself to have.

"I have a brother who's three years younger and lives in Colorado," she said. "I grew up with him and my parents. But that's it." To drive the point, she added, "I don't have a twin."

"Hmm." Monique sat back down on the stool, crossed her legs. "You don't sound really sure. I mean, I'm not a professional. *You're* the professional."

Julie kept staring, kept scanning, but God, they certainly did look alike. Even their eyes — from the distance, anyway: Monique's were the same hazel, smack between green and brown.

"What if I was to tell you your mother didn't know she was pregnant with twins?"

Julie shook her head.

"All sorts of shit can happen," Monique said. "Twins can be born weeks apart. Twins can have different *fathers* . . . Twins can be conceived within a couple of days. You can have one father of one twin, and then the woman has sex with a different man, and then there's another one *the next day.*"

"Those would be fraternal twins," Julie said. Her head was spinning. How had she missed it that morning?

She kept her back to you. Her hair hung in her face. She was naked.

Besides, she'd had more important things on her mind: Colton with another woman.

Ugh . . .

He was sleeping with this woman who looks exactly like you.

106

"Fraternal twins, right," Monique said. "I'm just giving you examples. The point is, it happens." Monique got close, now crouching in front of Julie, really freaking her out by staring right into her eyes. So close Julie could see the fine hairs on her jawline, a bit of dryness around the edges of her nose, that dimpled tip still slightly red from the cold.

"I know you," Monique said. "I know who you are. I know about the troubles you've had — everything. But you don't know me. You don't know anything about me."

CHAPTER TWENTY-ONE

"Got the van," Lindsay Cuthbert said, and dropped the file on Stamper's desk with a slap.

Cuthbert was the other plainclothes investigator for Oneida. You could call them partners, but no one really ever did. They ran their own investigations, but they also worked together on some of the same cases. Like this one.

"I looked at all white cargo vans going either direction on I-90, up to an hour out from the 911 call. Didn't even need to look that long. At 7:12, we've got one at the first toll west of Herkimer."

Stamper checked the image atop the file: a mostly overhead view of a white van. I-90 no longer had human-operated toll booths but computers that deducted funds from EZ-Pass accounts. The computer took pictures, too, but of license plates, with only a blurry, unusable look into the vehicle itself, through the windshield. He couldn't even see any humans in there. But Cuthbert was excited.

"Guess who owns a 2003 white Chevy Express?"

He pushed the picture aside to read the paperwork beneath. "*Flandreau?*"

"Yep. Registered to a one Warren J. Flandreau of Old Forge, New York."

Stamper thought about it. "It could be a coincidence," he said, despite knowing it was almost never a coincidence.

Cuthbert just looked at him, lips pursed, eyebrows raised, foot tapping a little.

"Okay. Yeah." He got up and grabbed his parka off the back of his chair.

Time to pay Warren Flandreau of Herkimer Brewing another visit.

* * *

The restaurant was busier than before, the waitstaff zigzagging through the busy dining room. The waitress from earlier, Brianna, glanced over before disappearing into the kitchen.

Warren Flandreau was sweating, and a little less cordial this time. He agreed to talk, but outside.

"Storm doesn't seem to be affecting business," Stamper said, gesturing to the crowded parking lot.

Flandreau lit a cigarette in the cold. "It's Central New York. If people stayed in every time it snowed, no one would ever go out."

"Mr. Flandreau, can you tell us where your cargo van was this morning? Around seven o'clock?"

"My van?" He blew smoke out of both nostrils.

Cuthbert held out a document. "Are you the owner of this vehicle, Mr. Flandreau?"

But Flandreau ignored it, instead trudging into the parking lot. Toward the back were a couple of dumpsters and a wooden fence that was uneven in places. The lot was stuffed with vehicles, right up to that fence, but no white van. "What the hell?"

"Mr. Flandreau," Cuthbert said, keeping up. "Can you look at this please?"

He kept scanning the lot. Finally, he flicked away the cigarette and took the paper. After a couple of seconds: "It looks like it. Where was it at seven?"

Cuthbert said, "Sir, your vehicle matches the description given to us by eyewitnesses. It was seen in front of Julie

Spreniker and Colton Rossi's shared home. And it was picked up on a traffic camera about ten minutes later."

"You've got to be kidding me," Flandreau said. "This is crazy." But he didn't deny ownership of the vehicle nor suggest there'd been a mistake, as Stamper had expected he might. "So where is it now? Because it's not here."

"Mr. Flandreau," Cuthbert said, "Do you understand what we're saying? Your vehicle — registered to you — was possibly used in the commission of a crime. The potential abduction of Spreniker and Rossi."

"The abduction . . . Jesus. Oh my God."

"We'd like to talk about where you were this morning."

"Where I was? In bed, sleeping. I'm here until after closing six nights a week, so I tried to sleep in a little this morning."

"Is there anyone who can corroborate that?"

He looked in at the restaurant through the door window, the words *Herkimer Brewing* bending across the glass, and didn't answer.

Stamper: "Are you married, Mr. Flandreau?"

"Divorced."

Stamper saw Brianna again, inside, sneaking a look at them, then hurrying away from the window.

"So was anyone with you this morning at seven o'clock?"

Flandreau turned and gave him a sharp look. "I have four vehicles registered in my name. My personal vehicle, my pickup truck, a motorcycle and my van. The van's been here, at the restaurant, where I usually keep it. Anyone could have taken it. Now — I'm sorry, but we're getting hit with an early dinner rush and I don't have a runner here yet — I'm it. I need to get back in there."

"I understand, Mr. Flandreau. So the van was parked over here?"

"Over there, yeah." He pointed to the spot in the far corner, now occupied by a new-looking Toyota Four-Runner.

"Any cameras on the parking lot?"

"No. Only camera is at the bar, on the cash register."

"Did you leave the keys in it?"

"Sure, yeah. Keys are always in it. Over the visor. That van is just basic, didn't even have seats in the back. Used it for deliveries for a while, during COVID. Lately, for construction work on the place."

"Any distinguishing marks on it, anything like that? Dents or cracks in the glass — anything?"

"It's in good shape. There used to be a decal on the side of it — the guy I bought it from had a carpet cleaning business and when I pulled the sticker off, it left a residue that never went away, no matter how much I washed it. It needs, you know, that Goo-gone stuff. I just never fully cleaned it off."

"Do you have a copy of the registration? We'll use the VIN and get more information."

"Um, maybe, somewhere in my office. Or maybe it's home . . . Officers, I really gotta get back. Can you come by in the morning?"

"Sure. Or maybe later tonight. Just one more thing. Colton Rossi — he knew the van was there, keys in it?"

"Yeah, of course."

"Anybody else? Staff? Regulars?"

"Yeah, absolutely. That vehicle is used on and off by half a dozen people."

Cuthbert jumped back in. "We'd like to know exactly who that half a dozen people are," she said.

"I mean, I'm just ball-parking. Literally anyone who works here could take it."

"But why would they? Why would anyone take it?"

"The cooks, for runs to the grocery store if we run out of anything. I had my contractor guy using it last week. Mostly we use it to deliver kegs. Look, I can give you a list of everyone who'd touched it in the past month if you want, when you come back for the registration. I gotta go, or shit's gonna implode in there."

No one moved.

"Unless you're arresting me."

Stamper and Cuthbert exchanged looks. Stamper said, "No, no. We'll be in touch."

* * *

111

A couple minutes later, in the car, Cuthbert was driving. "Well, that didn't really narrow it down."

"I think he had someone who could corroborate where he was but didn't want to say." Stamper pictured Brianna's big brown eyes.

"Spreniker isn't worth a lot of money or anything," Cuthbert said. "We checked. Less than ten grand between her checking account and deferred comp. And they're not even married yet, so there'd be no life insurance payout if it was something like that. Why else would Rossi have his own fiancée kidnapped?"

"What makes you think that's what I'm talking about?"

She smirked. "Please. You've liked Rossi for it from the moment the call came in."

"I don't even know the guy."

"Rock climber? Bartender? Dark hair that curls around his ears? Not an ounce of fat on him?"

"You're right — I hate him."

She laughed, then quickly sobered. "I'm not saying I don't have my sense of that, too. I'm just not seeing the motive. You know, you hire someone to kidnap your fiancée? And yourself, too? Why?"

"To make it look good. Or maybe he's just . . ." Stamper kept thinking about the guy's semi-celebrity. "Maybe they get turned loose after a couple of days and the whole thing was a big publicity stunt. The whole country gets talking about the abduction of this rock climber and his mousy fiancée. You've seen this guy's social media. He's not shy, he's ambitious."

Cuthbert was rubbing her lip, a sign she was considering it. "And whatever revenue that attention brings, he uses that to pay the guys in the van," she said, following up the idea. "It could work. But we're just making guesses here. We have nothing solid."

His phone buzzed, and he took the call.

"Investigator Stamper," said the duty officer back at the barracks. "I got a crazy message for you. You're gonna want to hear this."

CHAPTER TWENTY-TWO

Julie stared. And then she stared some more. It was impossible not to.

But — a twin? That her parents kept from her? All these years?

"We weren't poor when I was born," she reasoned. "It wasn't like my mother would give up one baby because she couldn't afford two. Or for any reason. It's crazy. It's not true."

Monique had been over near the kitchen sink, quietly talking to Keith when Julie had piped up. "Maybe it was for psychological reasons," she said. "Maybe there are things that happened back then you don't know about."

Julie considered her parents. Mother born in Saranac Lake to a large Irish-Catholic family. Father of German descent. He'd worked for a village water department. They hadn't been rich, but not destitute either. Not that she could remember.

Yet much of her childhood before her mother's illness was hazy, feeling like it belonged to someone else. Had she missed something this vital?

It's some kind of trick. And there are differences, too — she's not your twin. The way she walks, the sound of her voice — identical twins would share more than superficialities.

"We're not related. I can tell."

Monique leaned on the kitchen island. "I thought you were a therapist. Went to school."

"I am."

"Twins raised apart can grow up to be very different from each another. One rich, the other poor . . . One with the original mommy and daddy, the other one left to be raised in foster homes . . . You're going to act different, talk different, even look different."

Julie wanted to ask Colton what he thought, if he'd known all along — but that scared her. In some dark, twisty way, it felt plausible — more plausible, even, than Colton just having some random affair — that he'd slept with Monique *because* she was Julie's twin. Hadn't Keith made some comment along those lines?

Kinky.

A grin tugged up one side of Monique's mouth. She was make-up free but still beautiful.

Maybe that's why you don't believe it — you've never thought you were beautiful.

"You're wondering about us, aren't you?" Monique asked.

She meant her and Colton, but Julie didn't respond.

"You're thinking that even if your sex life didn't involve whips and chains, there's *some* sparkle to it — right? You're happy. You never caught his eye wandering . . ."

Well, that wasn't entirely true. Now and then, out on a date, maybe having dinner, Julie would notice Colton checking out other women. And then there was Brianna from the restaurant. Julie had no proof, but she felt like Brianna "got around." It had crossed her mind once, Colton coming home and showering at 4 a.m., that he was cleaning off more than the brewery smells. But she'd never had the courage to question him about it.

"Well," Monique said, clearly enjoying herself, "I'm here to tell you that it wasn't too hard. Not too hard at all to get him to stray." She walked over to Colton now, mussing his hair as she slowly circled around him.

Colton, for his part, stayed slumped, mute, zombified.

"What would *you* do, you know?" Monique asked. "If you were a man, flesh and blood, and someone came to you who looked exactly like your fiancée? You explain that you're her twin trying to reconnect with your long-lost sister — but it's precarious. It's a delicate thing, a reunion like that. He has to keep quiet about it. He can only meet with you in secret. And, you know, one thing leads to another. Lots of late nights together, all the sneaking around . . . And he sees how you're different. You're wilder, you're a little dangerous." She winked at Julie when she said, "Maybe you're a little fitter, too."

A twin, Julie thought — it would have its own special kind of thrill. Yes. In a horrible, nauseating way, she could see Colton going for it. And maybe, too, that kind of infidelity held its own perverted permission?

But she didn't ask this, didn't even want to hear about it, both because she was partly afraid of what Colton might say, but also because she was distracted. Keith had gone off to the back of the cabin, where he was rummaging around.

"He couldn't resist," Monique finished about Colton. She stopped at the island again and pulled her hair into a ponytail. In that moment, Julie made an assessment: Monique was well-to-do, even educated. But something was wrong with her.

She crossed to the door where there was a bag — it must've gotten here when she'd arrived with Michael. Julie had just been too stunned to notice.

A real habit with you.

"Where did Michael go?"

At the door, bent down to the bag, Monique produced a ball cap. Nothing fancy, battered blue and generic. It looked like the one Michael had been wearing earlier. She put it on as she stood and turned around.

"He had to leave. He's got a new job to do now."

Cryptic and unhelpful.

"Are we going somewhere?"

Monique didn't answer at first. In the ball cap, she looked even more like Julie.

"We are, yes. We'll be going soon, play our parts."

Julie glanced at Colton, expecting him to be staring at the floor, but he was suddenly alert again. Staring at Julie. Looking concerned.

"This is all a carefully devised plan," Monique said, sounding proud. "And we're going to follow through with it."

Keith came out of the back, a bag of his own over his shoulder. He set it down with a thump and pulled his gun from the rear of his waistband, aiming it loosely toward both Julie and Colton. "Okay," he said to Julie. "Get up. You're going with Monique."

Colton studied Keith like someone trying to interpret a foreign language. "Wait — what are you talking about? What about me?"

"You're staying here," Monique said.

Colton looked at her, growing frantic. "No — that wasn't what we agreed."

"There are a lot of things that had to change, baby."

"What do you mean? No."

"It has to be this way."

Colton's nerves bloomed into stark fear. When he faced Julie, his eyes were wild, his skin blotched with anxiety. "No," he said. "No, no."

"Come on, you knew this was coming," Keith said. "Say goodbye, or don't. But this is the end of the line for you."

Julie could register her fiancé's terror, and Keith's numbness — a solider inured to war and killing — but she couldn't quite process what he was actually talking about. Why would it be the end of the line for Colton? Were they going to just cut him loose? Send him out into the cold as punishment?

You know it's not that.

It hasn't been that for a long time.

Nothing is what you think it is.

Maybe Monique had discovered Julie was her long-lost twin and seduced Colton. The "punishment" in this whole thing might be directed the other way. Toward *her*.

"Wait," Monique said. "Wait, wait wait."

"What?" Some of Keith's humanness came back; he seemed annoyed.

"Did you do the van part yet?"

Keith thought about it. "No. We didn't do anything with the van."

"What do you mean you didn't do anything with the van?" She went to Colton and started untying his hands. "Jesus Christ. You needed to put his fucking prints in the van, Keith."

"His prints already are in the van."

"Well, so are yours. And Michael's. I told him this. Wipe down the prints and put *his*—" she pointed at Colton — "front and center. What kind of knot is this?"

Julie looked at the door as they argued. She was herself untied.

"We wore gloves," Keith said. He tucked the gun away. "And the van is used by a lot of people. Prints everywhere. Wiping it down didn't make sense."

Monique pointed at Colton. "But *his* prints."

"They're in there already. And it's not necessary. *He's* going to be here and the *van* is going to be here. That's all they're going to care about."

Julie edged a little closer to the kitchen island.

"You're sure you wore gloves?" Monique asked Keith.

"We had the plastic in the back, and we wore gloves up front."

She finally let it go. "All right. Okay. Jesus. All right. Let's do this and get on the road. We have to get ahead of the weather."

Keith noticed that Julie had changed position, now halfway between the kitchen and the front door. "Hey," he said, the gun coming back out. "Stop fucking moving."

She did, wincing at the gun pointed right at her, Keith's eyes gone cold again.

"Get going," Monique said to Julie. Of all things, it was so weird to have a version of yourself barking orders.

That's what you look like enraged.

That's what you look like when you've lost your mind.

"Just let me say goodbye. Please."

Monique seemed to calculate it. "Fine. Be quick."

Julie went to Colton, her knees spongy, legs shaking, and crouched in front of him. His body was tense, a coiled spring; he wanted to leap off the chair, to run away. But his legs were still tied.

He looked into her eyes. "Help," he said, and snot was running from his nose again, collecting in his mustache.

That stupid mustache.

"It's going to be okay," Julie said, feeling the tears sting her eyes.

"This wasn't . . . this isn't . . ."

"All right," Monique barked. "Enough, let's go."

"Don't leave me," Colton said. He sobbed, dropping his head. Barely able to speak, he lifted his face to hers. "I'm so sorry."

"It's okay." She leaned in and touched his face. The smell of fear on him was sharp and acrid. "Shh," she said.

On autopilot now, she stood and walked toward Monique, who waited by the door. "Put this on." She handed Julie a jacket. It was leather, loose, redolent of cigarettes. Then she opened the door.

Julie glanced back one last time.

Colton's whole body shook like he was having a seizure.

"Don't hurt him," Julie said.

Keith looked at her with that absence in his eyes. But, of course, he wasn't going to hurt Colton. This was just about scaring them. Colton had messed up. He'd gotten involved with some woman claiming to be Julie's twin sister. And now he was here. Tied up in a chair, snot dribbling. Watching his fiancée go out the door. But he would be okay.

She stepped outside. The snow was really coming down. When Monique shut the door behind them and Colton disappeared, Monique didn't say anything but indicated that Julie should walk in front of her.

So she did, through the big thick snowfall, toward the vehicles in the near distance. There was the van. With all the plastic in it.

And another vehicle that Julie didn't recognize, an older model Jeep Cherokee or something. They pushed on toward it, through the swirling snow.

They had nearly reached it when Julie heard a scream from the cabin behind her: "No! Keith, God, please, no! Stop, man, I'm your br—"

And then a gunshot. Julie stopped in her tracks. It felt like the shot had gone right through her, piercing her heart, shaking her ribcage.

A muffled thump from inside, and then everything was silent in the falling snow.

PART THREE

The Storm

CHAPTER TWENTY-THREE

The message from the duty officer was definitely interesting. A woman had called in from Verona, a town in the area, claiming she'd seen both Spreniker and Rossi at the Turning Stone Casino, part of Mohawk land in proximity.

The night before. When Spreniker was supposed to be in Buffalo.

Stamper called the woman back, the phone on speaker so Cuthbert could hear from her desk, which abutted his.

"Mrs. Burry," he said, when they had her on the line. "What time was this? To your best approximation."

"Well, it was about ten p.m. when I left," Burry said. "I never stay out past ten p.m., that's my rule. And it was just before I left, maybe fifteen minutes. So that's what I told the other officer. 9:45."

He wrote it down. "Great. And — I know you did this, too, already — but could you just describe them for me?"

She did, telling the investigators that Spreniker was elegant in a black cocktail dress, Rossi in a modern suit. They were playing blackjack when she saw them. "And you're sure it was them?" Stamper asked.

"Oh, yes. The young man and woman from the TV. Taken from their homes this morning. I saw them last night, no doubt about it."

"Sure, sure. Um, so what can you tell me about them, other than their appearance?"

"What do you mean?"

"Were they having a good time? Did it seem like they were up?"

"Oh, definitely not."

The witness's conviction took him aback. "Really? They didn't seem happy?"

"Well, no, I would say not. When I saw them, they seemed to be arguing. Well, maybe 'arguing' isn't the right word . . . they looked like they were in a fight. She seemed, I don't know, inconsolable. And he seemed like he didn't know the first thing to do about it."

"That's very helpful, thank you. Did you overhear anything?"

"I just saw them, and I can describe to you what it looked like, but I'm not an eavesdropper."

"Of course not."

Stamper hung up and sat back.

Cuthbert was the first to say something. "You want me to call Buffalo?"

He tapped his pen against his lips. "Spreniker was staying at the Regal Hyatt, according to her supervisor. She was there with about twenty other county employees."

Cuthbert picked up the desk phone. "I'm sure the hotel has cameras, too."

"While you're doing that, I'll call Gary Weintraub. See what he's got."

Weintraub worked for BCI, specializing in tracing and cracking phones.

"Good idea," Cuthbert said.

* * *

"Was just going to call you," Weintraub said to Stamper. "So, we did this three ways. We got Spreniker's number from her work, and historical CSLI is forthcoming. We tried to ping it, got nothing. Next thing we did was a tower dump for the period around seven o'clock this morning. And we got it — we saw her number showing up on that tower at 6:45, and then again at 7. Then we see it once more at 7:15."

"Same tower?"

"Same tower, yes. So then we did a geofence."

Stamper knew that meant a reverse location search. If a tower dump picked a specific time to get all CSLI data connected to a certain tower, a geofence looked at all users who were in a certain location at a certain time. When you mixed the two — tower dump and geofence — you could pinpoint a phone to a specific place and time.

"And what did you find there?"

"Well, that's a fair amount of data. Lots of users — I don't think you just want to go around questioning everyone who was within a half mile of Spreniker-Rossi home at seven this morning."

"No, I don't. But I got something for you to check it against."

He gave Weintraub the information on the EZ-Pass toll. Weintraub tapped some keys, then said, "Got a hit."

Stamper made a little fist pump in the air.

Weintraub said, "Yep, so my data corresponds with your 7:07 van hit at the EZ-Pass. That suggests she was in the van — but of course, that's not my call to make, that's yours."

"Right." Stamper rolled his eyes. Forensic guys were all the same — *Just the facts, ma'am.* He loved that about them. But this was exciting, good confirmation that Spreniker was in the van. At least, making it all the more likely.

"So we know where it is at 7:07, and you see it show up on the dump again at 7:15?"

"Yeah, that's it. 7:15. Nothing since then. Indicating either damaged, or battery-stripped, or maybe just completely out of range. But like I say . . ."

"My call, right." Stamper studied the Google map on his screen. Somewhere after 7:15 that morning, Julie Spreniker's phone disappeared. Eight minutes after the EZ-Pass, she was gone.

"Okay," Stamper said, "what else?"

"We've got content from both. For Spreniker, we reached out to the carrier, and they're getting it to us. For Rossi, whose phone we found at the house, we got around the biometric lock with GrayKey and have been going through recent calls and texts and social media. He has Instagram on his phone."

"Yeah," Stamper said, "We've been looking at that, but from the outside."

"Well, now you'll have his DMs. We'll send everything to you."

"Thanks, Gary, amazing work."

* * *

By the time Stamper finished his call with Weintraub, Cuthbert had spoken to the hotel in Buffalo and Spreniker's supervisor.

"Unfortunately, Spreniker was the only one to attend the conference from Herkimer County," Cuthbert said. "The event organizers are this mental health association for the state, and they gave me a list of attendees but can't confirm Spreniker was there or not. She checked in on day one — someone picked up a lanyard, anyway, with her name on it — but that's it."

"What about social media? Pictures taken, colleagues together at the lunch buffet, that kind of thing."

"Checking, yeah. There was a Facebook page for the event, and I've been looking, but so far not seeing her. The hotel has cameras, but they're wide-angle, overhead cameras for those rooms. What did Weintraub say?"

"He got into the phones and Rossi's Instagram."

They spent the next hour looking through all the messages. Colton had many friends, lots of DMs. Julie's life was simpler, and most of her communication was with colleagues and coworkers. Ninety percent of the texts between the engaged couple were about daily logistics — who was getting off work and when, who needed to pick up milk and bread from the store. The remaining ten percent were mostly frivolous; silly gifs and shared news items. But a few were heated, the couple trading harsh words.

"Money seems tight," Cuthbert said, still scrolling and reading. "A couple DMs between Colton and a friend about that."

"So they're gambling to try to make ends meet?"

"One of the messages makes it sound like she's threatening to leave."

"Really?"

"That one was about a week ago. Recent tensions."

They tried to add it all up. Either the woman who'd seen them at the casino was mistaken, even fabricating, or Spreniker had lied to her boss and taken a trip with Rossi to try and roll up a stake.

"He works, though," Stamper said. "Tuesdays, he's at the bar."

"Yeah, well, they just stayed around here, then. Went to Verona, maybe even left from there. I mean, what do we have, Louis? We have neighbors who saw a white van, a gun. Maybe this really *was* a burglary. The fight in the bedroom could have been between two men. One has a high-pitched voice; when he screams, the nurse neighbor thinks it's a woman. One goes out the window; the other goes out the front." Cuthbert kept thinking. "What if they owed someone? They borrowed money for the blackjack table and now these guys are here to collect. Only, Rossi and Spreniker are already long gone."

"In what car, though? Both their vehicles were there. And her phone was in the van."

A buzzing phone halted the conversation. Both of them checked their pockets, but it was Stamper's, actually sitting on the desk. "Hello?"

Trooper Taylor was loud, the way he got when he was excited. "A neighbor of Rossi and Spreniker's just came home from work. He's got something to show you. It blew my friggin' mind."

CHAPTER TWENTY-FOUR

What did you do?

She wasn't sure if she'd said the words aloud. All she knew was that she was running back to the cabin.

Keith — what did you just do?

"Stop!" Monique yelled, chasing after her, grabbing her. Julie yanked her arm away.

Colton — oh God, oh no . . .

Colton . . .

Monique grabbed her again, and Julie spun around and punched the woman in the face. Hadn't even expected it. Never hit another human being like that in her life, and suddenly she was Katie Taylor, U.S. women's boxing champ.

The blow snapped Monique's head back. She stumbled a few steps and Julie kept going, right up to the door, Colton's name blaring like an alarm in her head.

The man she'd spent the last half of a decade with. Planned her future with — someday kids and grandbabies . . .

The door swung open and Keith was standing there with the gun in his hand. He pressed the muzzle right up against her forehead and she winced and jerked back from the touch.

Blood stained his other hand. She tried to look past him and could only see a leg, Colton's leg, the rest of his body out of view. But he was down on the ground.

"What did you do?!" It came out in a scream.

Keith took a step forward and put the gun to her head again, and this time she didn't pull away. He said, "We should just do her right here."

But Monique was there, knocking the gun away with her hand, saying, "Are you fucking crazy?" She got in between them and scanned Julie's face as if checking for injury.

Monique's own nose was bleeding, but Julie didn't care. She shoved Monique aside and prepared to squeeze past Keith, but he caught her and wrestled her screaming to the ground. She could see all of Colton now, and his wide, open eyes, dead and staring, the blood leaking from his head — she could hear Keith breathing into her ear, saying: "It really doesn't matter — it really doesn't matter anymore."

But Monique was grabbing her again, hauling her away from Keith. She was strong, clamped onto Julie's arms as if with talons, and Julie's heels dragged through the snow as Monique pulled her back. She dropped Julie and then kicked her, hard, in the ribs, right at the diaphragm, expelling all of Julie's air. Julie curled into a ball, gasping and wheezing, and Monique said, "Stay, goddammit."

Julie barely registered it as Monique stormed over to Keith. "This is not the order of operations!"

"What order?" He was really yelling now, too, both of them unhinged. "This is a total clusterfuck! Everything we've done has been a mistake, right since this morning." He calmed some and said, "We should have aborted right then and there — and you know it."

Julie was finally able to draw breath, small and ragged, like sucking air through a keyhole. Her body spasmed and clenched and she tried again, a whooping inhalation, and got a little more air, breathing in snow with it.

"No, I don't," Monique said. Blood trickled from her nose. Digging around in her pocket, she came up with a used tissue and daubed. "I don't know that. It still works. It still all works."

"What about the phone? What about her fucking phone, Monique? That was supposed to be a hundred miles away."

"It's right where it's supposed to be. This works."

"You heard her," Keith said, pointing at Julie. "Everybody saw this morning. Neighbors saw."

"Part of the plan."

"Yeah, the plan was they saw a carpet cleaning company. Or they saw her vehicle drive off with what looked like her driving it. Nothing went like that. The whole fucking thing — it isn't going to work."

"Then why did you do what you just did?" She asked it while looking at Colton.

Her question stilled Keith, but not in a good way — he seemed ready to kill her, too, and took a step toward her.

Monique stepped back. She checked the bloody tissue, then held out her other hand toward Keith. "You gotta go all the way to the end."

"Don't fucking lecture me on endurance. You have no idea."

"I understand."

"He was trying to make a run for it. He'd untied his legs and he was trying to get away."

"Well . . . Now you have to move him."

Keith simmered and took a deep breath, looking at the open door, Colton beyond. "Fine. So I'll move him."

"Good. Just move him, arrange it, and we're all set. The new plan. Okay?"

Keith just breathed, exhalations spewing from his nostrils like a bull, snow falling thick around him, and said, "It's fine, Jesus." He went in and slammed the door.

It seemed like she wanted to go after him, but she glanced at Julie first, then at the door, and said, "Fuck."

Julie pulled another breath. Like needles in her lungs, but better.

"Get up."

When Julie didn't, Monique's expression turned angry. They looked alike, yes, they could pass as twins, sure — but if that was the way Julie looked when she was pissed . . . She was like some kind of demon when she came for Julie, and Julie winced, prepared for more kicks or worse, but Monique used that preternatural strength she had and hauled Julie up onto her feet.

"Walk."

"No."

The blow came out of nowhere against the back of Julie's head, hard enough to make her stumble. The next thing she knew, Monique had a handful of her hair and was forcing her to walk.

But not toward the cars, or the road.

Toward the shack on the hill.

CHAPTER TWENTY-FIVE

A reporter saw them coming.

"Whoa," Stamper said when they rounded the bend on Waverly Street, and Cuthbert, driving, put the vehicle in reverse.

The media scrum had grown in front of the townhouse. Stamper had asked to close the street, but there'd been too much pushback. Now, news vans crowded the whole area.

Cuthbert found parking on the next street over, and they walked back to Waverly — the north-south portion after the bend. The same reporter was hoofing it up the slight hill toward them, cameraman beside her, mounted and filming.

And there were more behind her.

"Excuse me," the first reporter said, as the investigators approached the alley. "Jacinda Myers, Channel 6 News — can you give us a comment on the situation?"

"We're going to hold a press conference," Cuthbert said, holding up a hand as if to ward them all off. Stamper lifted the crime-scene tape and she slipped through. At least no one had given them guff about closing the alley.

"When?" the reporter asked, but Cuthbert was still moving up the alley, sticking to the side.

Stamper lingered. "Soon. Our public relations person will send out the info."

She held a microphone near his face, recording. "Anything you can tell me? It's been nine hours. Are Julie Spreniker and Colton Rossi officially missing persons?"

"I can't really comment."

"That means there's been a crime. If they were just missing, you'd want us getting out the word, looking for them."

He started to say more as the cameraman twisted the focus ring on the lens, framing him up.

"Stamper!"

Cuthbert's voice was a hook, yanking him off stage. She was right — no talking to the press. Not yet. "See you then," he said to the reporter, and followed Cuthbert up the snowy alley.

* * *

The troopers had continued doing door-to-doors all day, getting statements. *Did you see anything? Hear anything? What kind of neighbors are they?* But it was still early evening, with most people yet to come home from work.

Except for a man named Shane Robbie, a UPS packer who got home from a shift that started before dawn.

Robbie had a Ring camera in his backyard, prompted by the rash of break-ins in the area a couple years before. "You just never know," he said, when they were standing in his living room. He wore a brown uniform and one of those lower back supports. "I check the footage every day when I come home."

The motion-activated camera worked with cellular technology and went to an app on his phone. It would alert him if someone was within range of his door. But he still checked it even if he hadn't been notified. Like he had today, and seen something very interesting.

The investigators crowded in with Taylor to watch as Robbie ran through the footage to the part he wanted to show them: Spreniker and her fiancé emerging from their backyard, hurrying into the alleyway.

And about five seconds later, a man in a baseball hat, chasing them.

Holy shit, Stamper thought, and grabbed the neighbor's phone. Realizing his impulsiveness, he asked, "May I?" and Robbie nodded.

They watched it again. Taylor looked on, pleased he'd found the neighbor.

The image was only so-so for a relatively cheap camera — but at least this hadn't happened at night, with everybody green-faced and black-eyed in the low-light footage. The resolution was good enough that he could see the fear and pain on their faces — not to mention Rossi was holding his shoulder and Spreniker was limping. Escaping the high window had apparently messed them up.

"How do we get this back to the office?" Stamper was asking anyone who knew, but the neighbor especially. "You can email this? Or we just download it from the phone somehow?"

"Um, so, it records to the Cloud. Basically, it's always going to the Cloud, but it's not saving unless there's some action, some motion. It actually goes back thirty seconds, so you can see what was going on just before the motion tripped it. Then it records automatically for two minutes."

"So how do you get it to us? Can you email it?"

"Yeah, or Dropbox it, I guess."

They exchanged information.

Stamper could barely contain himself. They had one of the assailants on camera. The hat covered a third of his face, and what was left wouldn't work for facial recognition software, but they still had his height, his clothes, the kind of gun he was holding. Maybe they could even get some tech guys working on the resolution — Stamper could almost make out what was on the hat. *O'Neill?*

"And I'll send you the second one, too," Robbie said.

"The second one?"

"Yeah, pretty weird because . . . well, I don't know. What happened, anyway?"

"What's 'the second one'? What do you mean?"

"The camera got activated again — another person came out. I kind of thought it was weird. Like it was a glitch. But then I figured it was just her sister, or something. I don't really know them; I thought it was just a guy and a girl living there."

"It is," Stamper said. "So, you saw another person come out? A second video? When? Can I see it?"

Robbie fiddled with his phone a second and brought it up. "Like I said, maybe her sister." He handed over the phone and Stamper, trying to be patient, took it and watched.

"But then the sister comes out, and she's so calm," Robbie said. "That's why I thought maybe the whole thing was some kind of weird . . . I don't know. Remember that show? *Punk'd?*"

They watched as a fourth person emerged from the back yard, looked both ways before stepping fully into the alley. And then she went to the left — in the opposite direction from Spreniker, Rossi and the man with the gun.

"What the hell?" Cuthbert breathed.

The woman was a dead ringer for Spreniker. In fact, if you hadn't seen the other video, you would have sworn it was her.

"Thank you," Stamper said, after a too-long pause. "This is very helpful."

"I got the alert on my phone this morning, but I don't always check them right away. I wish I did. I'm sorry."

"It's all right. We're just glad you have this."

"I was gonna call, but the, uh, officer here showed up knocking anyway."

Stamper was listening, but he'd started the video over again and was staring, his mind racing ahead.

* * *

134

He was driving too fast, Cuthbert holding onto the handle above the door.

"I'm never letting you drive again."

"Sorry." He slowed, just a little. "Spreniker doesn't have a sister."

"That we know of." Cuthbert was thumb-searching the internet on her phone with her free hand, looking for something they might've missed in the background check.

"It could have been Spreniker herself," Stamper continued. "You saw the time stamps. Between the first three people running off camera to the lookalike woman coming out was just over three minutes. That's enough for her to go back through the house and come back out."

"What? No way. You've walked it — it takes three minutes just to get around the block. And why do that?"

"I'm not saying it makes sense. I'm saying it's possible. She doesn't have a sister. Much less a twin. We would have seen it."

"Maybe," Cuthbert said. "But, come on. After jumping out the back window of her own house, and fleeing with her fiancé, looking terrified, a guy with a gun chasing them? She then *sprints* back to the house, changes her clothes and leaves again, this time without a limp? Or . . . we just missed that she had a sister."

"Yeah, I hear you." He slowed for a red light, tempted to blow it. He could run the lights and siren but decided against it. "The fact that this other — sister or whatever — goes out the *back*, that's interesting. Like she doesn't want to be seen."

"Or she's got her car parked up there on the next block, and it's just a quicker route."

"She's looking around when she comes out. Checking to make sure no one's watching."

They were both silent, then the light changed, and Stamper hit the gas. Cuthbert had to use a little force to overcome the Gs and sit up straight. "Maybe it's like a family thing. Twins that got separated at birth. It happens. Maybe they were part of some twin study."

"Oh God — no one would do that, not for all the money in the world."

Cuthbert wasn't so sure. "I think there are all kinds of people. Maybe you can't fathom it, but some young mother who's got no money, no prospects, gets offered a huge chunk of money to give up one of her twins?"

He gave her a look.

"Yeah, I know," she said, capitulating. "I couldn't do it."

"Let's just get to the office, look at the footage again." He took a big breath. "I mean, holy shit. We got one of them. We got one of them on camera."

"Yeah."

"Jesus. Really ran them out of there. I bet he put them in the van at the mouth of the alley. Drove off, then we got them at the toll six, seven minutes later." He gripped the wheel, feeling the excitement grow in his chest. "Where the hell are they?"

CHAPTER TWENTY-SIX

"Please," Julie said.

Colton's glazed, dead stare lingered in her mind. They'd killed him, and they were going to kill her, too.

Who were they? What was this? Some kind of twisted death cult? Members had to seek out their siblings to torture and kill them?

If she could just make sense of this, just figure it out, the nightmare would end. The masks would come off, the curtain would slide back and the applauding audience would get on their feet and cheer.

Julie's rational mind prevails again! As we've now just seen, ladies and gentlemen, logic and rational thinking will always be your saving grace in the end. Get to know your abductors. Plumb the depths for their childhood traumas and help them reprocess deep-seated emotions of guilt and shame. Understanding their shame and trauma is the key to understanding the game, and thus — to setting yourself free.

Let's hear it for Julie Sprenikerrrrrr!

The phantom applause died in her head. Through the storm, the snow coming down hard and slightly to the side, flakes getting smaller now, more granular, the shed like a painting. Gray and bluish in the otherwise monochrome landscape.

Run.

Yes. That old chestnut. Just run. Just run off into the woods in the middle of a snowstorm when you have no idea where you are, nothing to keep you warm, nothing to protect you.

They're going to put you in there and kill you.

No, she thought, in the end, it's not our rational selves which preserve us. It's our survival instinct. It's raw fear.

So she turned and she ran, sticking to the path in the snow, hurrying past the front door to the cabin. Past Colton, hidden on the other side. Toward the parked vehicles — the Jeep and the van. Maybe one of them had keys . . .

Monique was hot on her heels, yelling something at her, and yelling for Keith. Keith had the gun.

Julie reached the Jeep first. Found it open. Reached around the steering column and felt for dangling keys. Nothing there. She flipped down the visor, hoping a set would come tumbling out.

It didn't.

With just seconds to consider it: *you can either keep looking in the Jeep for keys — maybe the console or dashboard; maybe under the driver's seat — or you can move on to the van.*

Michael was gone. Colton said he'd had them. But would he take them with him?

Slipping and sliding in the snow, she moved around the front of the Jeep and lurched toward the van, bracing against it. It felt like she could fall over at any moment. She didn't trust her body; it wanted to betray her. Getting around to the driver's side didn't matter, though, because Monique was already there, and Keith was running over from the cabin.

Julie opened the van door anyway, and Monique just watched. There might've even been a smile ghosting her lips — she was enjoying this.

In the driver's seat, Julie felt the steering column, nothing again, and checked the visor. Reaching across for the glove compartment, she popped it open and fumbled around, but no love. The console between the two front seats was also empty.

Behind her, the plywood partition separated the front from the back.

Julie got a sort of mental grab, then, like a piece of a puzzle that wanted to slide into place. Something about her arriving here in the back of this van, with all of the plastic to protect surfaces against trace evidence. But now Monique, just standing there, looking darkly amused, didn't seem to care that Julie was getting her fingerprints and DNA all over the interior of the front of the van.

It's supposed to look self-inflicted.

Whatever this was, whether it was some cult initiation or something even crazier than that, Monique was staging things, framing them up to look a certain way.

"All right," Keith said. He stood at the driver's side window, his busted lip swollen and an angry purple. The window was up, glass between them, but she could hear him fine — there was nothing else to block the sound, no city traffic, no construction, no other human beings making any of their usual noise. She was all alone. "Come on out," he said.

No, Julie thought. *Why would I come out? Why would I do anything you say?*

She locked the door. Keith looked at Monique, who lost that faint smile. This wasn't part of the plan — Julie could sense it.

But then Keith, after a moment, reached for something out of sight. By the time Julie realized he was unlocking the door, it was too late. The door opened and she grabbed the handle and pulled. In a tug of war with him, but he was stronger. Finally, he wrenched the door free, and as she tried to scramble to the other side of the van, he reached in for her legs, started pulling her out.

"Careful!" Monique yelled.

With one hard yank, Julie was out, in free fall. Then she hit the ground, like slamming into granite, snow or not.

"God," Monique said. "I said to be careful."

She helped Julie up.

Keith said, "What the fuck does it matter? You want to be so ginger with her, and she's going to be obliterated."

"Her face, Keith."

"You know, you keep talking to me like I'm some piece of shit. Maybe I'll just get out of here. See what you do, then."

"Then you wouldn't get paid, would you?"

They stood there a moment, unspeaking, Monique holding on to Julie's arm.

"But you do whatever you gotta do."

"Yeah? Strand you here? Take my ride and leave?"

"I got your keys."

"I'll take the van. Or, I'll take them from you."

Monique laughed. A humorless sound. "That's it? That's what you think you got on me? You think I'm stupid? I've been planning this thing for months. So, you do what you gotta do, Keith, but I want you to think real hard about this: This is your cabin. You're who the police are going to look at, especially with the way things went. Who do you think they're gonna want to talk to?"

He stared at her — Julie could see him putting it together. "You're a fucking cunt."

"Sure. Now get her other arm, and be gentle. We're walking her up to the shack."

Keith spit to the side and glared some more, but he eventually did as Monique said. They carried Julie this way, her legs barely working, toward the tiny little dark shack on the hill.

Maybe if she just went limp, if she just went numb . . .

She thought of her mother. The first round of cancer, the way it changed all their lives. Then her brother. Her father. The two of them out there in Colorado. She should have visited more. Shouldn't have let things get in the way. *God, isn't that what people always think, in the end?*

Toward the shack. Through the snow. Trudging along, these two people carrying her. Colton dead. And now, for whatever reason — did it matter? — they were taking her to meet her own end.

140

Wasn't there some saying about being taken to the woodshed?

Your daddy was going to give you a spanking, that was the meaning. You were going to be punished. What barbaric pasts we had. What horrible creatures we could be, what suffering we inflicted and endured.

Maybe it was best that it came to an end. All the torment she'd seen. The people coming through her office with their long faces, their grief and their shame, draped over them like demons. Her mother, when the cancer returned with a vengeance.

"Get the door," Keith said. "I got her."

Well, wasn't it nice that Keith had come around? Keith had fallen in line. Whoever this Monique was, if she was Julie's true twin, she definitely had traits Julie herself had never possessed. And never would.

Monique opened the door. And she stared at Julie, and Julie stared back. Like looking in a mirror? It had been, at first. But the more she got to know this woman, the more her actions revealed of her, the less sense Julie had that they shared anything, much less genes.

The shed was full of junk, but it had been somewhat cleaned up, sorted and stacked against the back wall — shovels and rakes and some old lawn equipment, a few assorted soggy-looking boxes and half-squished gas cans — leaving a clear space in the middle of the room.

An old chair sat there, like something from an antique dining set, dirty and unloved, growing cobwebs.

Monique got that black-hearted smile on her face again, and then her gaze flicked to Keith and she nodded. Julie felt Keith give her a little shove into the room.

Julie bumped the light hanging from the center of the ceiling. It swung back and forth, shadows racing from one end of the room to the other, as Monique said, "Sit down."

And Julie did.

She felt calm, actually, in a way she never would have suspected.

Maybe it was because some part of her expected to be seeing her mother soon.

Did she believe in that?

Yes, she found she did.

And then Monique, from somewhere, pulled a knife.

CHAPTER TWENTY-SEVEN

"Dale Rossi," Stamper said.

"Who?" Cuthbert was staring at the screen, at a frozen image of the woman who'd come out of the townhouse three minutes and twenty-three seconds after the others had come and gone.

The lookalike was staring in the opposite direction Spreniker and Rossi — and the man in the ball cap — had taken. She gripped a reusable shopping bag against her chest and wore a gray zip-up fleece and khaki cargo pants. Boots on her feet.

"Dale Rossi," Stamper repeated. He turned his own computer toward her. "Colton Rossi's father."

The man in the mugshot was in his sixties, rough-looking, a big gray mustache.

"It was one of my first cases when I started with BCI, and it just touched the edges of the Falzone family. I remember this guy because he looks like the cowboy in *The Big Lebowski*. The one who orders the sarsaparilla in the bowling alley. Remember that?"

"He's connected?"

"The feds thought he was, yeah. They called me because apparently he had property in the zone. They never got the warrant to raid it, but I remember the guy, his name and a few things from his file: he's got at least five kids. Colton is one, and Colton's got two sisters we know about. But he's also got other kids from different relationships. And here's one of them."

Stamper tapped a key, and a new window opened. Keith Rossi. He compared this with a still image taken from Shane Robbie's ring camera.

Cuthbert saw similarity but knew it wasn't enough. The guy in the O'Neill hat could be almost anybody. The quality was poor, his face only partly visible. "Well," she said, "you talk to him?"

"Not yet. Just left a message. I've talked to the sisters, but I'm gonna call back, ask about Keith."

Stamper turned his screen back around. She could tell he was disappointed by her lack of excitement. But Cuthbert rarely got excited about much of anything. Life was too full of unintended consequences for that.

She liked Louis Stamper, even if he sometimes acted like God's gift. He was actually smart, and had an interesting perspective on life. She'd grown up in cow country in the northern part of the state — Potsdam, on her family's farm. Stamper was from downstate, near the city, and had dabbled in movie work.

On their first case together, he'd used pop trivia to help catch a serial killer. At least, he'd had a hunch that helped the FBI make a move that eventually led, one could say, to the catching of the killer. It seemed like he was always looking for that edge, that thing outside of the normative police work, that would crack the case. While she, for better or worse, plodded steadily along with standard procedure.

She let it go and refocused on her own screen, continuing to write down every detail about Spreniker's wardrobe from scouring social media. The woman was not very dressy or showy, nor given to exhibition — most images of her were on Rossi's Instagram page, not her own.

As Stamper had already discovered, Colton Rossi led a much more public life than his fiancée. He was flashier, too.

More outgoing. But it was taking too long to find what she was looking for, and it was time for the press conference.

* * *

Jim Bueller was senior investigator for the BCI, and their immediate supervisor. A tidy man, Bueller had started shaving his head when his hair thinned considerably. He wore Brooks Brothers suits and solid-color ties; never patterned. A picture of his wife and two sons — the younger had autism — sat on the file cabinet behind his desk.

After summoning them to his office, he closed the door, seeking a debriefing before the press conference. "Anything new?"

Cuthbert gave him the rundown: "No one has seen the van since this morning — the last image we have is from the bridge camera on Highway 8, where it was northbound. The next camera is in Cold Brook, but they never show up. There aren't too many options from there — Route 28 to Barneveld, and then maybe up into the Adirondacks. East would be back-tracking. Otherwise, it's secondary roads, dirt and gravel, in the Ferris Lake area. That just doesn't make too much sense if they went west on I-90, though . . ."

"Unless they wanted to get picked up on the toll," Stamper said.

Bueller wrinkled his forehead. "Why would they want that?"

"I dunno. It's how we got a picture, the reg, everything. Pretty stupid mistake, unless it wasn't a mistake. Because you can get to Cold Brook or Barneveld any number of ways."

They all thought about it a moment, then Bueller said, "And it's registered to Rossi's boss, correct? What happened with that?"

"Warren Flandreau told us anyone can take it. Keys were in it," Stamper answered.

"Who would know that?"

"Anyone who works at Herkimer Brewing, apparently. Or anyone who's friends with them, or knows about the vehicle — Flandreau says it's common knowledge. We're following it all up, talking to everyone. Troopers are canvassing for it, all around Black Creek, Ferris Lake."

"What else?" Bueller's gaze shifted between them. "What about this double of Spreniker's? What are we saying about this?"

Cuthbert took it: "We did a full background check, of course, and she has one brother in Colorado. I've been on the phone with the father — he's a bit of a handful. He's on his way here. He assures us that Ms. Spreniker does not have a twin sister. Or any sister."

"That he knows of."

"Well, yes, sir. That he knows of."

"Because," Bueller said, "you have this witness putting Spreniker at the casino last night . . ."

She nodded. "The witness seems solid, but we just don't have any corroboration yet." The Mohawk-owned casino was federal jurisdiction. "I've got a call in to tribal police."

Stamper added, "The witness also says that the pair of them looked unhappy. The woman in particular."

Bueller sat back and looked thoughtful, soaking up the information. "What about this conference Spreniker was supposed to attend? What are they saying?"

"No hard evidence she was there," Cuthbert said. "But a room in her name and someone signed for her lanyard."

"And where are we at with the phones?"

Stamper summarized about Weintraub getting Rossi's DMs, the messages about money and relationship troubles, and Bueller came up with a similar idea: "So they try to put something together at the casino but end up busted, maybe? Owing the wrong people? I mean, am I talking about two missing, abducted people, or two people on the run? At this point, this whole press conference is just an advertisement for the hotline."

Cuthbert said, "We absolutely considered that, but it just doesn't explain the second woman. Or, if it's Spreniker herself, why she would jump out the window, hurt herself, then double back, come out a second time."

"What do you think? Why does this woman come out later?"

"It's possible she was hiding," Cuthbert answered. "That she's related to Julie Spreniker and there's just no paperwork on her. Arlene Spreniker could have gone to the hospital, delivered one baby, then came home and delivered another. Not likely, but possible. She could have done it in secret so that even her husband didn't know. Or Julie."

Bueller looked at Stamper, as if knowing he'd supply the counterpoint.

"Or, they're not related, and she's just someone who happens to look very much like Spreniker. They say everyone has a double."

"They say that, but it's unscientific," Cuthbert observed.

"So if they're not related . . ." Bueller started.

"Either way, she's in on it, sir," Stamper said. "We're sure she has something to do with the intruders."

Bueller breathed a deep sigh. "Okay. Is that it?"

Stamper: "Preliminary testing looks like Spreniker left vomitus in the trash can. The forensic serology unit did a pepsin-assay in the field, using a fibrin blue-agarose gel plate. It can identify the presence of gastric fluid. There are differences in gastric emptying between men and women . . . sir, I'll spare you the details — all we know is that preliminary indications are that the vomitus was from a woman. DNA testing is being done, but that will take a while."

Bueller said, "Okay, so nothing there."

"Well, I think it was something. Not for public information, but it indicates something that could have been happening in the bedroom, something upsetting, prior to the intruders."

"Or that someone is sick."

He had them there. A silence formed, with Bueller looking around, thinking. "Okay, conference time. After it's done, I'm going to ask that both of you stick with this tonight. Is that possible?"

They glanced at each other, though one had nothing to do with the other's schedule. Stamper knew that his wife,

Cara, would be home from work, and she'd understand. Cuthbert had her own family with three kids.

She said, "Sir, I want to get back to the Spreniker house and take another look at a few specific things."

Stamper felt cued to say something equally affirmative. "And my current preoccupation is that Colton Rossi's father is Dale Rossi."

Bueller's eyebrows went up. "I remember the case. Rossi made a deal with the feds and walked, but before that happened, we were put on notice about a possible raid. I just don't remember where the raid was supposed to be. What location?"

"They never disclosed that. It was all pending. Need-to-know basis."

"They just had us on standby," Bueller remembered.

"Right."

"Where is Dale now?"

"None of the information we have on him leads anywhere — no working phone or current address. But I have a call in to the FBI. They said an agent would get back to me."

Bueller rolled his eyes, knowing that returning calls was very unlike the FBI.

Stamper said, "I think the man caught on the Ring camera could be Keith Rossi, one of Dale's other sons."

"Okay," Bueller said, after a thoughtful beat. "Let's keep this thing rolling."

CHAPTER TWENTY-EIGHT

The townhouse had two bedrooms. The first bedroom: busted door jamb, splintered wood, bedcovers dragged off the bed and tangled on the floor. All that had been bagged up and taken to the lab for analysis. Urine, semen, blood. Kay Howells, pathologist, was going through it. The window, open that morning, storm guard slid up and out of the way, had been closed after the crime-scene crew dusted for prints. Results were also pending.

No scarlet letters or stash of clues, but vomit in the trash can meant something. Together with social media messages about money problems, it suggested tumult in the young couple's life.

The second bedroom had been tidier to the point of being un-lived in. But, as Cuthbert had noticed, Spreniker kept the bulk of her clothes here. "I'm looking for brands, clothing type, things like that," she explained, riffling through it all. "The woman that came out of the house was wearing a brand-specific fleece, and I think I recognized the pants, too."

"Sounds good," he said. "I'm gonna go talk to Daubin."

* * *

The press conference had drawn off most of the news people, and the storm was keeping them from coming back. When Stamper crossed from the townhouse to the other side of the street, he was just a lone figure in the night.

A man came to the door holding a Coors Light, looking like he'd worked a hard day of construction in his paint-stained jeans and soiled white tee. Stamper introduced himself and asked for Daubin. "She's asleep," the man said, but Daubin came to the door, pulling a robe around herself, having overheard.

"No, it's okay," she said, after Stamper apologized. She squinted though it was almost full dark outside, her hair sticking up with static electricity. "I got work in three hours. Need to get some things done around here." She looked at the man beside her. "What are you doing, Trent? Did you take the dog out?"

"I just took him out," Trent said.

Daubin grabbed his Coors Light and had a big sip.

Great, Stamper thought.

She handed Trent back the beer, then surveyed the street as she spoke to Stamper. "You find those people yet?"

Trent said, "It's all over the news. Local and national."

"Actually," Stamper said, "I'm here with a quick follow-up about that. Angela, could I step in for a moment and just show you a picture?"

They let him in, snow drafting in before they shut the door behind him. Stamper pulled up the picture of Keith Rossi on the phone. "Either of you ever see this man before?"

Daubin gave it a good squint, like she needed glasses. "No," she said finally.

Trent shook his head. "No, don't know him."

Stamper flipped to another picture as Daubin asked, "Who is he?"

The next picture was the still image from the Ring camera. "How about this one — he look familiar?"

It took a second. "Oh . . . wait, I think so. Is that one of the guys from this morning?"

He reminded himself that she'd just been sleeping. Witnesses could be unreliable to begin with, notorious for getting crucial details wrong all the time, but a hard-working (and maybe hard-drinking) nurse who'd just been unconscious for several hours might struggle even more. "I believe it is." He waited to see if she made the connection between the two images he'd just shown her.

She didn't.

Then he showed her the first image again. "Would you be able to say if this is one of those two men you saw enter the Spreniker-Rossi house this morning?"

It dawned on her; her eyes widened and her mouth opened. "Ohhh," she said. "Yes. Yeah. That could definitely be him. Oh wow — who is he?"

"Thanks very much, ma'am." He nodded at the big man, who was finishing his beer. "Sir."

Trent grunted. Daubin pulled the robe a little tighter as Stamper let himself out into the cold.

* * *

So, not great.

Daubin had made the connection between the two images, but only after he'd suggested it. That didn't mean she was lying; it just wasn't as strong as he'd hoped. Not enough for a court order. If he was going to look at Keith Rossi, it had to be casual.

Back in the townhouse, he shook off the cold. The kitchen was chic, if a little small for him — he liked to cook and preferred a bigger workspace — but the hanging pots and pans over the island were a nice touch, a feature he'd always wanted. You could tell someone with culinary experience lived here: the blender was a Cuisinart, the cookware was cast iron or the top-of-the-line non-stick variety. All the appliances were modern and clean.

He moved into the living space to the left, below the second bedroom, his thoughts swinging back to the timeline

151

and likely order of events this morning. When the intruders came in, maybe there was no forced entry, but someone had encountered them. Spreniker or Rossi, walking back to the bedroom from the bathroom, maybe, saw the intruders just as they came in.

Because if the third person — the lookalike — had been the one to see them, it was unlikely she would have been allowed to just leave the property some ten minutes later. She could have been hiding, like Cuthbert suggested — or she could have known the intruders, like he thought. Maybe even been working with them.

That thing again, at the back of his mind . . .

His phone buzzed in his pocket and he took it out. "Stamper."

The woman on the line sounded hesitant. "Um, this is Jennifer Holt, returning your call."

Holt was one of Colton Rossi's two sisters, both older. Each lived out of state, one down in Florida, near Rossi's mother. Holt was in Maryland with her husband.

"Mrs. Holt, thanks for calling me back."

"I'm very sorry," she said, "it's been a crazy day. I didn't recognize your number and was in the middle of twenty things. But then a friend sent me a link to YouTube, to a press conference. I couldn't believe it. The whole thing is . . . shocking, honestly."

"I understand."

"You spoke with my sister?"

"I did, Wendy, yes. Earlier today."

"I mean — oh my God. What's happening? Is there something I can do?"

"I was hoping I could ask you a few questions."

"Um . . . of course."

Stamper overheard her talking to someone in the background, shushing them as one would a child. "Is now a good time?"

"Sorry, I know I just called you, but I thought I would have more time . . ." Her voice went muffled again as she spoke sternly to the child, or children. "I'm in the car," she explained. "The boys' basketball game ended early. But no — I want to talk to you. Let me know what I can do."

He dug his notepad out of his pocket and asked her the standard stuff, about her brother's state of mind, whether he seemed happy, if anything unusual had been going on in his life. Money trouble. If he had any enemies. She kept coming back with the same answer: "Colton and I don't talk too much."

When pressed, she elaborated. "I know he's probably got a mountain of debt from school, because that's what I've got, and his school cost more than mine did. I see his stuff on social media. Sometimes I'll comment on it. He's big into rock climbing. He was in a magazine. I hope that works out for him. Or he opens his own restaurant. He's always been such a good cook."

"And your sister said as much — but also not a lot of phone calls or get-togethers or anything. When's the last time you saw him?"

"Oh boy . . . Probably two years ago. Yeah. Over two years ago. I think we went to Thanksgiving in Florida to see Mom. And we hadn't seen each other in maybe two years before that."

They talked a little more, with Holt intermittently shushing her sons or hastily answering their questions. Stamper was delicate when asking about the father. Jennifer Holt said, "Dale? I don't have anything to do with Dale." Her tone had changed almost completely, from a concerned, caring sister to flat and cool as an estranged daughter. "He left us when we were young and never looked back. My mom raised us and did a great job, if you asked me. I'm the eldest."

"How about any of Dale's other kids? I'm especially interested in Keith Rossi. Do you know much about him? Colton ever talk about him, maybe?"

"No. Never. I mean, me and Wen, we didn't ever have anything to do with Keith. Dale got them together a couple of times when they were young — Colton and Keith — but

Mom didn't like it. No, Keith is just . . . he's just a name to me."

"One last question: To your knowledge, did Dale ever had property in this area, around Herkimer? The last known address I have for him was Rochester, and he's not there now. But I have reason to believe there was a property he owned in the area."

"You mean the cabin?"

Stamper thought: *Bingo.* "A cabin, yeah. Like, a wilderness cabin? Maybe like a hunting camp?"

"The only thing I know about a cabin, Colton said something about it once. Said Dale said he was going to give him a cabin when he died, him and his brothers. Colton said he never wanted anything to do with it."

"Do you know where this cabin is?"

"Ah, well, I might need to ask Wendy. She might remember. I don't know . . . what was it . . . I can't remember, sorry. I think it was up north of where you are — Herkimer, right?"

"Yes, ma'am. You don't happen to have an address? Or maybe Wendy would?"

Holt shouted at the kids in the backseat. "Oh, definitely not. Like I said, Colton told us about it a couple of years ago."

"It's all right." He'd search the townhouse. There had to be some paperwork. A deed, a bill, something. If he had to, he'd go to the fucking FBI. He felt a kind of vibration going through him, a sense of gaining ground.

Up north of Herkimer was the Ferris Lake Wild Forest region — forever wild state land, thick and deep.

You could really get lost up there.

CHAPTER TWENTY-NINE

The vehicles moved along in the darkness, going slow in the storm, lights flashing, everything eerily silent in the falling snow.

That buzz of excitement stayed with Stamper, tingling the base of his skull. But something heavier grew alongside it, a dread for what they might find.

They turned off from Route 30, which had been slick. The plows were out working, but this storm was really blanketing the region. The secondary road up the mountain was unplowed and unsalted. Cuthbert was grateful for four-wheel drive.

"Hang on," Stamper said. "Let me out a sec."

She slowed down and parked, forcing the troopers behind them to do the same.

He felt the wet kisses of snow on his face, getting into his eyes as he examined a shallower patch of snow off to the side of the road in the shape of a car. Something had been parked here, he thought. Footprints came from one direction, tire tracks led off in another, toward the main road, all of it barely discernible. He took a few pictures anyway, then got back in with Cuthbert.

The next seven-tenths of a mile were slow-going. The road was long and winding through snow-covered evergreens.

In the end, the FBI hadn't been so bad. They were actually monitoring the case and had planned to reach out. More importantly, they gave up the location of Dale Rossi's cabin when Stamper had asked.

It was more, now, than playing a hunch. Someone who'd looked a great deal like the half-brother of Colton Rossi was caught on video chasing people with a gun. And his father was a known associate of a regional organized crime family. To not follow this up — and proceed with an abundance of caution — would be ludicrous.

Again, though, the dread.

"I keep having these dreams."

Cuthbert felt herself bracing. In three years working together, they'd never gotten personal. But they'd never had a case so sudden and high-profile. It was testing them, pulling at their emotional fibers.

"I have kids," Stamper said, about his dreams. "And it's so vivid. You know? It's like I've been raising them for years. It feels like that."

Cuthbert cleared her throat when she felt something catch. "Maybe your subconscious is trying to tell you something."

He kept thinking about Jennifer Holt, never a free moment to herself. She'd had to call back an investigator on a case about her own brother while shushing boys in the backseat. Or Cuthbert's husband, a veritable homemaker who spent most of his time feeding children and cleaning up baby poo. There were reasons Stamper hadn't had kids yet.

And some of them, maybe . . .

Well, you saw certain things as a cop, things that made the whole idea of bringing life into the world seem a bit crazy.

The road bent around to the left, opening up to a small clearing with a log cabin and a couple of outbuildings.

"Holy shit," Cuthbert said.

The vehicle sitting under four inches of snow was the exact right dimensions to be a cargo van.

156

They got out, trudged to it and wiped away the snow to reveal a white paint job, the smudgy outline of a removed decal. And then Stamper's hand went to his gun.

*　*　*

Impressions in the snow suggested multiple people going in and out of the cabin. In one spot, what looked like drag marks. Two sets of footprints led to where tire tracks stretched down the road, and a single set led to another pair of tire tracks. Two separate parties had left? And not that long ago, given the rate of snowfall. What about the impressions on the road coming in?

"Blood!" It was Cuthbert, just ahead of him, calling out.

Stamper saw where she was pointing, a dark patch about the size of a football just beneath a top layer of snow. Copious footprints around it, the snow flattened. Like someone had lain there, hurt.

"All right," he said, licking his lips, looking around. The troopers were moving in on the cabin, some behind him, some flanking. They were all in danger of trampling evidence. But they had to check the cabin, and they had to keep safe.

As more troopers circled around back, he and Cuthbert waited by the southeast corner. When Trooper Taylor appeared at the opposite front corner, Stamper went toward the door, keeping low as he passed under the one window. He stopped short of crossing in front of the door, keeping to the side of it. Cuthbert approached until she was just on the other side of the window, and Taylor neared until he flanked the door with Stamper. The padding of snow helped them all to stay quiet as they got into position.

Stamper knocked.

"Ms. Spreniker? Mr. Rossi? Hello?"

No answer. He glanced back at Cuthbert and gave her the signal — she got low and then peeked in the window, careful to stay back now that they'd made themselves known. A little peek, then she risked a fuller look, cupping her hand against any ambient light. Stamper could see her scanning, her body crouched but springy.

And then everything froze.

After a second or two of Cuthbert still as a statue, she turned away from the glass. He saw it in her eyes before she even made the relevant hand gestures: Someone was in there, yes — but they weren't moving.

He knocked again, obligatory but pointless — "Ms. Spreniker? Mr. Rossi? This is Investigator Louis Stamper with the New York State Police. I'm coming in." He took the door and was somewhat surprised the latch easily lifted and the door swung inward.

Coppery blood scented the air, and worse things, too. "Hello?" He repeated his name and intention. Carefully, his heart hammering in his chest, strange memories of children he'd never raised lingering in his mind, Louis Stamper pushed the door all the way open and stepped into the room, aiming his gun, checking the corners, and Taylor was right behind him, shouting "State Police!" and Cuthbert was there after that.

Soon, half a dozen law enforcement members poured in behind them, but Stamper kind of blanked after he got into the cabin all the way and lowered his gun, his mind balking at what he saw.

"Ah, man," he said.

CHAPTER THIRTY

Those feelings, disliking Colton Rossi, prejudging him, swelled in his gut. Acrid, bilious guilt, a churning in his stomach he wanted to vomit out.

"All right," Stamper said, and his voice sounded strange to his ears, as if it belonged to someone else. "Nobody touch anything."

The troopers went through the space — most concerning was the loft in the back. It looked like Colton Rossi had committed suicide, but you never knew. Someone could still be here, so the troopers took the stairs in a kind of SWAT formation, going up to the loft with their firearms gripped like they were trained to grip them, shouting, "Okay, clear!" after they were up there for a couple of seconds.

"We need to clear the room . . . just clear the room," Cuthbert said.

Stamper and Cuthbert eased closer to Rossi, slumped in a chair, blood all around him. Near his feet, a handgun. Cuthbert sized it up: "Victim appears to be Colton Rossi. Fatal gunshot wound to the head. It looks self-inflicted. The round entered beneath the chin . . . I don't see an exit wound, but that could be because of all the hair . . ."

Stamper was grateful to her for talking; his vocal cords might have seized.

She inspected the ceiling, the wall, for signs of impact from a round that passed through, but saw nothing. It really depended on the caliber. She crouched beside the gun to better examine it. "Weapon looks like a Smith and Wesson M&P .22."

A compact semi-auto pistol, the Smith and Wesson .22 was a favorite for target shooting and used inexpensive .22 LR ammo. A .22 round wasn't very big, and if it entered a victim's head, it tended to stay in there.

"I'll call in for crime scene," she said to Stamper, who was carefully making his way toward the back of the cabin, beneath the loft.

"Okay," he said, "Good."

If her intuition was on, he was feeling a little sickened. Like her, he'd seen plenty of DBs so far on the job, but this was particularly gruesome. There was also blood in multiple places — a splash over by the door, for instance, and drops all over the floor.

The thing was, they couldn't leave the cabin without checking for Spreniker.

"Got something," Stamper called from the back. She was careful to follow in his footsteps.

The three troopers were coming down the stairs. Two others stood watch just inside the door. Cuthbert caught up to Stamper, saw what he was referring to: a homemade gun cabinet, the lock pried off. Using the edge of his shirt sleeve, he swung one of the doors open. Hunting rifles hung from straps, three of them. On top, cubbies for storing ammunition. Stamper pointed out the box of .22 LRs.

Rossi, apparently, had used a gun that was here. But he didn't have the combination to the cabinet and so had just torn it open.

* * *

160

Cuthbert tried to call the crime-scene crew, but regular cellular service was terrible, so she used the state police satellites. With the forensic team on the way, she joined the troopers and Stamper in searching the premises.

The first outbuilding contained shoveling equipment and lawn care stuff — Stamper yanked a tarp off a suspicious-looking object that turned out to be an old push-mower.

They also found a generator and several large deep-cycle batteries. The source of power for this off-grid cabin, maybe.

So far the wind had been quiet, the snow dumping straight down like sifted sugar, but now it picked up and drove the snow at an angle. Flakes caught in her lashes as Cuthbert followed Stamper up to the final outbuilding, a shed sitting several feet higher up the mountainside. The sun was long gone, darkness full and storming. Stamper was just a charcoal sketch in front of her — she shined her flashlight on his back just to make sure he was fully human, then huddled in her fur-lined parka as he pushed open the door to the shed.

In Cuthbert's head: *Please don't be her in there, please don't be her in there . . .*

The shed was small, maybe just twelve feet deep by eight feet wide. More yard care equipment, some logging materials — band saws and chain saws, much of it looking old and unused for some time.

Their flashlights picked it up: a concentration of blood in the middle of the floor. More blood spatter on the walls and the various equipment items.

She flipped her light up — even some blood on the ceiling. *God help us.*

Maybe this was what the investigators felt like when they first walked through scenes of the Manson Family murders. Blood outside of the body meant trouble — a small cut could stop a normal person in their tracks, get them headed to the medicine cabinet for a bandage and some Neosporin — but several ounces of it splashed around gave a sense of profound disruption, turned the mind into uncomprehending mush.

Someone had been hurt in this room, evidence of it everywhere, but the victim was not here.

They checked every corner, but it was a small space, and the longer they were in here, the greater they risked contaminating evidence, so they were soon back outside, the wind and snow whipping. Looking at each other, both of them thinking the next rational thing — either Rossi had relocated his fiancée's body — perhaps a shallow grave — or she might've not been dead yet and run off on her own. But there was no apparent blood trail. No tracks to follow.

Shining their flashlights over the snowy ground, they circled the cabin, him going one way and her the other, but nothing.

Julie Spreniker had vanished.

CHAPTER THIRTY-ONE

"He buried her," Cuthbert suggested, "and then the snow covered his tracks."

They sat in the vehicle, keeping warm and out of the weather.

"But she's up there somewhere," Cuthbert continued, looking out the foggy windshield. The dark trees in the distance. "She's buried somewhere up there, in a shallow grave. Or maybe she's just lying there. He dragged her into the woods and just left her . . ."

Stamper, without thinking, put his hand on Cuthbert's. He gave it a pat, and she took a cleansing breath. "Jesus, Lou," she said. "What a mess."

He thought a minute and said, "They had the fire going in there — you see that?"

"I did."

The wood stove had given off heat. "They had to have been there a while, enough to get that fire going to hot coals."

"They came straight here from the townhouse. But with or without the assailants? Did Colton drive just the two of them here? Or something else?"

"Angela Daubin saw man number one get back into the van and leave. Man number two came out the window right about the same time. Waverly curves around like that . . . The two of them got picked up. Then brought here."

"Okay . . ." Cuthbert said. "But then what? Where do they go from there? What happened to them? I'm just a simple country girl, but it looks like Colton Rossi brought Julie Spreniker to here to kill her and then himself. And that's that."

Stamper didn't know. And neither did she; she was guessing.

There was so much to do now, it was hard to break it all down, prioritize. They were going to have to go through the whole thing with the crime-scene crew, show them where they had come in, where the troopers had come in, so the police on scene could be eliminated from any trace evidence. An incident command would be set up somewhere in the vicinity but far enough away to preserve the scene. A search party would form, the area scoured for Spreniker. If Cuthbert was right, she wasn't far, and they'd find her before too long. But it was all going to have to happen at night, in the middle of a crazy blizzard, or it was going to have to wait until morning. That was Jim Bueller's call, or maybe someone above his pay grade.

"There would be a blood trail," Stamper said.

"What?"

"If that's Julie Spreniker's blood, and she ran off, we'd have found the trail. We looked. Everyone looked. There was nothing."

"The snow's covering it all up. Maybe she made a tourniquet."

"There were footprints leaving — there were tire tracks. You think Rossi and her weren't alone, right? So maybe the men could have been here and gone. What if it was two guys who work for the family in Utica?" He meant Falzone. "They set this up to look like a murder-suicide, but something went wrong?"

"Why?"

"Well, Colton was maybe in the wrong place at the wrong time, brother to the wrong guy. Or, maybe he was into something."

164

"Either way," Cuthbert said, "That means she's out here."

He thought about it. It definitely filled some of the holes. Perhaps even Warren Flandreau was involved, and that's how the van was connected. Maybe he ran a poker game out of the brewery on Sunday nights. Could be he was booking for some bigger games, too. The kinds with muscle-men who handled debts.

Cuthbert was quiet, staring out at the van. Stamper saw the tracks headed there, the drops of blood, and knew what she was thinking.

"Dammit," he said under his breath.

"Well, we gotta look," she said.

* * *

But the van was empty. No one and nothing in it. No rear seats, no carpeting, just bare metal. And for all the blood everywhere else, the back of the van looked clean.

In the front glove box was paperwork to officially iden-tify the owner as Warren J. Flandreau. They'd sweep the front area for traces of the driver, the gunman.

But if the two men had been here — and Stamper was more and more thinking they had — they were long gone.

* * *

It was late by the time Bueller showed up, going on one in the morning, Stamper yawning and getting fuzzy. "You should get home and get some rest," Bueller said. "Both of you."

It had taken extra time for the crime-scene crew to get there in the storm. It would take a while to get home, too — Stamper considered sleeping in the vehicle, but Cuthbert needed to get back.

Road crews were out working the storm, plows were going, but it was just one of those snows that kept coming, making the going slow. The investigators were too tired to talk anymore, too focused on the storm. Cuthbert hunched over the steering wheel, peering out with slitted eyes, while Stamper slumped against the passenger door, staring out.

Once they were back in normal cell tower range, his phone lit up with messages and he listened through his voicemails.

"Officer, ah, Stamper . . . This is Brianna Vincent. From Herkimer Brewing? I was wondering if . . . well, I just had something to talk to you about. You left me your card and, um . . . and then I saw you come back to the restaurant this afternoon . . . Anyway, please call me."

* * *

Cuthbert drove them back to the barracks — both of their personal vehicles were there — and Stamper said goodnight to her and started up his car.

After she drove off, red taillights fading into the black snow, he called Brianna Vincent. He hadn't told Cuthbert about the message. He wasn't keeping it from her, she just needed to get back to her family, and if she knew he was still working, she'd feel obligated.

It was late, but he had a feeling Brianna was not an early-to-bed-early-to-rise type. And she'd sounded urgent on the message.

"Hello?"

"Ms. Vincent, this is Investigator Stamper. Sorry for the hour."

"Oh, no . . . That's okay. Thank you for calling me back." Now that she had him on the phone, he wondered if he detected some hesitation.

"Is this about the van?" he asked.

"Ah, no. Though Warren told me about that. That's crazy . . . did you find it?"

"How can I help you, Ms. Vincent?"

"I, um . . . I don't know. I think . . ."

"Whatever it is, it's okay. All right? And anything you can tell me will be helpful, I'm sure."

166

She was quiet for a few seconds, music thumping in the background. "Um, so where do you live, Mr. Stamper?"

He wasn't in the habit of telling people. "I live in Holland Patent."

"Oh." She brightened up. "That's so cute up there. I love Holland Patent. I'm in Rome. So that's close?"

She might've thought he was home. "Not far," he said.

"Would you be willing to stop by? I could give you my address. I'll drop you a pin."

He took a breath, ready to say no. But he glanced at his watch. It was on the way. Whatever she wanted to tell him, she wanted to do it in person.

"Okay. I'll be there in twenty."

CHAPTER THIRTY-TWO

A cat nearly escaped when Brianna Vincent opened the door to her small rented house. Stamper moved to block its path as she quickly snatched it up. "Oh, Casper," she said to the all-black cat. "Bad kitty."

With the feline in her arms, she pushed the door open. He stepped off the porch and entered — it smelled like candles and cooking.

"He's the only one who tries to get out," she said, setting the cat down.

As it trotted off, Stamper said, "Maybe he resents the name."

She smiled. "He's my roommate's. She thought that was just hilarious to name a black cat Casper."

Music played from a small wireless speaker. Nina Simone, maybe. He was too tired to decide whether the whole cat thing was stupid or funny. He needed to get home.

"Can I take your coat?"

"I'm okay, thank you."

She wore form-fitting blue jeans and a white top with lacy sleeves, make-up darkening her eyes. She'd been waiting for him. But his stiffness was coming off poorly. She was looking like she regretted this. "You want to sit?" he asked.

She seemed relieved. "Sure, yeah."

He decided on the comfy red chair to his left and she sat across from him in a cushioned rocker. A braided rug stretched between them beneath a refinished coffee table. It all looked like rescued furniture.

"Can I get you something to drink?"

"Actually, water would be great."

She went to the kitchen where he watched her, framed by a pass-through window, take a drink of red wine. She seemed on the brink of nervousness. As she walked back into the room with the water she said, "I told Tori about you. My roommate."

"Tori, with the cat."

"Yeah."

He drank the water as Brianna sat down. Two more cats had appeared— an orange tabby, a gray one that looked like it had some Maine Coon in it.

"Just that you've been in commercials. And we, ah — we looked you up. You did some movies, too, and TV shows."

"Just a couple." The Maine cat came by for a nuzzle.

"I knew I recognized you. And it was more than the commercial. You were in that movie about Afghanistan. So how did you get into that? I'm sorry if that's too personal."

"It's okay." If her knowing him from his brief previous career helped let her guard down so she'd talk, he was fine with it. As the gray cat trotted off, he said, "My mother worked as a casting agent. That's it. And I got out because . . . I spent too much time waiting for the phone to ring."

The alcoholism part would keep for now.

"Does your mother still . . . ?"

"She passed away a few years ago."

"Oh, I'm so sorry."

"Thanks." He was prepared to say something about it if need be, but Brianna seemed ready to move on to the main subject.

She swept back her fine black hair and looked up at him, a final resolve in her gaze. "I just wanted to tell you, wanted to tell police, that I slept with Colton. While he was with Julie."

"Okay."

"Before they got engaged, though. But since they've been together." She took a deep breath. "I'm not proud of it, but it happened. And I thought, usually when police do this kind of thing, when you're investigating, especially if they've disappeared, him and Julie, or something happened, you're going to look at everything, right?"

He gave a soft nod.

"That's what I thought. If there are things hidden, they're going to look worse. So, this is full disclosure. I slept with him exactly twice. Once in August of last year and once in September, about two weeks after — it was Labor Day weekend."

When Stamper didn't say anything, she said, "Look, I know it's not an excuse, but it's a restaurant. I've worked in several. And everybody sleeps with everybody; it's just how it is. I'm not saying that's why I did it. I'm just saying . . . Oh God, this is coming out all wrong."

He'd had similar thoughts himself. "I'm not here to judge you, or anyone. I appreciate you being up front with this. You're right — it's better to get it all out, because we do look at everything."

She pulled herself back together, nodded and wiped her nose, sniffing back tears. Stamper reached into his pocket for a tissue but didn't have any. She just sniffed again and looked at him. "I don't know if it helps you."

"Everything helps. Do you think Julie knew?"

"I don't know. I think she . . . Maybe she was in denial, a little bit? About Colton? Is he okay? Can you tell me anything? You probably can't."

"Do you think, uh . . . You're the only one he's done this with?"

She looked at him for a long time and then slowly shook her head.

"Who else? Someone you know?"

"Well, that's the weird thing."

170

"What?"

"Would you like some more water?"

He looked at his glass. He'd emptied it without realizing. "I'm good."

But she rose from the chair and went to the kitchen and got her wine glass. The music switched to Pink Floyd, arguably their most iconic song: 'Comfortably Numb.'

"This song," Brianna said, and she began to gyrate a little, twirling around once.

"Ms. Vincent . . ."

"Some of the best lyrics ever put down on paper."

"Ms. Vincent . . . Brianna."

Her eyes opened and she focused on him, took a drink of the wine, and sat, a little heavily this time. He realized she'd been acting more sober than she was. Now she was letting down her guard.

"You were telling me about Colton."

"I'm sorry. It's been a long day. And Warren was an absolute wreck. He had me stay on through the dinner rush. I was there until ten. Twelve-hour shift. I mean, that place has been good to me, but Warren is starting to lose it."

"What do you mean?"

"I just mean he's . . . you know . . ."

Stamper drew a sharp breath. "Brianna, listen. Have you seen anything going on at Herkimer Brewing?"

"Anything illegal? Or immoral?" Her mouth curled into a half-smile. "It's the restaurant business, so it's all going on all the time. People cheating on their spouses, people doing drugs, people serving drunks their drinks."

"What about Colton getting into an altercation with someone? Anything like that?"

She scrunched up her face thinking about it. "No. I don't think so."

He pulled out his phone and went to the photo of Keith Rossi, showed it to her. "You ever seen this man?"

She gave it a long look, tilting her head. "Who is he? He's cute."

"Not at the restaurant? Anywhere?"

She shook her head and he put it away.

"Colton ever talk about his family?"

"No. You wouldn't know he had a family. He's kind of a narcissist. Sorry, but it's true. He might care for her in some way . . . Julie. I don't know. Maybe she can save him."

"How do you mean?"

"Hmm? Oh, I don't know."

"You were about to tell me something . . . That he was with other women, too."

She was staring off now, lost in thought.

"Brianna?"

Her focus came back. She finished the rest of her wine and studied the empty glass. A thin coating of translucent red still held. "I saw him outside, in the parking lot."

"Colton?"

She nodded. "Talking to someone, and I thought it was Julie. That's what was weird. It *looked* just like Julie. But it wasn't Julie. Her hair was different, she was taller, maybe . . . I don't know what that means."

Neither did he. But he was glad she told him.

He made his exit shortly after that. All the playfulness and flirtatiousness — if that's what it had been — had drained from Brianna by the end, and she only looked tired. He drove the rest of the way home thinking about Julie's twin, or lookalike. Even alter egos. He'd had a small part in a movie once about a man moonlighting as a serial killer, unaware of it in his daily life. He was still thinking about it when he crawled into bed next to Cara and put his arm around her.

She mumbled against him and snuggled into the spoon of his body.

After some time, he fell into a troubled sleep.

PART FOUR

24 Hours Gone

CHAPTER THIRTY-THREE

Messages blinked on Stamper's work phone, Post-It notes adorned the desk. He picked one up. Trooper Taylor had found a current address for Keith Rossi in Rochester, NY. Stamper tried the associated phone number, but it went straight to voicemail.

An email from another trooper contained background information on Angela Daubin, the nurse who had called 911. Not good. Daubin had worked for five different hospitals in five years, accused by two of stealing benzodiazepines for her personal use. She'd been to rehab twice.

"Shit," Stamper said.

Her statement was a big piece of the case. Ray Costa had seen the van drive away, but that was it. Daubin was the sole witness who could describe the two men arriving and going up the steps to Spreniker's front door. She'd identified Keith Rossi. It had been shaky, but it could have been enough to get a warrant and search his home.

Stamper opened the digital shared folder, checked the time code on the Daubin's 911 call against the Ring camera footage. It lined up — the man in front drove away just seconds after the man in back emerged from the gate.

Stamper rewatched the footage, from when Spreniker first stuck a foot out the window, then worked her way to hanging from the windowsill before she dropped. The camera lost sight of her behind the high fence. But, he noticed — she was already at the fence door, opening it, as Rossi started out the window.

She wasn't even waiting for him. Stamper could understand that: an armed intruder was in her home. It wasn't until Colton jumped, and got hurt, that she stopped.

Quite a bit of compassion on her part, especially if it was true they were fighting, like the messages suggested. Or, given what Brianna had said, if she'd just discovered Colton was sleeping with her sister.

But then the man with the gun appeared. And Stamper, leaning closer to the screen, saw something else interesting and paused the video.

He didn't yet have any photo documentation of the cabin crime scene, of the gun lying next to a dead Colton Rossi, but he had the picture in his mind, the knowledge of gun makes and models. That gun from the cabin had been a Smith and Wesson M&P .22.

A gun that looked just like the one carried by the man in the video.

* * *

With a fresh cup of coffee from the break room (though "fresh" was being kind), he thought it through: either Cuthbert was right, and Colton Rossi had managed to get the jump on these guys but then offed himself because he knew hell would follow. Or, Colton had been in league with them, setting something up, and it went bad. He then killed himself rather than deal with the fallout.

The whole thing could be Colton abducting his fiancée for the payout — Julie Spreniker had a good job working for the state that came with benefits. She had life insurance, but they weren't yet married. Colton Rossi was not the beneficiary.

He went back to the video and watched again as Spreniker seemed to reappear, as if by magic, to emerge from the back gate, look one way and the other, then exit camera left.

Stamper hit the space bar, and the video froze before she could disappear.

Cuthbert had explained her interest in Spreniker's dress style on the ride back from the cabin: "I want to know whose clothes this unknown female subject is wearing. Her own? Spreniker's? And what's the bundle she's carrying? It looks like more clothes in a bag to me. Something black."

The idea that the unknown woman might be trying to pose as Spreniker had implications that tickled the base of Stamper's neck. That was some crazy shit. But perhaps more likely than the alter ego idea.

Just as intriguing: she'd changed because she needed to blend in. Whatever was under her arm wasn't appropriate to be wearing around at seven o'clock in the morning.

Like maybe a cocktail dress.

After a moment, he texted Cuthbert.

What if they're in on it together?

Wherever she was, maybe sorting out what to do with the kids, Cuthbert was quick to respond:

Colton Rossi & Mystery Woman?

Yeah, he typed.

And, he figured, mystery woman was there already. In the townhouse. With Rossi.

It felt right, a thought so clear and crisp it might rival someone's idea of God talking to them.

She was there all along.

* * *

Cuthbert came in with donuts, snow on the box.

"Still coming down?" Stamper asked, about the snow.

"It's letting up a little."

176

As she took off her parka and booted up her system, he sussed out the chocolate glazed. "You're really amazing," he said, around a mouthful.

A minute later, they got down to business. "I think it goes like this: Julie Spreniker comes home early from her conference, just like her supervisor said, and discovers them in bed together. Maybe, alarmed and disgusted, Julie throws up in the corner trash bin."

Stamper waited as Cuthbert let this percolate.

"So did they know Spreniker was going to be early?" she asked.

"I don't think so." He had looked at the file with Colton Rossi's recent texts. Nothing between him and Spreniker since Tuesday afternoon, when she sent a picture of a man falling asleep in the middle of a lecture, with the caption, *He looks how I feel*. Rossi hadn't responded. In fact, his last message to her was Monday morning, the morning she left, a simple *Drive safe*.

"So if there was some plan, her coming in early wrecked it," Cuthbert said. "They weren't ready. Maybe why we have people coming out of the back window on camera."

"They're improvising," Stamper said.

It felt like something, and they both knew it. The air crackled in the small office.

But there was still so much that didn't fit and needed to be accounted for. Too much in his head to straighten out just yet.

There was a ping from Cuthbert's laptop.

"Blood came back," Cuthbert said, eyes back on her computer. "Kay Howells says not enough blood at the townhouse for a conclusive type. But the cabin is another story. No DNA yet, obviously, but it's a match for type. All over that shed on the hill — looking like Spreniker's blood."

He waited, as if he knew what was coming next.

"And they found a black cocktail dress, wadded up in the corner. I can't be sure, but I think that dress was in the bag she was carrying when she left the townhouse. No bag, though. Just the dress."

"So mystery woman was at the cabin, too?"

Cuthbert shrugged.

Meanwhile, out at the Rossi cabin, dog teams were out, search grids formed, helicopters covering wide swaths of the Southern Adirondacks. But so far, nothing.

If they'd buried Julie Spreniker somewhere out there, she wasn't turning up. And if she'd gotten away, she was likely dead from exposure.

CHAPTER THIRTY-FOUR

Death notices. Never fun. Stamper began with Colton Rossi's sisters, who wept and asked questions, and he told them what he could. Colton's mother, Ann-Marie Jacobs, lived in Florida. Her daughter, Colton's second oldest sister Hannah, asked to be the one to call her. Stamper was relieved.

Dale Rossi still wasn't answering.

Expecting Keith Rossi's voicemail to pick up per usual, Stamper was temporarily stunned when someone answered. "Hello?"

"Ah . . . is this Keith Rossi?"

"Who's this?"

"Mr. Rossi, this is Investigator Louis Stamper with the New York State Police. Can I ask you, uh, what you're aware of in respect to your half-brother, Colton Rossi, and his recent disappearance?"

There was commotion in the background on Rossi's end, like he was at a diner, someplace with people. "I saw it on TV. On my phone. Someone said there was a missing-person thing."

Stamper thought a moment. "Mr. Rossi, I regret to inform you that your brother Colton has been found dead."

He took the news silently, just the muffled din in the background coming through. After a few seconds, Stamper explained that a county coroner had made the pronouncement very early that morning. That things were moving slowly due to the weather, but that the body was in the process of being relocated to the morgue.

Keith didn't ask how he died. "I don't really have anything to do with my father's other family. We don't ever really see each other."

"I'm very sorry for your loss. Even if you weren't close."

"Okay. Well . . ." He seemed ready to hang up.

"Do you know when was the last time you saw Colton?"

"In person?" He let out a long breath. "Um, no. Years ago. I see him online sometimes."

"You guys don't text or anything?"

"No."

"And you live in Rochester?"

"Yes."

"Is that where you are now?"

Keith didn't respond. There was a burst of laughter in the background, distant.

"Mr. Rossi?"

"Is there anything else? You told me he's dead, I'm sorry to hear it. But I gotta go."

"Just real quick," Stamper said. "I've been trying to reach your father, too. Do you know where I can get in touch with him?"

"Who knows."

"Been a while since you talked to him, too?"

No response.

"I ask because, ah . . . well, your brother was found at a cabin in Ferris Lake." Stamper hesitated only briefly, listening for reaction, then continued. "Property records show your father has owned the land since 1981. There's pictures of him and you up there. You ever get up there, hunting and stuff like that?"

Keith remained silent a moment longer. "It's been a while."

"You were away for several years, I understand. You served."

180

A pause. "Yeah?"

"How's it been since you've been back?"

"You serious?"

"Okay . . . I'll ask you just this, just routine, need to cross you off my list: Can you tell me where you were yesterday morning?"

"At work. You think I had something to do with Colton going missing?"

"What do you do?"

"Construction, demo, whatever it takes."

"And you have people you worked with yesterday morning."

"Yep. All my guys."

"Okay, well, thanks for that info." Stamper let the silence sit for a moment, see where Keith might take it.

"How did it happen? Or, how did he die?"

Ah. At last.

"Well, right now we're still determining that."

Stamper swiveled in his chair a little and caught Cuthbert watching him, something in her eyes reading: *Easy, be careful.*

"And what about the, um . . . Colton's girlfriend?"

"Fiancée. The search is still underway."

Stamper was silent once more.

"Mr. Rossi, I appreciate your time."

"All right."

He ended it, looked at Cuthbert across the desk. She looked back, lifting her eyebrows. "That sounded interesting."

"Very interesting."

* * *

Warren Flandreau wasn't answering, either, but Stamper left a message: He'd like to see footage from the cash register camera, however far back it went.

State Police Lieutenant Ray Fergus, outranking Jim Bueller, made the decision to hold another press conference. It was important for the search and rescue efforts to continue, but there was also a death investigation that had opened: Colton Rossi had been found in the cabin. And two men seen by a witness entering his home — one caught on camera — were still at large.

The press ate it up. This was the one-two punch, the frosting on the cake: a missing white woman and a suspicious boyfriend in the mix. You couldn't sell the story fast enough.

"No comment," Cuthbert said, and hung up the desk phone. Her cell phone rang next and she scowled at what she saw on screen, then looked worried. "Oh shit," she said. "The father."

They'd tacitly agreed she was the better person to keep in touch with Spreniker's family — she just had a lighter touch and could be more sensitive than Stamper. But Thomas Spreniker had been monitoring the TV and was convinced his daughter was fighting for her life out there somewhere in the snow and cold, and he needed to be nearby. So he and Julie's brother, Jack, had just booked an early flight from Colorado. They would be landing in Albany later that evening, a two-hour time-zone lag slowing them up.

"We're doing everything we can," Cuthbert assured him over the phone. "Search crews have been out nonstop. We're going to find your daughter."

She glanced at Stamper and must've seen in his eyes what had to be asked, crazy as it might be to ask it. She waited for Spreniker to finish speaking, jotting something down as he did. "Well, I thank you again, sir. I just have one question. When we spoke yesterday, when I called you, I asked if Julie had a sister . . ."

She waited, listening. "Okay, how about anyone she ever mentioned — someone who might bear this very close resemblance?" Looking at Stamper, she shook her head. "Okay," she said into the phone, "thank you again . . ."

It took another two minutes to get him off the line. "He talked about a friend of Julie's," she said, "Annette Peters, who Julie went to college with and who lives in the area. She does social work, too."

"Do we know about Peters?"

"No, we didn't know about her. She left the clinic a few years ago, went into private practice."

"Okay then."

"He thinks maybe Julie is hiding out. That she got free of Colton and is hiding out with her friend."

Neither of them had to verbalize how unlikely it was.

"Worth a chat with Peters, though," Cuthbert said.

Stamper knew he was up and gathered his things to leave. Gun and badge, his heavy parka for the cold and snow.

"He says he has something to tell us about Julie," Cuthbert added about Thomas Spreniker. "But he feels it will be best only if he tells us in person."

Stamper stood there. "What?"

"I just said . . ."

"Right, yeah yeah." He started for the door, stopped. "But definitely no sister?"

"No sister. But something about who Julie is, her past."

Stamper thought about it. His hand on the door to leave, he lowered his head. "God," he said. His voice was a whisper. "Linds . . . we don't even know if she's still alive."

CHAPTER THIRTY-FIVE

Sixteen hours earlier

"Sit down," Monique ordered.

Julie, knowing it was futile to resist — Keith was just inside the door, blocking her exit — did as she was told. On a rickety chair in the middle of the shed.

"Lean back," Monique said. "I mean, tilt your head back."

Julie shook all over. She couldn't stop it. Sitting in the chair, she did as instructed, wondering why. *She'll cut your throat.* This was it, then. For the end of her life, it didn't feel like it should. No finality to it, just another moment to get through to something else.

Monique grabbed a handful of her hair, as if to steady her, then sliced with the knife. The cut was painful, but more surprising than anything else.

"Keep your head just like that," Monique said.

Julie did as told, touching her throat at the same time. The skin was intact. The place Monique had cut was the back of her head.

"Holy shit," Monique said. "Yep, bleeds like crazy. Look at that. You said there's a bandage? Gauze?"

"Yeah, there's a first-aid kit," Keith answered.

"Go get it, please."

Opening the door let in wind and swirling snow.

"Asshole," Monique muttered. "He's really such an arrogant prick." Monique moved her face into Julie's field of vision. There was a sound like rain drizzling in a bucket. "You thought I was going to kill you, huh? You thought you were gonna die in here?"

Everything — the pain in her leg, the terror she'd just felt of being killed in this shack, the confusion over what was happening now — it was all background to the other pain, which was everywhere, an unbearable mixture of anger and emptiness, thick grief and the deepest, coldest sense of loneliness.

For the loss of Colton, yes — but loneliness that such a world as this existed, in the crevasses where life stopped behaving by any sort of logic, or rules, and turned up the inexplicable: long-lost twins, hurtful affairs, senseless cold-blooded killings — all just waiting behind a door you open too early one morning.

She didn't even feel relief.

Monique had sliced her scalp, apparently, not her throat, but there was no exaltation at this.

Colton . . .

He was gone. She'd seen the emptiness of his wide and staring gaze. The heavy stillness in his body, the blood spreading from beneath his cheek, mashed against the wooden floor.

Keith had shot him in the head.

His own brother.

"Good God," Monique said. "Just an amazing amount of blood. And I only cut you like an inch across. A couple of millimeters deep. Won't even need stitches. But I gotta stop it, at some point. You're not a hemophiliac, I hope? Jesus, this just keeps going. Look at this. Wait, no, stay the way you are. Can you feel the blood coming out?"

It wasn't a question that needed answering. Monique was just chattering. If not nervous, anxious. Impatient. She had some plan — it was starting to take shape in Julie's mind, at least, pieces were starting to fit — and it was proving difficult to execute. Mistakes had been made.

Monique set down the small bucket she was using, then grabbed Julie's hair again. She pushed something against her scalp, and Julie winced. "Hold this. Keep pressure. God, that thing is still bleeding. But that's okay. Gonna fill this whole place with your blood."

A few seconds passed, and Julie thought she heard a door slam outside. Monique said, "In a way, I should thank you. You're giving me a second chance at life. Like a good twin."

Julie was forming her response when the door banged open and Keith came in on another swarming gust of flakes. "Fuck," he said, presumably about the scene. "He's not an axe murderer. He just kills her. Drags her—"

"Did you get the gauze?"

"I got it." He passed it to her. "We have to get going if we're going to get anywhere in this."

"I know that, Keith. We're not staying. There's absolutely no way we're staying. That's impossible."

"That's why I'm saying hurry up."

She sighed but kept her composure. "How much you think that is?"

"A pint?"

"I don't think that's a pint." To Julie: "Keep pressure."

"Here, I'll hold it." Keith took the towel from Julie and held it against her scalp, which was stinging now, throbbing with her pulse. He smelled of cigarettes, that funk a smoker gets when they return inside, but Julie was grateful for it — the metallic stink of her own blood was gagging.

They both stood behind her, checking and re-checking beneath the towel, occasionally bickering as they did, like an old married couple with psychopathy. They were using her in some crazy scheme, something Monique felt she needed in order to survive, apparently.

Julie's head throbbed as they finally wrapped a large bandage around it, everyone's breathing loud in the confined space, despite the storm banging outside. When Keith stood, his head hit the lightbulb. "Ow," he whined, and the bulb swung, making those moving funhouse shadows again.

"This is ridiculous," he said. "It's not going to work."

"Yes it is. This is better."

"With a gash in her head?"

"It'll look like anything. It'll look like a rock, or something."

"Take her car, drive off down I-90, get her on a couple of toll cameras, then, poof, she's gone. So much easier, so much better."

"Can you stop, please?"

"What difference does it make if she knows? I'm saying, it made sense."

"Stand her up with me. Come on, Julie, time to get on your feet."

There was something in Julie that meant to resist, but she knew it would only prolong things. Whatever they were trying to get away with — a murder-suicide, it seemed — wouldn't be undone by her little resistances, but by other, larger mistakes. And they both seemed to know it.

Keith took her outside. Monique stayed, and then just before the door closed, Julie saw her dip a small paintbrush into the cup of blood and start flinging it around inside of the shack.

Well, okay — a nice touch. You couldn't really fling blood around a room from a bucket; it would all splash out at once. So the paintbrush helped, and would look more like spatter from a beating.

Maybe they weren't so dumb after all.

* * *

Julie fell into the Jeep, scrambled to get up onto the seat, and Keith slammed the door closed before she had her legs in all the way. The door crashed against her right ankle, sharp and painful, causing her to cry out.

He took hold of the foot and shoved, then closed the door again.

Alone, she lay across the back seat. Her head pulsed from front to back in time with her frantic heartbeat, along with a new, throbbing pain, blaring up her right leg. She drew a shuddering breath.

The exhalation turned into an anguished cry. For Colton, for herself, for this long and insane day. It tapered off into sobs. For the first time since she'd been abducted that morning, dragged into the middle of nowhere to watch her fiancé die, to have strangers assault her, scream at her, slice into her and make her bleed, Julie wept.

It was cut short when the driver's side door opened and Monique got in. Keith, a moment later, got into the passenger side. He handed over the keys.

"Okay," Monique said, after starting the engine. "Here we go."

CHAPTER THIRTY-SIX

The windshield wipers whipped back and forth, caked with the snow they couldn't shake. Monique had stopped twice to clean the gunk before they were even out of the woods and onto an official road.

She occasionally spoke to Keith in the passenger seat beside her in low tones, Julie unable to make out the words over the engine.

The Jeep reeked of burnt oil and spoiled food. Keith had held the keys, suggesting it was his, yet Monique was driving. All part of a riddle Julie continued to work on, one that grew darker with each new chapter, each passing hour.

Had it really been seven o'clock this morning — just this morning — that the whole thing started? It seemed so much longer than that. There had been more life and death today than entire years of her life.

Except, maybe, the years her mother had been sick, the year she finally passed.

Mom . . .

Julie might go days without thinking of Arlene, then catch herself in a moment wondering what might have been. The path her life might've taken if things had been different.

She called up her mother's image now, her smile, the way her hair fell wavy to her shoulders.

Did you have another daughter you never told me about?

Arlene's eyes glittered with secrets. Every mother had at least one — but this? It felt close to impossible.

After a while, Julie drifted into a troubled doze. Awake since three that morning, battered and beaten, mentally and emotionally shocked, her body was finally shutting down. She was still lying across the seat, the way Keith had left her; suddenly it was the perfect repose, the most perfectly comfortable bed . . .

* * *

The car stopped and the door opened. She'd been dipping in and out of consciousness. Now she grew fully alert. The back hatch opened next, letting in a blast of arctic air. There was a crackling sound, like plastic.

Afraid to sit up, she did anyway, watching as Keith moved away from the vehicle toward a parking lot. He carried something with him, a Walmart store glowing in the near distance.

Her pulse picked up and she swallowed around her tongue, dry as rock salt. Civilization. People. A fucking Walmart . . .

Keith shrank to a dark shape in the storm, snow driving at an angle, flakes turned into black pebbles under the high arc lights. He stopped at a trash can, removed the lid, stuffed whatever he was holding down inside. Then he started toward a vehicle in proximity.

"Hey — lay down." Monique hit the brakes and threw the car in park, staring at Julie in the rear-view mirror. She had just started to pull away from having dropped Keith off, now she faced Julie. "I said lay . . . the fuck . . . down."

Maybe it was the nap, or the signs of life around her, or that she'd just had enough of this shit. Julie continued to ignore the command. Sitting sideways in the back seat, she watched Keith's vehicle start to move as she spoke. "Why did you say you were my twin?"

"Oh, Jesus. Give me a break."

"Just answer me."

"I told you to lay down back there. Do you want to test me?" And as she enunciated the last words, she reached for a handful of Julie's hair above the gauze wrap and yanked her head back.

Normally, Julie might submit. But she grabbed Monique's forearm and dug in her thumb as hard as she could. Monique yelped and let go. Julie tried the door: locked and childproof — the latch bent back, but the door stayed shut.

Monique put it in gear and hit the gas. "Bitch!" They got going a little too fast, fishtailing in the parking lot.

Julie saw Keith turn to look — he was twenty yards away now, about to get into the other vehicle — but then he was gone. Monique bumped over a curb and they were out of the parking lot, back on the road. A truck swerved to avoid them and blared its horn.

Monique charged on. Julie thought maybe she recognized where they were. This wasn't the Walmart in Herkimer, off Highway 5, but the one between Dolgeville and Oppenheim.

We're going east. Utica is west, Albany is east. Troy, Cohoes, Interstate 87.

"Don't you fucking try anything like that again," Monique said. She sounded angry, but less confident than before.

Julie felt a surge of something — hope, maybe — but was careful with it. Her assessment of Monique was that while she was already street tough, she was desperate, too. Enough to see this through.

And that made her very dangerous, indeed.

Things were quiet for a while. There was nothing out here, not even streetlights now, and Monique was going slow again, thirty miles an hour on the speedometer. Julie still hadn't lain down like she'd been told.

"Why don't you take I-90?" she suggested. "These back roads are going to be shit."

She's staying off the interstate.

191

Maybe she didn't want to be caught on camera — the tolls. Not anymore. Keith had made a comment about driving Julie's car. The plan had always been to disappear her, it seemed. But it had changed to include the appearance of Colton killing her at the cabin instead.

"I'm gonna take off my shoe and beat you with it if you don't lay down."

Julie didn't think she would. Keith had said something about that, too — not harming her.

"It's dark," Julie reasoned. "It's a blizzard."

"You're in my mirror."

"Oh. Sorry." She shifted right — now she had a better angle on Monique, too, could see her full profile, amber in the dashboard lights. This imposter, this woman who looked nearly identical.

"You said we were twins," Julie persisted. "You guys had a whole conversation about it. You said I was in denial."

Monique sighed — demonstratively, so Julie knew she was exasperated. "We fucking look like twins," she said at last. "That's the whole point."

Julie felt relief at that, and from an unexpected place — a kind of blame she'd been holding against her parents, as if they could have kept something from her all of this time that was so major and so vital. She hadn't really believed it . . . but she'd believed it just enough to feel that anger toward them.

Now that Monique admitted the lie, the tension loosened in her chest as she mentally apologized to her parents.

The rest of the emotion — forgiving herself — she'd have to deal with later. "The whole point of what?"

"I should have drugged you. That was the original idea."

"What original idea?"

"You weren't supposed to *come home*. Not until four. And then it would have been nice and calm. I even bought chloroform. We would have grabbed you when you came in. You know, came in, set your bag down, put your keys in the little dish . . ."

"I don't have a dish."

"Then rolled you up."

"Rolled me up?" But she could picture it: the oriental rug in the entryway.

"In the carpet," Monique confirmed. "Plastic first, then the carpet — my idea. Then they would have carried you out in their hats and overalls like a couple of workers taking a rug in to be cleaned."

Julie was going numb with the effort to process it all. "You said I was the key to giving you a second chance. How does this do that?"

Monique didn't answer, but things were connecting in Julie's mind. The final pieces fitting together forming a grisly picture.

"No one would believe I disappeared," she said. "I have a good life. I don't want to go anywhere."

"I was going to take your car. I was gonna hit the first and second tolls west on I-90, then leave the car at a truck stop in Constantia. From there, when the vehicle was found, cops would assume you'd dumped your car and hitched a ride with a trucker. North to Canada, further west, whatever. Just another missing person."

"But why? Why would I?"

Monique's eyes found her in the mirror, but only briefly. She leaned forward, peering over the steering wheel to battle the storm and the greasy roads. Her headlights probed the darkness; the road was a flat white surface, not even tracks of other vehicles to follow.

"Everybody's got a reason to run," she said.

CHAPTER THIRTY-SEVEN

Annette Peters was tall and blonde. Stamper looked up into her eyes when shaking her hand. She offered him the second chair in her private office — comfy, well-padded, but the kind that kept your back straight and head up.

"I left the clinic two years ago," Annette said. "Went into practice for myself. They were very nice to let me keep a couple of my clients."

He noticed the artwork on the walls — two abstract paintings that evoked calm feelings, even though he couldn't say what they were about. A winding road through the woods? Seahorses? Pleasantly purple, though, with subtle hints of green.

"I love it here," Annette said. "Really is a nice space. Not too expensive, either."

"Did Julie ever talk about going into private practice?"

"No. Not really." Annette didn't elaborate.

"So, but you two have kept in touch."

"Oh yeah," she said, becoming more animated. "We see each other for lunch a lot. We sometimes go for a run, or in the winter we cross-country ski. This year, we started snow-shoeing. There are trails right around here — it's convenient."

Sitting in the chair, and even though Annette was the one doing the sharing, Stamper suddenly felt like a subject.

Her clear blue eyes seemed to shoot right through to the back of his skull.

But then she blinked, disrupting the illusion, snapping him out of it.

"Can you recall the last time you and Julie spoke?" he asked. "Or saw each other?"

"Same time — it was last Friday. Our usual lunchtime meet-up."

"What did you do?"

"The snowshoes."

"Any contact since then?"

"We texted a little when she was at the conference. Just a couple of minor things." Those clear eyes betrayed some secret, it seemed, something going grayer just there at the back of her gaze.

"Anything she was worried about? Maybe between her and Colton?"

"No. Nothing like that."

"You think she would tell you if there was anything?"

She considered it. "I do."

She might've said more, he thought, but years of being a therapist had taught her the art of discretion.

Right now, it was public information that Julie was missing and that Colton Rossi had been determined deceased. The details, of course, were being withheld, which left everyone free to make up stories in their minds. Which, from a cop's perspective, could sometimes be helpful and revealing. If you wanted to know what people thought, you wanted to let them talk. But a therapist like Annette Peters was trained to keep her thoughts to herself.

"What I'm hoping," Stamper said carefully, "is to get your feeling as her friend — even if she didn't say anything specific — how did things appear to you?"

She took a deep breath, let it out. "Well, you know how it is. You think a friend has a normal life, and then something drastic happens, like today, and suddenly everyone has a theory. 'I always wondered about him.' That kind of thing."

"Hindsight," Stamper agreed.

"It can play tricks on you. But, you know, from what little I saw, they were pretty textbook happy. Both outdoorsy, hard-working, liked the same movies. That kind of thing." She frowned and shook her head, as if warding off some emotion. "This thing . . . it's just so surprising. You don't think something like this is ever going to happen to someone you know. It's true what they say."

"It is true." He shifted back to something Annette had just said, remembering how Julie's supervisor had called her unadventurous, or something close.

"They did a lot of outdoor stuff together?"

"Well, yeah. I mean, Julie isn't necessarily a rock-climbing enthusiast. But she has that athletic background."

"Athletic background?"

"She was an athlete in high school. She downplays it, but by my understanding she was the best swimmer on the swim team, selected to go to the state championships, everything."

"Wow. What happened?"

"Well, that's another story, I guess." Annette's gaze bounced off. She had hit a soft spot. "Probably best told by Julie."

"Please, any little thing . . ."

She took a breath, let it out slowly. "Julie had a few challenges in life, just like we all do, and they made her who she is." Annette found his eyes and smiled. "Could I be more vague? Sorry, I just . . . If you really think it will help, I don't know how it will, but there's this: when Julie's mother got sick, she went through a very hard time."

Seemed natural enough, Stamper thought.

"She wasn't able to be the same sort of girl she wanted to be. Her whole family dynamic changed. Julie had to give up her sport. Or, felt she did. But it seemed to pass, her mother seemed to beat it. And then it came back, aggressively. Cancer is such hell. Devastating. And this time, when Julie lost her mother . . . It took its toll on her mental health. She had a psychotic break."

Stamper felt himself sitting up a little straighter.

Annette continued, "A friend called 911, worried that she was going to hurt herself, or hurt someone else."

Oh, wow. Now this is something.

"Do you know who made the call?"

"No, sorry. I never asked." Annette sighed. It clearly pained her to talk about as much as it pained her to know her friend was missing, maybe in deep trouble. "When her mother finally . . . passed, Julie saw someone, a therapist, and I think that's what led her into this field."

"I can appreciate that," Stamper said.

Annette searched the space in front of her as she found her words. "Julie still carries some limiting beliefs about herself."

It seemed obvious what it meant, but with psychology, you never knew.

"She's hard on herself. She pushes. It's different than Colton. He pushes himself to climb higher, faster, get more Instagram followers. She's much more internal. No one really knows what she's after. I don't even think I do." Annette smiled a little, but she was still gazing into some middle distance, her finger on her chin, lightly rubbing. She seemed to come out of it. "God, I hope you find her soon. Is there anything you're able to tell me? At all?"

It was Stamper's turn to smile grimly. "Just that we're doing everything we can."

CHAPTER THIRTY-EIGHT

The roads were still bad late into Thursday morning. The blizzard had stopped, plows had scraped and salted, but wind made cyclones of snow, whiting out the day. When Stamper's phone rang, he answered it through the hands-free vehicle system.

Cuthbert sounded like she was walking somewhere. "How did it go with Annette Peters?"

"Spreniker has had some emotional instability in the past."

"Such as?"

He relayed Annette's story, emphasizing *psychotic break*. "And there was a 911 call. It'd be long gone, but someone was pretty worried about her."

"Okay. Listen — I just got off with the facial recognition people. They can't make any IDs off the Ring camera, it's just not enough. Like we thought, too far away, too pixelated."

"Damn."

"Yeah, but — so what I did, I had them run a picture of Spreniker to see if there were any hits."

"Ooh, that's smart." He started to pump the brakes as he approached a traffic light, its red eye blurry in the maelstrom.

"Well — smart enough that we've got eight results."

"Eight?"

"Narrowed down from an initial 54, all within the United States. I hand-picked these eight, but if you asked me, there are only three that really look like her. Like dead-on for her."

"And that's only people who are in the system."

"Yes, true. Megan Chenoweth, Ann Rusk, Katelyn Graham."

"And the winner is?"

"Considering that Chenoweth is in Wisconsin and Rusk in California, I focused on Graham, from Rockland County."

He knew where that was — it abutted Westchester County, his own home turf, just north of New York City. "Well, we don't know that proximity matters," he said. "It's the twenty-first century. There are jets."

"True. But I spoke with Chenoweth."

"You could have led with that."

"I could have, yeah." Cuthbert got in a car, or so it sounded. The walking noises cut off, a door slammed.

"Well, don't keep me in suspense — did you talk to the other two?"

"Left messages with Rusk and Graham. So, we'll see. But Graham is real interesting."

"Runs a charity soup kitchen?"

"Close. The Southern District of New York is about to hit her with embezzlement charges, her family's own company. Pharmaceutical company in the low billions. They're loaded. But meanwhile, she's in the system for a DUI, a possession charge, indecent exposure, assault."

Stamper whistled.

"Yeah. She's a handful. The fact that she's in this kind of trouble, that she's a dead ringer for Spreniker, and she may have just shown up on a neighbor's Ring camera in Spreniker's clothes . . ."

"You followed up with that?"

"Spreniker has more pants and another full-zip that are the same brand. It's nothing definitive, it's only circumstantial, but for my money, those are Spreniker's clothes our female unsub is wearing when she hightails it out of there, just before Taylor shows up. She was there at the house."

"In a black cocktail dress," Stamper said.

"I think we're right about that, yeah. And then she put on Julie's clothes and ran. It's camouflage, I guess, but where it's leading . . . I don't know."

Stamper thought he might — thought Cuthbert might, too — but it was too soon for either of them to give it words.

But they could have a look at Katelyn Graham. They could do that.

Though, first . . .

* * *

Warren Flandreau looked thick and red, as if all the attention over Colton Rossi was giving him high blood pressure. It didn't help that he was now down a bartender and seemed generally understaffed. "I debated closing," he said. "I just didn't know what was right."

Stamper surveyed the packed dining room, three-deep at the bar, though it was barely two in the afternoon. In addition to the local drama, New York was still in a state of emergency, with schools, county and state facilities — and many businesses — closed.

Flandreau wiped sweat from his brow with a handker-chief. "I just can't believe this."

Stamper didn't know if he was talking about Rossi's death or the uptick in business.

"He was more than just an employee. He was . . ." Flandreau was quiet a moment, just staring wide, uncompre-hending of it all. He blinked. "Anyway, I've got that list for you. Everyone who knew about the van or would have access to the van. I was up until three last night thinking about it."

He pulled a piece of paper from his back pocket and handed it to Stamper.

200

Giving it a quick scan, he recognized Brianna Vincent's name. But no Keith Rossi.

He stuck the paper away. "You got my message about the video?"

Flandreau nodded. "Yeah, we'll need to go down to my office."

Some customers watched as he led Stamper toward the stairs; one pointed at Stamper while mouthing something to a friend.

Downstairs in the tiny office, he showed Stamper the cash register video. "It feeds live — that's what's going on right now. It stores up two weeks of footage and then deletes."

Stamper could see the same people he'd just noticed. "The whole two weeks?"

"No, just a day. A day at a time. So, like, at the end of today, the computer will delete the very first day from fourteen days ago. And then tomorrow, it will delete the day fourteen days prior to that. Does that make sense?"

"Sure," Stamper lied. He sat down and feathered his hands over the keyboard like he knew what to do next. "So when was Mr. Rossi's last shift?"

Flandreau took him through Rossi's entire schedule from the past two weeks.

Afterward, Flandreau lingered. Sitting in the other chair in the room, he fixed Stamper with a pained, honest gaze. "What happened?"

"Well, we're still determining that."

The big man's eyes ticked to the computer screen. "So, on that — you're looking to see if something happened at the bar? Do I need—"

"A lawyer? I don't think so." He fished out his phone — now was as good a time as any — and brought up an image of Katelyn Graham, which he held out. "Ever seen this woman before?"

Flandreau looked confused. "That's . . . Julie?"

"Looks like her, doesn't it? Actually, this is someone else."

"I mean, wow. I woulda thought that was her."

"I know, I hear ya." Stamper flipped to another picture before Flandreau could ask more questions. "How about him?"

"Oh yeah, I've seen him a couple of times."

"Really?" Stamper let out a held breath. "When?"

"First time, maybe a few months ago. Then maybe like a week ago."

"What were the circumstances?"

"Just . . . at the bar. Having a drink."

"With anyone?"

"I don't think so. I don't remember."

"But you remember him?"

"I do. Who is he?"

"He's Colton Rossi's brother."

"Oh. I didn't know Colton had a brother." Flandreau looked away, a bit wistful, maybe a bit confused.

"What about him stood out, though?" Stamper asked. "What makes you remember him?"

"I don't know." His gaze returned to Stamper. "My brother, Terry, was in the military. He's got muscles, he wears those Grunt-style T-shirts. This guy . . . he had that look. Like he was a normal-enough guy, but you didn't want to say the wrong thing to him."

CHAPTER THIRTY-NINE

I should have drugged you.

Monique had planned to use chloroform, an anesthetic. To bundle Julie's limp body into a carpet and carry her out the front door.

Why?

She'd made allusions to escaping her life. Thanking Julie for the chance to start over.

"They'll do an autopsy," Julie blurted. "Whatever you plan to do to me, they'll know I'm not you."

Monique's eyes in the mirror. "No, they won't."

It was confirmation. Of course, it had always been there in Julie's mind — she'd expected death when they'd hauled her up to the shed on the hill. But now she understood it was to stage her attempted murder and subsequent disappearance. Initially, they'd meant to disappear her quietly, but things had changed. She'd come home early. Colton had tried to back out. So they'd set things up at the cabin to look like he'd tried to kill her, then himself. This part now, this would be to kill her for real.

"We'll have different blood types. They can check DNA."

She wasn't sure about the last part. But, the blood.

"I'm O-positive," Monique said. "Most common blood type. You?"

Julie's heart sank. Hers was the same.

Cause an accident. Right now; jump into the front seat and steer the car off the road. Get out and run.

The tension pooled in her gut. Even though this was a back road and the weather was bad — okay, horrible — there would be someone along.

The other option was to play possum until they were closer to people again, which would have to be at some point in the near future. Julie resigned to studying the roadside for signs, anything that confirmed or changed where she thought they were headed.

"So, you're not my twin," she said. Her lips tingled with anxiety. "But you look exactly like me. How did you find me?"

"You were in a magazine. Michael came into the living room one day, dropped it in my lap. Said, 'You're never gonna fucking believe this.'"

Climbing Magazine. Patagonia, six months ago. She remembered feeling out of place, nervous with all the professional climbers and photography. But she'd wound up in the main group photo with Colton and several other climbers, with their significant others, too. A two-page spread, middle of the issue.

"And Mike said, 'That's our way out, right there.'"

"Way out of what?"

But Monique wasn't answering that. "It took time to put together," was all she said. She seemed proud, wanting to gloat even, but the intense driving was distracting her.

So much remained unexplained. How had Keith factored in? Where had Michael gone?

And then there was that ache in the back of Julie's heart, a hard, cold weight that hadn't gone away since that morning. Monique had seduced Colton. It was the only thing that made sense. She'd gotten him into bed and then leveraged him, threatened to end his marriage before it began. Or worse. Maybe she had other things on Colton, things Julie didn't know about.

But there were still things that bothered her, didn't seem to fit. "When Michael showed up, he grabbed you. Put his hand over your mouth and carried you away . . ."

"He thought things were falling apart and was afraid of what I might say. We were still reacting to you showing up. And, honestly, he didn't like how close I'd gotten with Colton."

"And later? With a bag on your head?"

"Just having fun. I knew you saw me get grabbed by Michael, and I figured I'd take advantage of that, show up at the cabin later, play the part of a victim."

"You know, I say this as a licensed mental health therapist with years of experience — you're crazy."

Monique laughed, a humorless grunting.

Julie wasn't finished. "I'm sure you lied to him." She meant Colton.

Monique shrugged.

"What did you tell him? Did you tell him we were sisters? That was your way in?"

"First of all, you think you know your man? You know nothing. That's what I know. That's true about them all. They're all horny pigs. You don't even own a slinky cocktail dress. I had to use my own. You weren't exactly, you know, driving him crazy."

"You lied to him. Promised him something."

Her eyebrows went up in the rearview mirror. "I promised him a way out. Just like I needed a way out, so did he. Sorry to be the one to have to tell you — but he wasn't happy. He was excited by the whole thing with me. He didn't jump into it right away — Keith had to work on him a bit before he'd even see me. But then he did. We gave him a whole different pitch — yeah, I lied to him. Promised him money for his restaurant."

That stung. It was all horrible to hear, but the idea that he'd done any of this to get his dream off the ground, it was a bitter pill.

"Plus, we told him he'd get even more famous from all the media attention. And then there was me — I'd be dead from suicide, and all my troubles would be dead with me."

"I don't believe you," Julie said, through the tears starring her vision. "All you've done is lie, Monique. Your life is one big lie — even your death is going to be a lie."

Dead from suicide.

She'd heard it, it resonated deep, but knowing your own end was hard for the mind to take.

She focused her energy elsewhere.

"'Monique' . . . That's not even your real name, is it?"

After a moment: "It's all you'll ever know me as."

"Well, Monique, you're a fucking psychopath."

"You know what Colton said to me? He said the relationship was boring. You were so broken, so unambitious. There was nothing even to hold onto. The whole thing was too vanilla. You may have been somebody once, he said, someone exciting. But you'd become the most predictable person he'd ever met."

And that's when Julie pulled the knife.

CHAPTER FORTY

"Where did you get that?"

Julie didn't answer her. First, because it didn't matter. Second, because she was afraid any sound she made would betray how terrified she was. Doing her best to hold the knife steady, the right way up, took all of her focus. Could she really stab someone? Really thrust out and plunge this blade into flesh?

What was the alternative?

"You saucy bitch," Monique said. She had to return her attention to the road, but she said with a sort of admiration: "I didn't know you had it in you."

"Stop the car."

"Stop the car? In this?"

"Stop the car."

But Monique didn't, of course. She just kept driving, calling Julie's bluff. More and more, Julie got the sense that Monique was a criminal. Beyond the obvious — that her life was very different from Julie's, and that having a paring knife pointed at her wasn't exactly a big day.

It was Keith who had been using it to cut up the apple. He'd left it sitting out on the kitchen island, and she'd grabbed it during his argument with Monique. Saying goodbye to Colton, she'd tucked it in her sock, terrified it was going to cut her ever since. It hadn't.

"There's nowhere to stop," Monique said. "Seriously. I can't tell the middle of the road from the side."

"Plows are concentrating on main roads," Julie said. "You can just stop the car. All you have to do is press on the brake." Now that her words were coming, she was much steadier than expected.

"And then I'll just get out," Monique said. "And you'll drive off."

"Something like that. Yes."

"You really think you're going to use that little thing?" Monique cocked an eye at her in the mirror. It made Julie think of some kind of animal. Like a bird with talons, looking over.

That was the full bluff call. Yes, it was a small knife. It probably looked ridiculous, the way she was holding it two-handed, a battered woman with a huge white bandage around her head, thrusting a tiny paring knife.

But she said, "Maybe all I have to do is stick it in just under your jaw. In the soft spot where your artery is pulsing right now. Just one little stab, and that would be it."

It seemed to have an effect. Monique swallowed, and that eye went away, her gaze riveting back to the road. The wipers were going, the snow diving at the windshield, the speedometer still cradling the needle at 25 mph.

Julie grabbed the back of the passenger seat.

"What are you doing? Hey, hey — you're gonna wreck us!"

It wasn't easy keeping the knife pointed at Monique, as she climbed into the front seat. Julie's body was stiff and moving painful. She was half terrified she might slip and cut herself — the other half terrified of what she might need to do. Violent, ghastly, a last resort. But she got into the passenger seat, keeping one leg tucked up beneath her, her right foot down in the footwell.

The Jeep had a temperature readout on the dash: well below freezing and probably dropping. Just eight o'clock, it would be dark for another eleven hours or so. She'd seen a road sign for NY-29 and before that she'd made out the words Lassellsville Fire House, maybe two or three miles ago. There'd been a few lighted houses back from the road, fuzzy glows in the stormy dark, then long stretches of nothing. The roads were nearly empty but for the occasional glimpse of headlights, far behind them, when the road was straight.

"Stop the car."

Monique stayed tucked against the wheel, hands at ten and two, peering out, her jaw set. *Is this what I look like when* I'm *being stubborn?* It was a silly thing to wonder, but the uncanniness of their physical similarities hadn't faded. There were still moments of surreality, a dizzying second or two where Julie felt like she really was looking at herself, that she'd detached somehow and was watching this all from some disembodied distance.

I've never seen this woman before in my life.

Colton, in the beginning, acting like she was a stranger.

What sense did that make? Clearly, they all knew who she was. The whole point of this was because of who she was, what she looked like. Julie had mulled this point over so many times and still came back to the same conclusion: in the end, Colton regretted what he'd done and wanted to pull out. So desperate to put a stop to things, he'd tried to deny the very facts that had set everything in motion: who she was, who she looked like. As if the sheer insistence of his denial would have some magical effect.

That bird's-eye came back. Like Monique was watching her but still managing to stare at the road, too.

They were east of Herkimer, she thought, somewhere between Oppenheim and Rockford, maybe. No — Rock*wood*. The next big town was, what? Saratoga Springs, some fifty miles away? At the rate they were going, two hours to get there. And then what?

She kept the knife aimed, not so close that a bump in the road would cause an inadvertent stabbing, but near enough that she would only have to stiffen her arm, just give a little jab forward . . .

After a few seconds, Monique said, "Jesus. Can you put that thing away? Okay?"

Julie stayed tense. "I don't think so."

Monique took a hand off the wheel and made as if to slide it under her thigh.

"Put that hand back."

Monique returned the hand, showing Julie it was empty. "Touchy, touchy."

"I'm reaching under your leg," Julie said.

"No, you're not."

She put the knife within inches of Monique's soft neck. "I said, I am going to reach under your leg."

Monique swallowed again. Licked her dry lips. Just breathed.

Julie reached under her thigh, careful to keep the small knife steady, and grabbed the hard shaft of Monique's own knife — the one she'd used to cut Julie's scalp. She dropped it in the footwell beside her. "You're all done," she said. "This is all over. You're going to stop the car now, and you're going to get out. Or I'm going to slice your throat open."

"You won't do it."

"I will."

The car started going faster.

"Slow down . . ."

"You really haven't thought this through. I'm the one who's put all of this together. Obviously, I'm crazy enough to have done all of this. You think it's game over because you have a fruit knife pointed at me? You're not as smart as you think."

Julie glanced at the speedometer, the needle climbing to forty. The tires kept slipping, the engine racing whenever they did.

"What do you think I'm going to do? Give it all up when I'm this close?"

She had a point. There was no turning back now. Julie knew Monique wouldn't stop until she'd seen it through.

So where did that leave things?

The speedometer wiggled past forty miles per hour. Forty-five. The back end of the Jeep had started side-sliding.

"Okay! Okay!" Julie dropped her weapon in the footwell and grabbed onto the dashboard and the back of the seat, gritted her teeth and held on. "I've let go of the knife."

But the back end gave out and they started into a spin.

"Whoa," Monique said. She might've been laughing. "Here we go!"

The headlights swept along, picking up a post-rail fence, maybe a pasture beyond, a tree, and then they were coming back around, still doing forty, at least.

The Jeep dipped to the right, sliding as it rotated, pulled towards a ditch running along the edge of the road.

But somehow the vehicle stayed on the snowy tarmac. It swung around a full three-hundred-and-sixty degrees. Monique pumped the brakes and started to turn into the skid. With a practiced movement, she spun the wheel back in the other direction, but too late. Doing thirty now, they went off the road on the right side now and crashed into the fence. Metal shrieked and wood splintered. The Jeep bounced back, then came to an abrupt stop, throwing both of the occupants forward with the momentum.

When everything settled, Julie saw Monique lunge across, her eyes on the knives. Julie dove for them, too, and the two women collided.

Monique cried out in pain and then grabbed Julie by the throat. She swore at her, and then she hit her, blowing Julie's porch light.

CHAPTER FORTY-ONE

Thomas Spreniker arrived at the state trooper barracks in Oneida with his son, Jack, at his side. They had not stopped since they boarded the plane in Denver some four hours before, plus two for the time change.

Stamper had expected a pushy man, red-faced and barrel-chested. At one point, Spreniker may have lived up to it, but grief and time had done some work on him. He looked seventy-five instead of sixty.

"We're doing everything we can to find your daughter," Cuthbert assured him.

They went through all the expected back and forth, but it wasn't long before Spreniker had exhausted his questions, albeit with few satisfactory answers. As far as the police knew, and as far as the police could say, Julie was missing from a cabin in the Ferris Lake wilderness area owned by Dale Rossi, Colton's father.

"And what's he saying?"

"We haven't been able to contact Mr. Rossi," Stamper answered.

"I don't understand. I thought this was a home invasion, and that Julie and Colton were taken. That's what the news was saying all day."

"Of course, Mr. Spreniker," Cuthbert said. "It can be confusing. We're not sure how it all fits together, but we're working on it."

"Just call me Tom." He wore brown slacks and a navy Polo shirt, Nike sneakers on his feet. A step down from business casual — the outfit of a state employee retired and traveling.

Beside him in sweatpants and Crocs, big arms and a wide back, Jack Spreniker seemed more like hired muscle than a son. A stoic personal trainer, at best.

"But why would someone take my sister and Colton to his father's cabin?" he now asked. "It must be someone in the family?"

Stamper hazarded he probably wanted to implicate Dale Rossi himself, but thought the better of it.

He laid out pictures of all Colton Rossi's known siblings. "Maybe you can help us with something."

Tom looked them over. "Who are they?"

"Colton's sisters, and also his brother."

"Brother? Colton doesn't have a brother."

"Apparently, he does. Dale Rossi's child with another woman."

They watched him for a reaction.

Jack finally stirred, leaning in to get a look at the photo of Keith.

"You recognize him?" Stamper asked.

"No," Jack said.

"Have you talked to him?" Tom asked.

Stamper glanced at Cuthbert. "I have. He claims they weren't close. They were together a few brief times as kids, but then Colton's mother wanted Colton to keep away from Dale. Dale gave them both access to the hunting cabin, though."

Tom smoothed back his floppy gray hair. "Did he say where he was? Does he have an alibi?"

Another glance between the investigators. "We're looking into it."

"Why are we talking about Colton?" Jack asked, chest muscles twitching. "Why aren't we talking about my sister?"

Cuthbert put her hand on Stamper's arm before he could answer. "Because, Jack . . . Tom . . . the more we understand about what happened — with both your sister and her fiancé — the better equipped we are to look for her. But I would like to know more about Julie. What can you tell me about what her life has been like the past couple of years? Has she seemed happy? Has she had any issues that she might've talked with you about? Anything bothering her?"

The men looked at each other, not saying something.

Tom finally answered. "We're not as close these days."

"Can you tell us what that means?"

His gaze was defensive, emotional. "It means Julie and I haven't spoken for years."

CHAPTER FORTY-TWO

The woman looked like she could be Julie's twin sister. Same small nose, same complexion, only the hair color was different. This woman's was a reddish blonde.

She'd given Julie a long look at first, like someone appraising a piece of furniture at a flea market. Now she removed her jacket — puffy and black with a fur-lined hood — and draped it over the stool where Keith had been sitting.

He was behind her, and Julie registered the mild amusement on his face. She'd thought he'd gone out for a cigarette.

The woman stood in front of Julie and folded her arms. She wore skin-tight snow pants, a fashionable sweater, like some villain in an '80s movie about a ski resort. The closer Julie looked the more differences she saw in the woman's face. Her mouth was a little wider than Julie's. She might've been a couple of inches taller, too, but she was wearing thick-soled knee-high boots.

"Yeah?" Keith made the word a question.

"Yeah," the woman said. The word was breathy, pleased. "You're right — she's perfect."

It seemed like they were waiting for Julie to say something. She checked Colton for a reaction, but as usual, he wasn't looking at her. She wasn't sure he had a face.

Finally, she found her voice. "Who are you?"

"You don't recognize me?" The woman's huge smile seemed practiced, like a model's.

She's prettier than me, Julie thought. It was such a wildly incongruous thought, but there it was.

"I don't . . ." Julie started. "You look like me."

"Yes, I do," the woman said, widening her eyes. She bent toward Julie and wagged her finger. "That's exactly right. Keith, you didn't tell me she was so smart."

The woman turned to him, grinning, taking her attention off Julie for just a second. Keith stood by like a sentinel. Although now he looked like her father when he was younger, when he'd worked for the school, and his hair was still thick and brown.

And when the woman turned back to Julie, Julie recognized her mother's face, her pretty eyes, hazel like Julie's, if maybe a little lighter.

She took off her hair, the same way she'd taken off her coat, in fact dropping it right on top, bald beneath, gleaming like a cue ball.

Those eyes narrowed a bit, still assessing. Then she turned away to wander around the cabin. "Place it in some lonely vale and set the echoes ringing," she said.

Keith shrugged. "There's no telling where the world is going to go from here: America is four corporations in a trench coat, and the pyramids can't save us."

Suddenly the woman clapped her hands and squealed with delight. "Oh, this is going to be so perfect!"

She picked up her jacket and shrugged into it. Her hair was back, even though Julie hadn't seen her return it to her head. And she looked like Julie again.

When the woman got down in front of Julie's face, it was truly like looking in a mirror. And then, even more uncanny: Julie felt her thoughts transfer to the woman in front of her, so that she was both in the woman's head, looking back at herself, and sitting there, tied to the chair. This stranger.

"But when you were a little baby," the woman said, "still in your mother's womb, I was there with you. And you ate me."

Her face broke into a toothy grin for a moment as she gazed at herself. Her voice was stereophonic, booming all around. "I'm not a

216

twin. I'm you, Julie-boolie. You sucked me right up." She made a loud slurping sound, then grinned some more. "And now I'm gonna eat you."

* * *

Julie woke with a breath caught in her chest, then let it out with a moan. There was only darkness, and a thrumming vibration all around her. She tried to move, but the space was small and her hands were tied behind her back. She fought against the rising claustrophobia.

Monique had put her in the trunk.

But it's a Jeep. There is no trunk.

It must mean she was in some other vehicle.

The Jeep had gone off road. Even if someone had stopped, why would they agree to put her in the trunk?

America is four corporations in a trench coat.

The dream, which had quickly dissipated on waking, came slowly back.

Keith.

The headlights way behind them.

All this time, she'd assumed Keith had gone off somewhere else after Monique had dropped him in that parking lot.

But he'd been picking up another vehicle. One with ample trunk space.

Oh God, the knife.

She'd taken a huge risk when she snatched it from the kitchen island. She'd managed to keep it concealed, even when they'd taken her up to the shed. She'd been prepared to use it, stab them both and run, but they hadn't tried to kill her.

Maybe she should have done something after that, but she'd worried about making her situation even worse. If she'd taken the knife out as Keith led her to the Jeep, she might have fumbled it and blown her chance. Better they drive her out of there, get closer to civilization, then act.

But she'd messed that up, too.

Don't think that. You're doing the best you can.

Maybe.

And that dream. Her father, her mother.

You ate me . . .

It was just a dream. It meant nothing: an indigestion of the mind. Dreams were thoughts running wild when the world wasn't there to organize and box them in.

Julie's consciousness flickered. Her head throbbed as she fought to stay awake.

"It's gonna be okay."

The sound of her voice, flattened by the enclosed space, was a lonely, scary thing. Fear churned in her stomach and squeezed around her jaw and neck.

The car thumped over something, hard enough that Julie felt airborne a second. Either they'd run over some debris in the road or taken a speed bump too fast. But they seemed to be accelerating again, the pitch of the engine getting higher. The interstate now, that's what it felt like. Going somewhere far away.

CHAPTER FORTY-THREE

"Mr. Spreniker," Cuthbert said, "you told us you had something to share. You flew all the way out here."

Tom's eyes got a sharp look. "To help. Of course I did. Because we're not speaking doesn't mean I'm not still her father: she's still my daughter."

They waited.

He settled. "I got sick several years ago. I was still living in our house in Saranac Lake. Julie came to see me just about every weekend. It was a few years after Arlene died. And I wasn't taking her loss very well."

Tom glanced at his son, still sitting beside him, silent and resolute. "I saw Julie going through it all over again: Giving up her life for a sick parent. And I just couldn't bear it. She didn't want me to go, but I reached out to Jack in Colorado, told him what was going on. Jack has obligations, of course, but his . . . his life is simpler."

Stamper looked at the younger man. *Work, gym, home. Simple.*

"He suggested I come out and stay with him for a while. So I sold the old house, moved out to Colorado. That was almost five years ago."

Cuthbert asked, "And Julie just stopped talking to you? Why?"

"Not at first. We had an argument."

"Can you talk about that?"

He looked at them both. "Before I left, Julie was busy with her schooling. It was draining for her to keep coming up to take care of me. And she was starting to see a young man."

"Colton," Cuthbert confirmed.

"Yes." Tom seemed to lose himself in his thoughts.

"Tom, anything you can tell us right now could help us find your daughter," Stamper pushed. "Anything."

It was a shopworn line, but it worked, because it was true. The smallest details were often the ones that put the other pieces in place.

The older man consulted his son again with a quick look and then studied his hands as he replied. "I was worried about her."

"Why?"

"Because she . . . she was showing signs."

"Of?"

He sighed — talking about it seemed to make him uncomfortable. "She was showing signs of past behavior."

"She had to give up swimming," Stamper prompted, thinking about the meeting with Annette Peters. "Is that right?"

A spark in Tom's eyes — Stamper had touched on a family secret, of sorts. "She gave up a lot more than that. The first time Arlene got sick, I was not in the best shape. I didn't handle it well. I was drinking. I didn't always make the best choices, say the right things. Julie was young, just fourteen. She had a boyfriend — Mason, I think his name was. Mason Ridgell. She stopped seeing him, stopped swimming, stopped everything to help take care of Arlene."

He looked into a corner as tears started to spill down his cheeks. He wiped them off. "It was my fault. I pulled myself together. And Arlene recovered that first time. But Julie . . . I don't know. She never went back to the way things were. I said she couldn't use her mother as an excuse to hide from her life. And I said something similar when she was taking care of me recently. I told her she was scared."

He let that hang in the room for a moment.

"Why would you say that? What did you think she was afraid of?"

"Julie was in her early twenties when Arlene's cancer came back. And this time, she did more than withdraw from boyfriends and sports. Arlene's death affected her so much that she eventually had to see somebody. A therapist."

It was what Annette Peters had said. Stamper noticed Jack shift in his seat, searching for a place to rest his gaze. He seemed to settle on studying his fingernails.

"That makes sense to me," Cuthbert said. "She was going through something incredibly difficult."

Tom's eyes became hard to read as he stared at each of the investigators sitting across from him. "Why aren't you out there looking for her?"

Stamper leaned forward. "Sir, we've had teams out looking for your daughter since ten p.m. last night. Hundreds of people who walked the woods all night in the storm. If there's something about Julie's life that could help us narrow down where to look for her, I think we need to hear it. That's what you're here for. That's why you came."

He took a moment to gather himself.

"You need to consider that maybe things aren't just what you're thinking, here. Julie has had some real challenges with her mental health. It's possible she might be . . ." He didn't finish.

Stamper pictured the woman coming out of the house in cargo pants and a zip-up fleece. At one point, he'd wondered if it could have been Spreniker herself, having doubled back.

"Could you explain what you mean?" Cuthbert jumped in. "Her mother died and she had a hard time and you told her she was using it as an excuse to stop pursuing certain things. What are you suggesting?"

"When Arlene was first diagnosed, Julie was young. And she was under a lot of pressure. She was the best swimmer in the state — everyone knew it. But she never went to the championships. She said she had knee pain, but every doctor we saw could find nothing. Her grades started slipping — I found unfinished homework in the trash. She wanted to help with her mother, that was true. And it was my fault for not being more capable at the time. But I believed she also was scared. Afraid of something happening. Afraid of getting hurt, dying. She was doing whatever she could to sabotage herself."

He let that settle.

"Did you take her to see someone at that time?" Cuthbert asked.

"No. Our family doctor said it all would pass. And Arlene's cancer went into remission. We thought everything would go back to normal. Julie graduated high school — just not valedictorian, like everyone had expected, but middle of her class. Not only had she been lying about her grades, but her senior year, she said she was back with Mason again. Only, we never saw them together — no one did, not even her friends. I don't know if it was to get attention or to avoid attention." He cleared his throat and shifted his body weight. "It seemed to smooth out some — she went to college, she traveled, she got her master's. But then Arlene died . . . It was a couple of days after the funeral. I came back for a walk. I heard Julie in the kitchen, talking. Arguing like someone was there. I figured maybe Jack was back early from work — but he wasn't. She was sitting alone at the kitchen table, the phone was on the other side of the room, on the counter by the sink. I knew she hadn't been on it. And then she looked at me, and she started to sob and she wouldn't stop. She said they were coming for her."

"Who?" Cuthbert asked quietly.

"She didn't say. She didn't know." He shook his head. "She found the therapist after that. She didn't talk about it to me, but I know she had some kind of breakdown."

Another silence developed. Stamper thought about Annette Peters saying *psychotic break*. He looked at Cuthbert.

She was good at appearing neutral, but he knew her: she was having a hard time buying what Tom Spreniker was selling.

And what was that? The idea that Julie was having another breakdown, now? Making things up?

That she'd killed her own fiancé?

Caught him cheating?

Keith Rossi was in on it with her?

Maybe Tom didn't mean to imply that, but it was out there now.

Stamper pulled a breath, wondering what exactly to say next, when someone knocked.

Trooper Taylor had cracked the door and was leaning in. "Sorry to interrupt. But you guys wanted this right away: I got more information on Katelyn and Trevor Graham. I've got phone numbers for you."

CHAPTER FORTY-FOUR

Katelyn's voice mail picked up without ringing and Stamper left a message.

But Trevor Graham answered on the second ring. "Hello?"

Stamper sat up a little straighter, set down the pen he'd been playing with. "Mr. Graham, uh, this is Investigator Louis Stamper with the New York State Police, how are you today, sir?"

"Okay . . . How can I help you?"

"Sir, I just have a couple of questions in relation to a missing person case we're working on."

"Missing person?"

"Yes, sir."

After a long pause, "Jesus. She's only been gone a day. How? I didn't call in a missing person's report."

The confusion blurred Stamper's thoughts. "I'm, sorry — who are you talking about, sir?"

"You're not talking about Katie? Oh, God, I'm sorry. I thought you were talking about my wife."

"Why would I be talking about your wife?"

"Because she . . . Okay, I see. Sorry. She's over in Vermont, seeing some friends. She needed to get away. Jeez, you gave me a heart attack there for a minute."

"I'm sorry, yeah, sorry about that. No, I'm calling in regard to a different missing person case. So . . . Katie, you say, is in Vermont?"

"Yes, sir."

"She needed to get away?"

"I mean, yeah. She just wanted to take a trip up there, get some air, enjoy a little time away. That's all."

"But you can't confirm that she's there?"

"Oh, no, I can confirm it, yeah. Which was why your call threw me." He laughed, and it sounded brittle. "She got there last night. Which is good, because I guess we're getting some weather. You must be getting it now?"

"I didn't say where I was, sir."

"Well, you said New York . . ."

"Right, okay, yeah."

"So . . . who is this about?"

"This is about a missing woman. I'm here in Herkimer, New York. Does the name Julie Spreniker mean anything to you?"

A brief pause. "I think I saw something about that on the news." It was true, the story had gone national. Now Graham was the one confused. "So — why would you be calling me?"

"Mr. Graham, your wife came up on a list of people who look very much like the missing woman. We're just getting a sense of where everyone is, so we don't have any false sightings." It was total bullshit, and not very convincing.

Graham seemed to buy it, though. "Oh, okay. Yeah, that makes sense. Well, Katie's been in Vermont since last night. Near St. Johnsbury. I heard from her on her way up."

"What time would that have been, sir?"

"Uh, hold on . . . gonna put you on speaker so I can . . ." The pitch of his voice changed, got tinny. "Okay, looking at my messages. Yeah, so the last message came from her at about eight o'clock."

"About eight o'clock?"

"8:08."

Stamper wrote it down. "And the message?"

"Uh, 'Hey babe, long drive, here now, talk soon.' So it sounds like she couldn't be mistaken for your missing woman. She wasn't anywhere near where you are."

He didn't respond for a second, then said, "Yes, right. Well, thank you very much, sir. I appreciate it."

"You bet." Graham added, "Good luck."

Stamper hung up and thought about it. Either the guy was lying and was part of the act, or he was telling the truth and Katelyn Graham was miles away from Herkimer, visiting friends. In that case, the woman on the video was either someone else or was, in fact, Julie Spreniker herself, carrying out some kind of weird delusion.

Like maybe she'd done when her mother died.

CHAPTER FORTY-FIVE

"Colton?"

"I know."

Voices in her head. A liminal state between waking and sleep.

"Colton, what . . . ?"

"I'm sorry, Julie. I'm really sorry."

"What is going on?" She was back in the cabin again. In a chair from which she could never escape. She'd known, even while it was happening, that some part of her would always be here. This was Trauma, big T. The kind you had to work to reprocess, if you ever could. *"Colton, please tell me what is going on!"*

Instead of answering right away, he watched the door. Like he was worried Keith was going to return, upset by the noise.

But no one came.

And Colton, she now realized, was standing by the kitchen island, eating an apple, cutting it up with a small knife.

"What's going on is you," Colton-Keith said. *"You and all of your problems."*

"What are you talking about?" But something was stitching ideas together in the back of her mind.

Julie looked past Colton at the sign in the kitchen.

If any little word of ours can make one life the brighter . . .

"You made this all up," Colton said, and popped a wedge of apple into his mouth.

"No, I didn't."

"So you just happen to come home early from your conference, found me in bed with someone who looked exactly like you?"

"You said you'd never seen me before."

"I've been dealing with your problems for five years!" His voice bounced off the walls, and he walked toward her, the apple gone now, a hole opening beneath his chin, blooming red again. "For five years, babe. And bringing you up here, to the cabin, this always helped mellow you out."

If any little song of ours can make one heart the lighter . . .

Blood ran from Colton's neck, pattering down to the floor.

"But not this time," he said. "This time, you couldn't let go of it. All the fucking fantasies and games. Pretending you're this other person, this Monique woman. Spending all that money on a dress!"

Julie looked down at herself in a black cocktail dress.

God help us speak that little word and take our bit of singing . . .

"But it had to end," dream-Colton said, and now he was Michael, with those wide-set eyes, a shark moving through shallow waters. "I didn't want to be anybody else. I didn't want to be 'Michael.' And I pushed back. But then you took it all the way."

And drop it in some lonely vale and set the echoes ringing.

He changed back to Colton again, on the floor, those eyes wide and staring now. And in her hand, not a knife, but a gun, a wisp of smoke snaking out of the barrel.

* * *

Julie came to again. The vehicle had stopped moving. She'd been in a dreaming doze, half remembering, half inventing things in her mind. Now it was slipping away, as dreams do, rapidly down the drain of her subconscious.

The vehicle has stopped.

She tensed, listening, sensing. It was still running, but definitely no longer in motion.

You're crazy, you know.

No, she didn't know. She didn't understand where such an accusation would come from, either. Some protective part of herself, maybe. Would it be easier to think none of this was happening? Sure. All things considered, it would be preferable that she was strapped to a bed somewhere in an institution, drooling as she tripped on this wild and elaborate fantasy in her mind.

None of this is actually happening.

Of course it was. Nothing could be realer than the ache settling into her muscles from being in this fetal position, lying against the hard base of this trunk. They didn't exactly line these things with cushions.

And nothing could be more direct and crisp than her sense of the car rising slightly on its shocks as someone got out, and the vehicle weighed less.

She listened for the sound of footsteps; maybe they were muffled by the snow, but it was dead quiet. Still, she waited for the trunk to open, for hands to reach in and grab her.

It's not so far-fetched . . . you've had issues before.

Okay, maybe there was a coincidence that she lost it for a time when her mother died. That she talked to her mother for a while afterward, even though she wasn't there.

Each time one of her parents had gotten sick, she'd put her life on hold to help them, and in the process, yes, she might've done some damage.

Big T or small t — you be the judge.

Coincidences aside, though, people committed heinous crimes every day. Husbands killed wives for the money. People tried to disappear from the law, or from abusive exes, you name it. That was true, too.

But the more she waited for someone to come open the trunk and end her suspense, the more she prosecuted herself like this.

And an image formed, as clear and detailed in her mind as if she were seeing it projected on the underside of the trunk lid: Her — or at least, someone who looked exactly like her — sitting at a familiar bar. The Herkimer Brewing

Company. The same hanging wine glasses. The same sheen to the lacquered bar surface, the greens and whites of the glowing bottles on the three-tiered shelves beside the register. All those taps, frothing with home-brewed dark brown ales, amber lagers and hoppy gold pilsners.

And there she was, at the far corner, nursing a gin and tonic. Pinching the little red straw, swirling the drink gently around as she snuck long looks at the bartender. The insanely cute guy with a full head of wavy-curly hair, like Harry Styles before the buzz cut. Rock-climber muscles moving beneath his crisp white shirt, nimble fingers pulling those taps, scooping the ice, squeezing the lemon wedges, cute little mustache.

Colton Rossi.

He sounded like a movie star. And he *was* something of a celebrity, too. He had an impressive Instagram following, but it was a magazine where she'd first seen him. A magazine called *Climbing*, and he was down in Patagonia with a bunch of other climbers and his arm around a young woman that must be his girlfriend . . .

No. That woman is you.

But she persisted: *The woman is his fiancée, the one that was in his bed this morning, the one who you chased out of the house.*

He even said it:

I've never seen this woman before in my life.

Because she was a stalker. A lonely single woman who went to the local brewery and lusted over the perfect young bartender.

A woman who became so desperate she finally followed him home one night. Sat outside until dawn and then went in, found him in bed with his fiancée. And from there, concocted some intricate fantasy about a twin sister of hers coming in to do harm to them both.

You're a psychotherapist, Julie, you know what this is.

You've had another psychotic break.

The trunk opened, flooding her with fear. She recoiled and squinted and held up her hand to ward off anyone coming for her, anyone trying to hurt her.

But there was no one. Just the open trunk, the dark sky above. She'd bumped something, an emergency latch release, apparently.

The stars were out. The storm had passed and the sky was clear. A dim light shone somewhere far away, off to one side.

The wind blew across the open space. It curled through the trunk, tousled her hair. Icy cold, raising her skin with goosebumps.

"Hello?"

Her voice sounded unfamiliar, alien.

There was no one there.

Carefully, cautiously, tensed for a blow — or at least some kind of surprise — she gripped the edges of the trunk and started to haul herself out.

"Hello?" she called again. She put one foot down on the snowy ground. Then the other.

And no one answered.

CHAPTER FORTY-SIX

Starving, they ordered food at a roadside diner. But the press recognized them and chased them off.

They ate in the car, overlooking the Mohawk River.

"So what do you think?"

"Good burger," Stamper answered.

"I've had better."

He had a final bite and cleaned his hands with a napkin. "You know, that dream I had . . ."

He knew that Cuthbert was asking about the case. The two investigators rarely brought their personal lives to work. Maybe mention of a birthday, or some other life event, but nothing heavy. But it had been on his mind and he knew she'd have good advice.

"Cara wants to have kids," he told Cuthbert at last. "She's thirty-four, and I think she feels the window is closing. Or thinks it is."

Cuthbert was silent, thinking it better to listen and keep any ideas to herself.

He scratched the salt-and-pepper beard stubble on his neck. "My parents had four kids. I'm the fourth. My dad and I were talking, some Christmas or something, and everyone is there, and it's just chaos, kids everywhere. Anyway, he said,

'Once you get the big wheel turning, Lou, you can't just jump off.'"

"Some people do." It sounded like Cuthbert was speaking from experience. She got a cold look in her eyes, but then it cleared. "But you show up, Louis. My guess is you'd keep showing up."

There was a silence. After smiling sheepishly and glancing at her, he said, "Thanks."

"Don't mention it."

* * *

There were twenty cops in the room. Julie Spreniker had been missing now for thirty-six hours, counting from the home invasion. The general feeling was that she'd been already picked at by coyotes.

"But search crews are still working around the clock," Bueller said from the podium. "Mostly unpaid volunteers who need to stay diligent and feel their efforts are worthwhile. So what we're about to discuss needs to stay here, in this room." He eyed the group, making sure he had everyone's full attention. "There are reasons to think Julie Spreniker might not be up on that hill, not up in those woods."

After a moment, he continued, "Our working theory is that Colton Rossi attempted to kill her, then killed himself. Maybe he thought she was dead, maybe she got away. In either case, his body was found at the scene, with wounds that are mostly consistent with a self-inflicted GSW. But there's enough evidence to dispute that, according to our pathologist on this, Kay Howells."

Howells, a middle-aged woman with chin-length red hair and a round face, stood and faced the room. "First, no powder burns on the hand. That's kind of a big one. Another is that the angle is a little off from what you'd usually expect to see in this type of death by suicide, wherein the victim shoots themself under the chin. Additionally, though possibly unrelated, the decedent had signs of assault. Contusion on the cheek from blunt force, lip laceration and swelling, and periorbital hematoma. A black eye, in layman's terms," she added, answering the confused looks.

"Thank you, Kay," said Bueller, resuming. "The fact that we haven't found Spreniker yet, alive or dead, doesn't necessarily upend the theory either, but it creates doubt. And, of course, there's the apparent home abduction, throwing a big wrench into things."

He tapped a key on the laptop beside him and asked an officer to dim the lights. The first projected image on the large screen showed Rossi and Spreniker on a rock-climbing trip, looking happy.

Bueller clicked another key and the new image was a still take from the night's Ring camera video. The woman leaving with the bag in her hand. "There are two alternatives to the murder-suicide theory. One: that this was some kind of a set-up, staged to look like a murder-suicide for reasons we haven't quite yet ironed out, but that includes a woman who looks very much like Spreniker, possibly working with two other men." He searched the room until he found Stamper. "Louis, where are we with this?"

Stamper felt the eyes on him.

"We've spoken with Spreniker's father," he said, standing, "and with one of her friends. We've looked back at her college years, and into her childhood. Ms. Spreniker had some issues with mental health back in high school, and again after her mother died. We're not clear exactly what form these took, but from what we've gathered from her colleague and her family, it seems she'd had some fantasies, some delusions."

"She's delusional?" It was one of the other cops.

"There's no indication that she'd been struggling with her mental health recently. I'm only saying that some of the pieces don't fit with the main inquiries, here. It's possible that she's having a reaction to a major life event."

"Like what?"

"There is some evidence that Colton Rossi cheated on her."

Stamper watched the information work through the group. As major life events went, infidelity was right up there, along with bereavement, getting fired, and they knew it. "I'm not saying that we're certain of anything, but with the mental health history and the possibility of infidelity . . . It's possible that Spreniker herself hired a couple of guys to abduct and murder Colton Rossi."

As the room started to react, he added quickly, "Including his half-brother, Keith Rossi, who may resent him deeply for getting stuck with the biological father as his parent. Dale Rossi, someone we know to be a violent offender.

"According to this theory, Spreniker will show up in a couple of days with a story about how she narrowly escaped her own murder."

People were really grappling with it now, talking to each other.

"We've checked her bank records," Stamper said, above the noise. "No purchases made since three days ago, no activity at all, really, no plane tickets purchased in the recent past, but there was a substantial withdrawal of two thousand dollars a little less than a month ago, so she could be paying for things in cash."

He let the room settle before finishing.

"Basically, in this version of events, we have a deeply troubled woman who may have experienced a transformative life event. Wherever she is right now, she could be suffering the fallout of her own revenge gone awry. And it's possible she could be having some sort of mental health crisis." He looked at Cuthbert, knowing she disapproved of this theory, but he had to put it out there. "She may not even be sure of what's real," he said.

CHAPTER FORTY-SEVEN

The vehicle was unoccupied. Engine running, no one in it. The light off to the side: a gas station. Closed, empty, just some beer signs flickering with popsicle neon light. The snow kept coming down. The area had yet to be plowed — maybe a good foot and a half had piled up.

She was alone.

Where had everybody gone?

I told you. You've made all of this up. There's nothing and no one out here but you and all the crazy shit in your head . . .

And then she saw the shape of a man emerge from along-side the gas station, and he looked like he was zipping up his pants.

Seeing her, he stopped, then hurried toward her.

"What are you doing? Ah, man, this fucking car . . ."

Julie ran.

She ran away from the closed gas station. The man caught her, gripped her in a bear hug and she screamed. But the nearest house was a good quarter of a mile away. The snow swallowed the sounds she made, and her legs barely worked — she'd been scrunched in the trunk for hours now, it seemed, and her aches and pains had only worsened, her muscles turned to gristle.

He started dragging her back to the car. He was breathing a little heavy and saying, incredulous, "Fucking trunk opens from the inside. I mean, Jesus."

Keith Rossi. Colton's brother and murderer.

She screamed again — she'd scream herself hoarse if it came to that. He clamped a hand over her mouth and she bit him. He yelped and loosened his grip on her enough that she broke the hold and ran again. This time she ran harder, and faster, her legs warming up a bit, limp not as bad.

About a quarter mile up the road — dear God could it be true — were headlights, pushing through the storm.

She waved frantically but then he reached her. Once more wrapping her in his iron-bar arms, he walked her back to the gas station and the car, and she stared at the headlights and screamed at them to hurry. But the lights turned slowly off onto a secondary road and disappeared.

"Stop it," he hissed. "Stop it, goddammit. Or I'm gonna fucking hurt you."

"Don't put me back in there." Her voice cracked from the strain. "Please. I can't breathe in there."

"Oh yeah? And you're going to behave?"

She wondered where Monique was, or when she'd been switched to this car. And their surroundings seemed even more desolate than the Southern Adirondacks.

"Please," she repeated. "I'll behave." *I'll do anything. Just don't put me back there in the dark. With my thoughts. With just my horrible thoughts.*

She was shivering, too, wearing only that thin leather jacket, not much underneath, still just sneakers on her feet. "It's cold," she said.

"So what. Cold is good. Preserves you like meat." But it lacked real conviction or malice. They'd reached the back of the car now, and he was poised to put her in.

"I'll do anything you want," she said. "The trunk pops open anyway. It's not gonna work."

She had him there.

He looked around at the snowscape, deeply void of people. Whited out memories of a world.

"Fine," Keith said at last. "You'll sit up front with me where I can keep an eye on you. But you do anything . . ."

"I won't. Keep my hands tied. Tie them to my legs so I can't signal anybody. I don't care. I just need to get warm."

* * *

Ten minutes later, driving in silence, he put on the radio. White noise blared for a moment, but he turned down the volume and scanned until he found a classical station. It was crackling, the signal in and out, but she thought maybe it was Bach, *Suite No. 3 in D Major*.

Keith was wearing leather gloves.

No he isn't. None of this is happening either.

Sure, it was. She was sitting here in this luxury car — it even smelled new — and Keith was driving. And yes, those were driving gloves.

You saw him get dropped off. He left, he's gone. Why would Monique turn you over to him? Where is the Jeep?

She didn't have an answer. Outside, there was still nothing around. Just rolling country in the dark, everything blanketed white. They seemed to be heading out of the storm, though, perhaps having gotten ahead of it at last.

Occasionally, Keith's phone would light up with a subtle vibration, and he would read it. Once, he texted back, keeping one hand on the wheel.

Monique, Julie figured. She felt like a prisoner on death row, just sitting here, awaiting a terrible fate.

"You fucked up my Jeep," Keith said.

She waited.

"I mean — you really went after her with a knife? Where did you even get it?"

"When you were cutting the apple. You left it."

He shook his head. "Jesus."

Half a minute of silence.

"Keith . . ."

"Don't."

"Don't what?"

"I can sense you warming up your psychobabble."

She thought a moment. "Colton never said much to me about his father."

"Don't talk about him. Either of them."

"Why not?"

"Because I fucking said so."

The fear was a living thing in her body, a sickness in her veins. Sitting within arm's reach of someone who'd just murdered his brother, she said, "You won't hurt me."

"That's some confidence talking."

"You need me unharmed. At least, you can't do anything that would contradict whatever plan you guys have."

He was silent a moment, his jaw twitching. "What if the plan was a terrible car accident? You think it would matter what I did to you right now? I could beat the shit out of you and no one would know."

She swallowed over a hard lump in her throat. "You need my body found, and you need it in good enough shape that they assume it's her. That it's Monique."

A quick glance. Then he kept his eyes on the road.

"Keith, just stop this car and turn around, and I'll do anything."

She watched him for a reaction, but he was stoic. Didn't scoff, didn't get angry. She could see the resemblance to Colton now — they both had that strong Roman nose, the same shape to their ears. The likeness to her dead fiancé pierced her.

"How could you do it?"

He knew what she meant. "I never had a problem with it."

"It's your brother."

"Colton had it good. He had a good life. He got to go off with little Ann-Marie. Raised in the suburbs, went to college, got his little rock-climbing fame going. Got you."

239

Keith gave her a sharp look, then continued. "But my mom . . . she didn't fight back the way Ann-Marie did. She didn't leave the way she did. My mom stayed. She just let him beat her, beat me."

"I'm sorry."

"I didn't go to college. I enlisted. Colton was my big brother. He never even tried to help. He acted like I didn't exist."

"What you're feeling, what you have — you know millions of people struggle the same way. Whether it was your father, or it was war—"

"I've tried all that." Keith's jaw tightened.

Julie bit back the rest of what she was going to say. You needed to want help and Keith clearly wasn't interested. She waited a minute, deciding on a different tack.

"Is she paying you?" Julie started. "You can have my savings . . ."

But Keith only smirked, suggesting he knew she didn't have much to show for herself.

Julie tried again. "If she needed a place to stage the murder-suicide, why not at the townhouse? And why do it at all, especially if she wants to disappear? People are going to notice. This will be news. It probably already is. I know you said things were supposed to happen the way they did, but later when Monique got there you seemed—"

He cut her off with a gesture, slicing his hand through the air. "Look, Plan A was you decide to leave Colton, drive off and disappear. In reality, we would have smuggled you out of the house, driven your car west and abandoned it. To the world, it would look like you left and Colton shot himself."

She dared to sneak in a question. "Shot himself with what? We don't have a gun."

"Colton has access to all the guns at the cabin. Just needed to get him there. So the story would be, he drives up there and kills himself. When we switched to Plan B, I said just use the van to get to the cabin. Perfect abduction vehicle — already had the partition in it. I think someone used it to haul some chickens at one point. And if it got seen by tolls, neighbors, fine. It would fit the new narrative." He looked almost proud of himself. "I said we should put in the plastic because the van would stay at the cabin, and when police went through it, we didn't want them finding evidence of you in the back. We wanted it to look like you two rode up front together. And Monique was always saying we needed to minimize what happened to you, what you came into contact with. So it's been bumpers and bubble wrap for you all the way."

Julie hardly felt like that described things.

"So she needed you for the cabin," Julie said. "And to get close to him? I didn't even know he had a brother. How could you help her get close to him when you were estranged? You were some bully that used to smother him in hay bales when he was a kid."

Another look. She had offended him. It wasn't really the question she wanted to ask, though, was it? Close, but not quite.

The static-laced music changed. Chopin. *Nocturne No. 20 in C-Sharp Minor.*

"How did Monique know to contact you?" That was the question. "How did she know Colton had a half-brother when even I didn't?

"She didn't," Keith said, and Julie stopped breathing. "I knew Michael from way back. We were in school for just a couple of years. But I knew who he was, followed his life a little bit, knew they were in the pharmaceutical business — or her family was, really. And everything that was going on with Monique being in legal trouble with her family. Facing likely prison time." He paused and she slowly inhaled. "The whole thing was my idea: use you to escape. But they came up with the details, and said they needed me."

"So you saw the magazine first. And told them."

His silence answered.

"And *everything* was your idea?" She pictured Colton on the floor, glassy dead eyes.

"I said no at first."

241

When he didn't elaborate, she said, "But then they offered you money." She could barely choke out the words. "How much?"

"A million. Half up front, half when it's over."

A million dollars, she thought. *To kill your own brother.*

"You're better off, anyway," he said. "Colton was a selfish prick. He would have made you miserable. Look how easy it was for her to seduce him. She barely had to try."

"And now you're going to kill me, right?" Her voice sounded strange in her ears again. The words like another language. "Or is she going to do it?"

He didn't answer. He kept his hands at ten and two on the wheel, focusing on the road. Like Monique had. *Where was she?*

"Why did you say — why did you both say — she was my twin sister?"

"That was her idea. She wanted to meet Colton but needed a story first. The coincidence of her looks — it only worked, she said, if she started by saying she was your sister. I didn't know she was going to show up to the cabin in a dress, though." He laughed a little. "She sort of played you in that dress. Went to the casino, lost a bunch of money, got upset. I think it was kind of a half-baked idea, but Monique thinks she's smart. I don't know. She's ballsy, though. I mean, here we all are."

For a while, neither of them spoke.

"It still doesn't make sense," Julie said. "It's going to be news. All of it. You don't think people will put it together?"

"No, actually. I don't. It's separate police jurisdictions. And, honestly, we both live in this world, with endless bad news everywhere every day. You think anyone is going to notice that one woman way over here happened to look like some other woman way over there, in totally unrelated events?"

Julie felt herself slipping into a kind of fugue. She was so tired, so exhausted, and in pain, and being taken farther and farther from home, from everything she knew.

There wasn't much else. She watched the night gradually brighten to morning. Not only had they outrun the storm, the sky was clear, the sun shining through evergreen trees as it rose.

They'd been driving too long to still be in the Adirondacks, Julie thought. They had to be somewhere like Vermont.

Vermont: population 600,000, where no one can hear you scream.

They drove for a while longer, passing a sign that might've said Black River Chasm.

When Keith spoke again, the topic seemed out of the blue.

"I asked you about God."

"I remember."

"My old man, Dale, he put me in Sunday school — just a place for me to go for a couple of hours and be out of his hair. And there was this nun, right, who taught the class. She talked about angels. But the way she talked about them, they were these scary creatures, huge and muscular with giant wings. I never forgot that. So when we were in Afghanistan, I named our Humvees *Azrael, Gabriel, Sariel.*" He nodded a little to himself. "We called ourselves the Furious Angels."

And then he fell silent again, just driving with his gloved hands.

They came to a bridge. As they rolled across it, going slow, Julie saw a massive waterfall in the distance, dropping down a hundred feet or more to the river far below. Keith seemed careful where to park the car, stopping it just past the bridge on the side of the road. He also seemed wary that someone might be around. But it was early, and there'd just been a huge storm, so maybe no one was.

When he turned off the engine, the radio died, too. The white noise of rushing water filled the silence.

He leaned into the back, came up with a plastic bag stuffed with clothes.

"Put these on."

She didn't move.

"Just do it, Julie. There's no way out of this."

The panic started to close in again, a phantom strangulation. Her ears thrummed. Was it blood, or the river she heard?

"I'll scream," she said.

"That's fine." But she saw him check the mirrors. What time was it? Maybe six. Someone would be along. There was a chance. Wasn't it supposed to be an overpopulated world?

Not here. This was the land time forgot.

"Put them on, or I'll do it for you."

She could hardly see, she was so nervous. But she didn't budge.

Fight, flight, or freeze.

Keith grabbed her, pulled her to him, and as she struggled against him, she thought of her mother, saw her face clear as if she was floating above her.

Keith was squeezing her around the neck. His hands were metal jaws. Her vision started to dim, her mind leaping forward to a certain near future: Keith putting her in Monique's clothes, dragging her to the edge of the bridge, and throwing her off.

She saw herself plummeting to the river far below, crashing into the icy, churning water, jagged with sharp rocks. And disappearing. This time forever.

PART FIVE

Furious Angels

CHAPTER FORTY-EIGHT

"Louis," someone said. "Stamper, wake up."

It was Cuthbert. Apparently, he'd nodded off after the meeting.

She looked around at the door. "Good thing it was me coming in and not someone else," she said, sitting at her desk.

He put both feet on the floor and sat up, pawing at his face and neck. "Just needed a quick reboot," he said, trying to make light of it.

But she wasn't biting.

She was mad at him.

Well, if not mad at him, disappointed. And he hated that.

"Look, I don't think she's delusional," he said, about Julie Spreniker. "I don't think she hired Keith Rossi to kill her fiancé, none of it. I think she's been targeted, and Keith Rossi is in it."

Cuthbert said, "I do, too."

No shit.

But he was glad to be back on the same page with her. Especially since she was usually right.

Three minutes later, Taylor knocked on the door. "I ran the name Katelyn Graham through missing persons, local and county police, departments of public safety," he said.

"Just got a hit in Caledonia County, Vermont. Apparently a vehicle was found registered to Katelyn Graham."

"Oh boy," Stamper said.

"No one in it, no keys. Park ranger came across it sitting by the bridge at Black River Chasm. They're searching for Graham."

* * *

It took five hours by car. Stamper could have put the lights on and made it in four, but most of Vermont was back roads, unplowed and unsalted. By the time he got to Black River, the whole circus was out, lights flashing off the surrounding evergreens. Police and fire and rescue to rival Ferris Lake.

He found incident command in a white tent, teeming with state and county officers, parks people, volunteer leaders, and sought out Sergeant Dumain, the man in charge.

"That vehicle is registered to Katelyn Graham, New York," Dumain said, referring to a nice-looking black Audi parked nearby, roped off with caution tape.

"You think she went into the water? Jumped?" Huge work lights running on generators illuminated the bridge and the surrounding forest. The river was below, out of sight.

"It very much looks that way," Dumain said. Dumain was big, with bushy sideburns and watchful cop eyes. "Car doesn't seem to have anything wrong with it. It's got half a tank of gas, and keys were found on the bridge. It's still possible she flagged a ride for some reason, got picked up. Or that she just went off into the woods. This is Groton State Park, about as remote as it gets. Why are you interested?"

Stamper gave an abridged version. He'd already talked to Caledonia County and the Vermont State Police several times on the drive, just trying to stay updated. Besides, his theory was just a theory, an idea forming in the back of his mind since first seeing the Julie Spreniker lookalike, but with nothing solid to give it real shape.

He went to the bridge, showed his badge to the deputy there, and went under the tape.

Black River was impressive, to say the least. A sidewinding snake far below, black with white frothing edges. He stood staring a minute until he sensed someone approach — a woman in a dark-green ranger uniform, thick black parka on top.

"How deep is it?" Stamper asked her, after they made introductions.

"Gets deep in places. Fifteen, twenty feet. It's high right now. We had some warming last week which melted snowpack, really giving it some volume."

"You ever have people jump?"

She got a look. "Unfortunately, yes. Once every few years. Some people want to raise the sidewalls on the bridge, or put up some fencing, but it's such a popular tourist spot. It's a sandstone gorge, 500 million years old. We're talking Cambrian. It's amazingly ancient."

"Looks fast," he said.

She peered over the edge with him. "It is. Especially now."

"If someone were to have jumped in . . ."

"They'd be washed downstream pretty quickly."

"I don't suppose you have a map?"

She did, in her truck. Spreading it out on the hood, she pointed out where they were, at the chasm, and where the river wound up, many miles away, dumping into the Connecticut River that formed the border of New Hampshire.

He did some mental calculations. He and Cuthbert had gotten to the Ferris Lake cabin around 9 p.m. the night before. The tracks leading out had been fresh, maybe a couple of hours old. Driving in that blizzard, doing twenty-five, conservatively, it would have taken someone ten hours to make the trip from there to here.

"Let's say she went in the river at six this morning," Stamper said. "What time was the vehicle noticed?"

"It was me that called it in," the ranger said. "I saw it earlier in the day — we have a pull-off right over there. But when I came back through hours later, it was still there. When I looked around on the bridge, I found the keys. Right over there."

A yellow evidence marker noted the spot, though the keys were no longer there, likely bagged and taken for analysis. "So I ran the plate, called it in to county. That was at eight a.m."

"So, you're searching downriver. How far?"

"Well, put it this way: If someone went into that river and got carried along, and it's been—" she checked her watch "—almost eighteen hours, she could be anywhere between here and South Ryegate."

He checked the map — South Ryegate was ten miles away. It was a lot of area to cover.

"There are falls and eddies along the river that could trap a person. I've seen it happen, rushing water pinning someone beneath the surface, right in place. So in addition to scouring the river banks, we've had divers in there all day, with stretches of class two and class three rapids."

"It doesn't sound easy," Stamper said, noticing movement behind the barricade. Three black SUVs were pulling up. Police had one lane open for traffic, but these people didn't seem to want to pass through. A couple of the doors even opened in unison, like something out of a movie. Feds?

No — the first to get out was a man wearing jeans, a ski parka and a slouched beanie hat, all of it expensive-looking. He strode toward the bridge as an older woman emerged, more slowly, from the rear vehicle.

The man made it almost to the bridge before police intercepted him. He tried to push through, but they held him back.

"Let me go, let me go!" His face was flushed with anger, maybe fear. But they held him.

"Trevor," the woman called. "That's not going to help." She was more formally dressed, in a long black coat.

Stamper nodded goodbye to the ranger and headed over for a closer look.

Dumain approached Trevor as the cops held him. "You're the husband?"

"Yeah, yeah yeah," he answered, still speaking fast. "That's her car. That's Katelyn's car. I can see her leather jacket in there."

"Sir, I'm going to need you to calm down." Dumain patted the air.

"Is she down there?"

"Sir, let's talk over here." Dumain pushed his barrel chest toward Trevor. "Step over here please, sir."

Stamper followed them into the tent. Dumain gave him a quick glance, then introduced himself to the woman as she came in: Evelyn Cade, Katelyn's mother. "My husband's in the car," she said. "He's just on a call."

Stamper recognized the name. Katelyn Graham was born Katelyn Cade, and the Cades were wealthy owners of a major drug company.

Dumain stayed focused on Trevor. "Sir, what can you tell me about where your wife was the past couple of days?"

"The cottage. We have a place up near St. Johnsbury. On Old Route 2. She was coming up here for a long weekend."

"Where was she coming from, sir?"

"I've already told the police all of this, I . . . We live in South Nyack. In Rockland County."

"Okay," Dumain said, "And when did she leave?"

"Wednesday morning."

"And did she arrive at the house?"

"She did. At least, she said so in a text. It was eight o'clock Wednesday night. 8:08."

Stamper remembered the time from his own chat with Trevor Graham.

Dumain glanced at Evelyn Cade, as if inviting her to chime in. "How was she when she left?"

"Not good," Trevor answered. "Honestly, not good."

Evelyn, in a softly hoarse voice, did speak up: "My daughter is facing litigation. She has two—"

But Trevor cut her off. "They're railroading their own daughter, accusing her of things she would never do."

An older man entered in a black coat, his white hair swept back, his face gaunt and blotchy. Phillip Cade. "What's going on? Where's Katie? Where's my daughter?"

It went on for a while, and Stamper stayed back. It seemed Trevor Graham and the Cades were used to getting their own way. They didn't stop until they'd persuaded the police to let them look over the bridge and investigate Katelyn's car.

He took Dumain aside when they'd left. "Sergeant, like I told you on the phone, we have a missing person in Herkimer County, New York who's . . . well, a veritable twin of Katelyn Graham's. Julie Spreniker has been missing for over thirty-six hours now, and I'm just chasing down everything I can. Graham popped up for us because of a possible second woman involved in the abduction . . ."

Dumain seemed to understand, but he was distracted by the case before him. The family now out there, mucking around in his crime scene.

"Have you been able to look at phone records, yet?" Stamper asked.

"We have. Coverage is tricky at best in northern Vermont. It's missing altogether from many places. Graham had a carrier that's not popular up here, but we followed it up. Her phone pings from South Nyack Wednesday morning. It travels north, to this area, and shows up a couple of times later the same day. Until there's nothing, as of six o'clock this morning. When we're pretty sure she went into that water."

Searchers had first covered the immediate area and the river just below, Dumain explained. More searchers had been downriver for hours now. Several teams had started over ten miles away and had been working their way back upriver, although the searchers had emphasized the first mile of the river moving away from the bridge. Dumain seemed sure they'd find her eventually.

Two missing women now, Stamper thought.

When the time was right — just before they got back in their gleaming SUVs — he approached Katelyn Graham's family. When he called out Trevor's name, the man looked Louis up and down with suspicion. He had wide-set eyes, a slightly crooked nose, and an unfriendly look.

Stamper formed a grim smile as he re-introduced himself. "We spoke on the phone earlier today."

"Oh, yeah. You're here?"

Katelyn's mother and father edged closer.

"Still looking for the same missing woman I was looking for when I called you. Haven't found her." He waited until the parents were close enough to hear for sure and said, "She looks just like Katelyn, is the thing."

He held up a picture on his phone, the professional headshot they'd been using of Julie Spreniker.

Trevor looked at it, scowled, but then made a dismissive face. "Huh. I guess she does, yeah. Well, good luck." He started climbing into the SUV.

Stamper was unsatisfied. "It's just, when we spoke earlier, something wasn't right."

Trevor waited, looking annoyed.

"When I told you about Julie Spreniker — that's the woman — you said you saw it on the news."

"Yeah?"

"But you didn't seem to understand why I was calling you."

Trevor glanced at the parents, hovering close.

"It just seems like if you saw Julie Spreniker on the news," Stamper pressed on, "a dead ringer for Katelyn, you would've had some idea why I was calling. You would have thought it was a coincidence, at least."

Trevor stared, a sinew of muscle pulsing in his jaw. Then he smiled a little. "Look, Detective . . .?"

"Stamper."

"Investigator Stamper. I honestly don't think they look that much alike. And it's a big world. I'm sorry, but it's been a difficult time, with a lot going on, and now I have to go."

Getting into the SUV beside him, he shut the door and disappeared behind tinted glass.

Stamper turned to the parents, but they were already getting back into their own vehicle. The caravan pulled out, turned in the road, and the first and second vehicle roared off, leaving him in a swirl of agitated snow.

Great.

But the third vehicle stopped, and the dark window came down.

Evelyn Cade peered out. "We'll be staying up at the country house," she said.

And then the window went up as the SUV drove away in the oncoming dusk.

CHAPTER FORTY-NINE

The Cade family "country house" was situated on a 105-acre parcel of land, a stone-slate-and-copper European-style retreat with five bedrooms and eight bathrooms. In the dark and cold, the place still managed to look inviting, built into a hillside and presiding over a presently frozen pond, cleared of snow for ice-skating or hockey.

After checking in at a sleek intercom panel, the gate buzzed open and Stamper drove up the gently winding drive to the main entrance. He glanced at his phone — barely any service. Even the GPS had been intermittent, guiding him through the dark countryside to an address he'd gotten from Dumain.

The Cades home was well known in the region, and he could see why. At first, the shapes on the sloping front lawn seemed like real animals — but the three deer were iron statues.

The man who stepped out of the front door to meet him claimed he was the Cades' personal assistant. Stamper counted at least one gun on him, tucked discreetly beneath his suit jacket.

Armed assistants, too. This family wasn't messing around.

He directed Stamper to park behind one of the dark SUVs beneath a luxurious curved carport, then showed him inside. The Cades were cozied up in a solarium, its wall of windows overlooking low dark mountains in the distance. Flames popped and sizzled from a giant open fireplace. Phillip Cade looked like he'd been crying.

"Thank you, Charlie," Evelyn said to the assistant, who'd led Stamper into the room. Charlie had offered to take Stamper's coat, and he'd turned it over. Now his gun was showing on his hip holster.

"Please, have a seat," Evelyn said. "Charlie will get you anything you need. Coffee? Water? I'd offer the wine, but it seems you're on duty?"

Stamper noted the open bottle on the table, half gone, glasses empty.

"Yes. No, thank you," he said, and Evelyn smiled at Charlie, who left.

Two white, half-moon couches faced each other, per-pendicular to the fireplace. Evelyn and Phillip sat down on one — sitting a little apart from each other, not touching — and Stamper took the other. Phillip wiped his eyes with a delicate-looking handkerchief. Trevor Graham was MIA.

"Thank you for coming," Evelyn said. "It's been a very long day, and we were a bit overwhelmed by all the activity at the bridge. This whole thing has been a lot for us, as I'm sure you can imagine."

"I'm sorry, it must be very difficult."

"It is. We have yet to have many satisfactory answers. It will be good to talk."

"Where is Mr. Graham?"

"Trevor is staying at the cottage," she said. "It's right back there." She pointed through the vast windows. Stamper leaned forward to get a better angle — there, in the snowy near distance, was a much smaller building glowing against the blackness of the hills beyond. "He arrived back shortly after we did and didn't speak to us. He went straight there. They have always preferred to rough it out in the cottage."

One thing about great wealth, Stamper thought — amazing levels of insulation.

Evelyn got a hard glint in her eye then, something almost devious. "You had something interesting things to say at the bridge. It seemed you were implying something."

"In all honesty, ma'am — it was a bit overwhelming for me, too."

For a moment she only studied him, as if determining for herself whether he thought he was clever. "You've come a long way. To travel this far — and in the midst of your own missing person case — you must have something you can share. Perhaps you could tell us what you're thinking? Or at least, what you and Trevor discussed when you called him yesterday?" And she raised her eyebrows, as if knowing something confidential.

"Yes, I called him in the evening. Your daughter's name came up in a database search, through a kind of reverse facial recognition. In layman's terms, we used AI to identify people that are a 95 percent facial match for someone else, but basically we asked the program to find anyone who looked just like our missing person."

"And because Katie has a record . . ."

"Yes, ma'am, she was in the database."

Phillip Cade suddenly stood, seeming emotional again, shaking his head. "This isn't going to help us, Lynn."

"Phillip, sit down."

"Katie is out there, she's out there in the . . ." He couldn't finish his sentence and walked away, overcome.

Evelyn let him go. He hurried out of the room and they could hear him walking away, coughing, maybe crying. Eventually his footfalls faded into the house. Evelyn turned her attention back to Stamper but remained silent. He looked into the fire a moment, then back to her.

"Your daughter is being investigated. Can you tell me about that?"

"It's all very difficult, as you can imagine, but we have to separate family from business. My husband thinks she can do no wrong. He blames us for this. He thinks that we pushed her to this point. He's always blamed us for Katie's misfortunes. Blamed me, really. For Katie running away from school. Her trouble finding a career she wanted. For her subsequent actions. When we cut off her allowance, she started to take money from the company. And regrettably, the evidence against her bears out, whether Phillip likes it or not. I love my daughter, but I wouldn't be much of a mother if I let her lie to me, steal from us, and I did nothing."

"So, she's been indicted and is facing prosecution."

"The trial starts four months from today, in fact."

"That's a lot of pressure."

"Of course. But we're talking about over a hundred million dollars. Gone over the course of several years. Invested, I'm sure, and all hidden — Katie was always smart. If she's convicted, she'd not only face prison time, but she'd have to pay it all back."

Evelyn fell silent then, her own gaze wandering to the fire. She'd come just short of saying what was in Stamper's head, what had been in his head for a while now: Katelyn Graham had wanted to disappear.

* * *

He made the trip through the cold up to the cottage on the hill. The whole thing reminded him, in a perverse way, of the Rossi place. A study in stark contrasts, but compared to the huge, pristine house, the cottage felt like the shack on the hill.

There, of course, had been all that blood inside, but no Julie Spreniker. Here, though, the path was lighted. And instead of a fleet of state troopers, he had an armed assistant accompanying him. Charlie stepped up onto the porch of the homestead-style cottage and knocked on the formidable wooden door.

When Trevor opened up, his eyes were bleary, as if from sleep. "You again. Can I help you? I told you everything I know."

Stamper looked up at the big man beside him. "Charlie, okay if we do this in private?"

"You know your way back." The assistant turned and walked off toward the main house, where Stamper could see the fire flickering through the solarium windows. He thought he glimpsed a figure looking back at him, then it moved away.

"Can I come in?"

Trevor sighed but opened the door wider and Stamper stepped in. Wow, if this was "roughing it" in the cottage . . . The space was generous, must've been close to a thousand square feet, its own fireplace going. Trevor led them into the large kitchen, flicking on the light. It was all steel and stone. He wore pajama bottoms, maybe silk, in a deep-charcoal gray. His upper half was bare, several tribal tattoos across his defined muscles. He opened the fridge and pulled out a beer, then slapped off the cap against the counter.

"You want one?"

"No, thanks. I can't stay long." Stamper got the sense that Trevor Graham had married into his wealth. That he was still part hustler, and that he knew his way around a fight.

Trevor watched him while taking a long sip from the bottle. Then he wiped his mouth with the back of his hand. "So you're here from New York State?"

Trevor made it sound like a question, but, Stamper reflected, he already knew where he was from. Stamper had said so this afternoon by the bridge. He was stalling.

"Yeah, took the drive over when I heard about Katelyn. Listen, sorry if I was a little bit rude earlier. I just . . . this case in New York has got us all scratching our heads."

"Yeah?"

"Yeah. And now this thing with your wife. How long have you been married?"

Trevor set the beer down and unconsciously sucked at his lower lip a second before saying, "Hey, look. I don't want to come off rude either, right? But it's late, and my wife might have just . . . I don't feel like talking about our lives right now to you. I've been talking to police all day."

"It is late," Stamper said, making a point to check his phone. He also noticed that the one bar of cell coverage had reduced to a full No Service.

"So, you know, I mean . . ."

"Yeah, I hear you. Of course. It's just — I'm married, too. And I thought, if my wife was missing, if maybe she'd jumped off a bridge, or there was foul play . . . I'd be up all night. No question about it." Stamper looked at the pajama bottoms and let the implication hang in the air. "You got a phone in here? A landline?"

Trevor's eyes narrowed with mistrust and growing dislike. But he wasn't afraid, which was interesting. "No. Landline down at the house, though."

"So if there're any updates, the police can call down there, right, leave you a message? And, then what — I guess Charlie would walk up here, to let you know? Or do you have cell service?"

Trevor didn't answer, just stared Stamper down, that nerve firing in his jaw. "I think I've been as cordial as I'm gonna be," he said finally. "I don't have anything else to say. I can't help you with your case. And if you want to ask anything else about me, or Katie, or our lives . . ."

Stamper raised his hands in peace. "We can do it tomorrow. Sure. Well, I appreciate your time. Sorry to bother you this late." He paused at the door. "Sleep well."

He found his own way back to the parking area, just like he'd told Charlie he would.

* * *

Deciding whether he wanted to find somewhere to bag out for the night, or make the drive all the way back, wasn't much of a debate. He was exhausted, it had passed midnight, and he didn't want to leave. Not now.

After inhaling a couple of terrible fast-food sandwiches from a twenty-four-hour gas station, he called Cara from the hotel room phone and told her what he could. Then he got on the Wi-Fi and messaged Cuthbert to see if she was around.

Five minutes later, she was talking to him on the landline.

"I did some research, and you're not going to believe this, but there's precedent for this. This happened before, or something just like it, in the Czech Republic."

"Oh, well, there you go."

She ignored his sarcasm, saying, "A few years ago, a woman who apparently wanted to disappear from her life found someone online who looked just like her — a social-media influencer type. Somehow, she convinced this woman to meet up in person, then killed her, and staged it to look like it was *her*."

"How come we didn't know about that?"

"Maybe because it was Eastern Europe. But it's happened in the US, too, in Utah: a woman not only found her doppelganger and killed her, but then entered her life."

"Really."

"For three years," Cuthbert said. "She had everybody fooled — neighbors, coworkers, everyone. It wasn't until the doppelganger's mother came back into the picture that the truth came out. They'd been estranged, but she finally found her and arrived on the doorstep — of course, the mother knew straightaway it wasn't her daughter."

It was hard to wrap his mind around. "So both these women tricked everyone who knew—"

"No," Cuthbert interrupted. "The woman in the Czech Republic didn't try to impersonate her lookalike. She just needed the body, I guess. To fake her own death."

"Damn."

He was grateful to talk about it all with Cuthbert but soon ended the call. The pink elephants were starting to appear.

He ended up sleeping atop the comforter, fully clothed, something he hadn't done since his drinking days, and didn't move until the hotel phone rang again, this time at just past six in the morning.

"Louis Stamper?"

He made some unintelligible sounds in response.

"It's Sergeant Dumain. You're a hard man to reach — phone just goes to voicemail, but I tracked you down." There was commotion in the background, chatter and ringing phones. "We got quite a situation over here. Katelyn Graham showed up early this morning and was admitted to the emergency room."

CHAPTER FIFTY

Stamper pulled up to the hospital in St. Johnsbury twenty minutes later, found an available spot, and headed for the main entrance. A few reporters gave him the eye as he walked past, like they might smell a cop, but he made it inside before anyone started recording.

Katelyn Graham had already been moved from the emergency room to the critical access wing. Stamper found a group of uniformed cops in the hallway, Dumain a head taller than the rest.

"She showed up last night around four a.m.," the sergeant said. "Had a phone on her that was completely dead, and a small wallet with a couple of credit cards and a driver's license. Driver's license and credit cards are for a Katelyn Harlow Graham, thirty-two years old, South Nyack, New York."

"What's she saying?"

"Nothing. She's not talking to anyone. The truck driver that dropped her off spoke briefly with one of the nurses. He didn't stick around long enough for us to talk to him. But he said he picked her up at P&H Truck Stop."

"Where's that?"

"Well, that's about a mile downriver from the bridge at Black River Chasm."

"She didn't say anything to him?"

"All he told the nurse was where he picked her up and that she was bleeding, looked like she'd been beaten with a baseball bat. I wished he woulda called the police right then and there, but some of these truckers, they don't want to get involved with police, and he didn't even leave any way to be contacted. Anyway, I remembered you being a New York investigator with a missing person's case — that Julie Spreniker woman — and you'd been over there, looking around. So I called you."

"I appreciate it. You call anyone else?"

"Well, the family, yeah. The husband, Travis, I think . . ."

"Trevor."

"Right. And the parents."

Stamper looked around. "They're not here yet?"

"Just you."

"They'll be coming. Probably followed by a lot more media, too, and interested public."

"We can handle it."

"Is she . . . can I go in?"

Dumain looked around, as if searching for hospital staff. But the nurses' station was a ways down and they were alone.

"She's stable, but she's a bit banged up. Bandage around her head, swollen eye . . . You can maybe get in and out, but you'll have to be quick."

* * *

The truck driver had said a baseball bat, but it was worse: the woman in the bed looked like she'd been mugged by a mob and dragged across concrete. A white bandage wrapped her head and crossed her left eye. Lacerations along her jaw, chin, and nose, stitches and butterfly-bandaged. Blood seeped through the gauze covering her left ear. They'd dressed her in a hospital gown, but Stamper saw a clump of clothes in the corner that would need to be sent to a lab asap.

He smiled down at her, and she watched him approach with her one available eye.

262

"Hi," he said, moving slowly, almost gingerly, like she might easily be spooked. He kept his voice low as he spoke. "How are you feeling?"

She didn't say anything for a moment, just watched until he reached the foot of the bed, where he stopped. It was a stupid question anyway.

"Can you talk at all?"

She made no response. Behind the dried blood and bandages, her expression was impossible to read. "I'm Louis. I work with the New York State Police. I've been asked to find a woman named Julie Spreniker. Have you ever heard that name?"

She remained motionless, just watching.

He eyed the pile of clothes on the chair in proximity. "Do you remember anything about what happened to you?"

She seemed to think back, her gaze drifting to the window. The snow had finally stopped, completely, but not before blanketing everything in white. And then she started to cry.

"Whoa, whoa," Stamper said, and started hunting around for a tissue. As he was pulling some from the box in the corner to give to her, a doctor hurried into the room, face full of concern.

"No, no, no," the doctor said. "She needs to rest."

"I just have a couple more quick questions." Stamper handed the woman the tissue as he spoke.

"I understand that. But they'll have to wait."

The doctor held out an arm for him to leave. There was no point fighting it.

"I'll be back," he said to the woman.

The doctor ushered him into the hall. "She's had multiple head traumas. Not only is she concussed, her CT scan shows subdural hematoma, and she's still hypothermic. She's in no shape to talk to you."

"What else can you tell me about her injuries? Anything unusual?"

"She looks like she fell off a bridge," the doctor said with perfect deadpan. "Excuse me, I have to go."

Stamper was left standing in the hallway. Dumain and the cops had migrated to the lobby where they crowded around. Outside the glass doors, the crowd of onlookers and press had grown.

And then, pushing their way through: the Cades.

CHAPTER FIFTY-ONE

Stamper was mildly surprised to see Trevor Graham along with Evelyn and Philip Cade. He wore sunglasses despite being indoors, his clothes and jacket again expensive-looking.

A nurse showed the family into the room while Stamper waited in the hallway. They'd been in there barely a minute when his phone rang — Cuthbert said that Tom and Jack Spreniker were likely on their way up.

"They might not even be able to get in to see her," Stamper said. "They're only letting in immediate family right now, and as far as everyone here is concerned, that's Katelyn Graham in the room."

"What did you think when you saw her?"

"Honestly? I couldn't tell. She's in real rough shape. Could be either of them. Listen, I gotta go — they're coming back out already."

Evelyn walked fast, pulling her husband by the arm. She glanced at Stamper as she went past, something like embarrassment, anger, fear, all mixing on her face. Phillip, for his part, once again had tears in his eyes.

Trevor Graham emerged from the room next, started after the Cades, but Stamper blocked his path. "Hey, just a few words."

Trevor stopped, looking not too happy about it.

"Remember, I have that missing person in New York."

"I don't know what to tell you. Maybe she's the woman in that room."

Stamper felt himself exhale. "That's not your wife?"

"I don't know who that is, but that's not Katie."

"How do you know?"

Trevor was inscrutable behind those dark sunglasses. "A husband knows his wife, and that's not her."

"Don't go anywhere," Stamper said.

Trevor started down the hall.

"Hey!" Stamper called, but Trevor went out the door and into the growing throng of reporters.

* * *

"I need to get back in there," he said to the nurse.

She held up her clipboard for him to see. "Sir. We admitted a 'Katelyn Graham.' And the doctor's orders are only immediate family right n—"

"Be that as it may," Stamper said, pointing at the door where Trevor Graham and the Cades had walked out, "they came in claiming to be the immediate family, but they just said it's not her. It's not Katelyn Graham."

He pulled up Julie's picture on his phone and thrust it at the nurse, who looked briefly horrified.

Dumain materialized at his elbow, softly speaking into his ear. "Investigator. Come on, let's go talk about his."

"Do you see?" Stamper ignored the other man. He pushed the phone closer to the nurse's face. "Do you see this woman? This is who's lying in the bed over there. Julie Spreniker. She was abducted, taken from her home—"

"Stamper, put that away." Dumain's voice was calm, but there was an edge to it. He was pulling at his arm now, trying to get him to move along. "We don't know that."

Stamper yanked his arm free as he responded to the sergeant. "You need to arrest Trevor Graham right now. Put him in a box, let me talk to him."

266

Dumain reared back a little, not used to being talked to that way. Stamper knew he had no jurisdiction in Vermont, but there seemed to be a crime being committed right under everyone's noses and nothing was being done about it.

"Sir," the nurse said, "I can only go according to hospital pol—"

"Fuck it," he said, and started to the hospital room, the nurse calling, "Sir! Sir!"

He stopped just short of going in, his eye drawn to the camera in the ceiling, pointing down at him.

Dumain was about to grab him again, but Stamper held up his hands in peace. Bullying a nurse, barging into this person's room — it wouldn't do any good. Whether she was Katelyn Graham or Julie Spreniker, she needed to heal. Any more questions from him would have to wait.

"All right," he said. "All right."

* * *

He called Cuthbert again from the hotel, pacing the room as he talked.

"The search is still going at Ferris Lake," she confirmed. "Still no sign of Spreniker, alive or dead. But they found her phone."

"Where?"

"In the shed with all the blood. Battery drained."

Forensics on the van had also come back: Spreniker's fingerprints were everywhere in the front, including the steering wheel.

He called Dumain. Katelyn Graham's car was being processed, too. Some prints on the steering wheel had already been identified as hers. "You'd think there'd be more," Dumain said, "but our crime-scene guys told me it looked a little wiped down."

Dumain seemed all right with Stamper, no hard feelings about the hospital. Stamper stopped pacing and sat on the double bed.

"Yeah," he said about the uncannily clean vehicle, "because Spreniker was probably in that car. Driven by Trevor Graham, maybe, or Keith Rossi. Anybody see a man walking alongside the road early yesterday morning, not far from the bridge?"

"Not that's been reported."

"She was supposed to die," Stamper said. "That's what I think. She wasn't supposed to make it through like this. This was all supposed to look like Katelyn Graham jumped to her death."

Dumain grunted, as if unsure.

"If you'd found a body, you'd presume it was her, just like the hospital thought it was her. No reason to look further when you had the car and the license. Those clothes in the corner of the hospital room are Graham's."

"How do you know that?"

"About the clothes? I looked at them. Burberry sweatshirt, Versace jeans. Not Julie Spreniker's brands. My partner Lindsay would attest."

Dumain withheld comment. Either way, it didn't make the case. Someone could say they were stolen. Trevor Graham might.

"Can you pick him up?" Stamper asked.

"Graham?"

"Yeah."

"We don't have anything. What are we picking him up on?"

"Just to talk. His wife is missing, a woman in her clothes just washed up at a truck stop. I've got her possibly on video coming out of that same woman's house in Herkimer, minutes after her abduction. It's enough."

"He won't come quietly," Dumain said after a moment.

"So let him come loudly."

"He'll just lawyer up."

"If he does, he does."

"He's probably on his way back to New York."

"Nah, he'll stay around here. They might go — the Cades — but he won't. He'll stay."

"All right. Let me think about it."

"Don't take too long."

CHAPTER FIFTY-TWO

It was hard to sleep. Almost as hard as staying awake. But when she closed her eyes, she saw a face: her own face, like looking in a mirror.

And water.

So much rushing water, so cold.

Keith would appear, and Michael, and they would be watching her. Keith would sit on the stool in the cabin, munching on an apple, piercing her with his eyes. Michael was always in the background, stalking over the floorboards, pacing like a lion in a cage. Waiting to see what she would do.

What she would say.

What she would tell the people that were showing up. Like the man who said his name was Louis. He was good-looking, a guy who could be an actor. Maybe not a leading man, but a handsome extra. He'd wanted to know what she could remember.

But her thoughts were so jumbled. Time had lost all meaning. What was today? She had no idea. She only knew she was supposed to do something. To say something. To play her part. To be somebody they wanted her to be.

And who was that?

She didn't know. She was unsure of how she'd gotten here, to this room, hooked up to these machines. Unsure what was coming next. So she'd remained silent.

Would they find her?

* * *

Stamper was in the waiting room when Tom and Jack Spreniker arrived at the hospital. They listened as Stamper explained the situation.

Tom trembled with anger and emotion, glaring at him with red-rimmed eyes. "Is that her in there? You tell me if that's her. If that's Julie. I don't care if we break the door down, you can just arrest us if you have to. You tell me."

"I can't be sure," Stamper said.

Dumain arrived then and led a robust discussion with everybody trying to keep their cool. He sent a trooper to check to see how the woman was doing, if she was awake. The trooper returned with a nurse, who was clearly unhappy with proceedings. But she agreed to let the Spreniker men into the room. Stamper joined them.

"Honey?" Tom Spreniker approached the bed cautiously, like Stamper had done a few hours earlier, as if any sudden movement might do her harm.

She looked over. Stamper saw her eye had cleared some, the white was showing through again. Her dry lips pursed, and she croaked a word. "Daddy?"

He moved more quickly to her, but then embraced her carefully. "Oh, honey. Oh, it's so good to see you . . ."

Jack stood near, stoic and unemotional.

The reunion went on like that for a while, and then Tom Spreniker moved back from the bed a little. He seemed to forget Stamper or his son were in the room. "Honey, what happened?"

Her voice was hoarse, barely audible. Stamper imagined she'd done her fair share of screaming in the last twenty-four hours. More — she'd probably swallowed lungfuls of frigid river water.

"I don't remember everything, but . . . Colton . . ." She turned her head and started to cry. Stamper remembered where the tissues were and handed her one. She looked at him, seemed to recognize his face.

"Hi," he said. "I was here earlier. I'm—"

"Louis."

"That's right."

"You've been looking for me."

"I have."

"Is Colton . . . ? Is he really . . . ?"

Her eye leaked tears. She didn't bother to dab it with the tissue, just stared at him, waiting, and he nodded.

"All right," Tom Spreniker said. "Maybe this isn't the best time, Detective."

"It's okay," Stamper said to him. "You're very lucky," he told Julie. "I'm glad you're here."

He walked out after that, not wanting to cause anymore hurt, not wanting to upset the father.

You're very lucky.

We sometimes say silly things in stressful situations, Stamper reflected as he settled into one of the hard plastic waiting room chairs. Julie Spreniker wasn't lucky. She'd been precisely very unlucky, given all that had happened to her. And she'd probably have survivor's guilt over the loss of her fiancé.

But she was alive.

What he'd meant was, that river, that height, that fall . . .

Her survival was a miracle.

* * *

He'd been sitting in the waiting room a few minutes when Jack Spreniker came out. The beefy young man saw him. "Can you talk?"

271

Stamper, surprised, said yes. "Here? Somewhere else?"

They went to the cafeteria for some burnt coffee and a stale bagel, Stamper sneaking furtive glances at Julie's brother while they sipped and munched. Finally, Jack started with a question.

"You think that's Julie?"

In truth, Stamper had been going over it, asking himself if it could be Katelyn Graham masquerading as her. Out in the world, she'd have to hide, never be seen in public. The woman in that room was going to have scarring, an altered appearance. If Graham was posing as Spreniker, she could live and breathe and move freely. It could be to buy some time, to finish up a few things before she disappeared all over again.

Jack was waiting for an answer.

"If it is your sister, she survived something probably nobody on Earth could survive. It's a high bridge, then class three rapids, pools that suck you down, jagged rocks. That's the part that's a little hard to reconcile right now. Plus, the time. If she went in the river yesterday morning, where's she been?"

"But what's the alternative? It's a woman claiming to be her, okay, this woman who was trying to kill her to fake her own death, then what?"

"I don't know. It wouldn't make any sense, I guess."

For the first time in years, he thought about having a drink. Maybe it was the long days, maybe it was this case. Maybe it was the bad feeling he had, that this thing wasn't going to end happily.

"If anyone could survive it, it would be Julie," Jack Spreniker said.

"What makes you say that?"

"Because I'm her little brother," Jack said. "You ever been to Saranac Lake?"

Stamper shook his head.

"There's a high cliff called Bluff Rock," Jack explained, "a massive glacial erratic. Only the boldest kids ever jumped

272

from the top. Julie did, years ago. A sheer straight drop into the water from seventy feet.

"She was like that back in the day. She was very . . . very much alive, took risks. And, yeah, she was captain of the swim team," Jack reminded Stamper. "The people that knew, they were saying she had more lane than they'd seen in years. That she was going to wind up at the Olympics." His eyes went shiny. But then he snuffed it back, blinked a couple of times to compose himself. "This bridge, it's how high?"

"The bridge is over a hundred feet above the river."

"And those are class three rapids?"

"That's what I've been told."

None of it seemed to douse his confidence. "If anybody could survive that, let me tell you what — it's my sister, Julie."

* * *

All of that water.

She remembered the bridge now. She remembered Keith bringing her up to the edge, how she'd fought against him, how she'd screamed. Her pleas had echoed down through the chasm before being swallowed up by the rushing whitewater.

Nothing in a thousand lifetimes could have prepared her for what came next. All she knew was that she was being lifted up, pushed over the edge, dropped like unwanted cargo to the river below.

She'd been more or less horizontal, her legs bicycling and arms flailing for balance, the rising air tearing away her scream. But at some point, the muscle memory had kicked in. She'd adjusted her body in order to straighten out, held her breath, and prayed wherever she'd landed wasn't on top of a rock. She'd plunged into it like a sword, into the depths of all the frigid, violent water.

Down and down, the momentum carried her until she had finally equalized, and then she kicked for the surface. Before she could break through into the air, the powerful water tried to toss and tumble her. The freezing cold was like a million needles piercing down to the bone. She had to let it take her, while fighting to break free. She managed to snatch one breath, and then another, and open her eyes long enough to see all the white rapids, to see the rocks and avoid them.

But not all of them. She swam hard with the flow, guiding herself through, but she couldn't escape them all. Knees and elbows scraped. The rocks pummeled her ribs, her forearms, her face. Julie swam mostly submerged, snatching breaths to the side, catching glimpses of her course, for half a mile, her limbs increasingly numb. She crashed over one waterfall that tried to drag her under, then another. Each time she had to swim hard for the surface, to escape the powerful suction, a black hole under the surface.

Finally, the river slowed enough that she could keep her head just above water and start to see one of the banks.

Everything hurt, her knee already twisted from jumping through the window, her shoulders shredded, lungs burning, eyes and mouth and ears filled with water, the terrible cold seeping deeper into her muscles, shutting them down, getting into her bones.

She would never make it.

Yes, I will.

All those months in the pool — those *years* — everything she'd given the sport until her mother got sick. She knew how to move through the water.

The trips up through the locks to Lower Saranac, jumping from Bluff, she'd always been able to do it, always been the bravest, the first, and it had never left her. She'd swum these strokes before. She had the endurance.

And a mile or so downriver, the current was slow enough she was able to swim for the shore, to crawl up into the snow there, frozen, bleeding, broken. And from there she ran limping into the forest, her breath coming in ragged bursts, heat rising around her head, her body steaming as she clawed through the branches until she saw the small abandoned camper and climbed inside. Didn't know how long she was there, only knew that she'd been able to crawl under some mice-tattered blankets and shiver herself to sleep.

It was night when she reemerged and stumbled away from the camper. She wouldn't have gone far, would have considered staying right there if it hadn't been for the lights in the distance. She'd hurried toward them and into the parking lot, where the big trucks sat rumbling in the cold. . .

CHAPTER FIFTY-THREE

Stamper was right — Trevor Graham had stayed — but Dumain was also right: it wasn't going to be easy getting in to see him. First, they had to deal with Charlie, who had stayed with Trevor at the house, and not gone with the Cades.

"Do you have a warrant?" Charlie asked. He pulled on his ear lobe, bored. His gun bulged under his suit jacket.

"We just want to speak to Mr. Graham."

"Mr. Graham is not here. Would you like me to leave him a message?"

Stamper looked at Dumain, who shrugged. They didn't have a court order, they couldn't force their way in. Stamper muttered an expletive and walked away. But when Dumain and his deputies got back in their cars, he lingered a minute.

The mansion glowed in the twilight. She was in there, somewhere, he knew it. Hiding in all that 12,000 square feet. In the library, the indoor pool, the circular wine cellar. The cottage out back.

Stamper wandered to the side of the building, scoping it out. There was no way of getting around. A fence stretched from the eastern edge of the main building to the tree line some fifty yards away. But the forest was dense and too far away to see into the smaller building anyway.

Circling the house, he admired the arched carport again as he walked through. The carport wasn't the only place for vehicles. On the far side of the complex was a three-bay garage.

He stretched up to look through the first door's windows, which sat just above eye level.

"Hello there," he said.

The Jeep looked pretty banged up, like it had been in a recent accident. A crumpled front right quarter panel, the bumper crimped there, hanging a bit at the end. The headlight was smashed. Might even have had a crack in the windshield.

Evaluating the damage, he dug out his phone, but the cell coverage was impossible. He hurried down to Dumain, waiting in the turn-around driveway in front of the main entrance.

"I need you to make a call." Dumain dialed the number and handed the phone over.

"Louis, what—" Cuthbert sounded far away.

"I need the file on Keith Rossi. The license plate of the vehicle registered in his name."

Two minutes later, she rattled off the numbers and letters and promised to text them across. He thanked her and handed the phone back to Dumain, who punched in the number for the local judge. It was enough for a court order.

Stamper ran to the front door, he waved at the cameras covering the entryway and then made a gesture of signing a piece of paper. *Search warrant, baby.*

This time when the big assistant answered, Stamper had a message. "Yeah, I know they're not here — like you said. Which is fine. We've got a warrant on the way. We're going to search the entire place, soon as the paperwork gets here. Shouldn't be long." He looked back at Dumain, who gave him a thumbs up.

Stamper smiled up at Charlie.

Somewhere in the house, a door slammed. Then a whirring sound broke the still night air — a garage door going up — and a black SUV crunched over the gravel into view.

"You gotta be kidding me."

He ran to his own vehicle and jumped behind the wheel.

Through the dark and snowy roads, he chased the SUV. Dumain and the others were behind him, lights flaring. The roads were still bad, slick as shit, and the SUV lost control, clipped a tree and flipped.

Stamper pumped the brakes and managed to stop without colliding. He came up on the other vehicle with his gun drawn. Trevor Graham was trying to open the door with everything upside-down. But a passenger had already escaped and was running. Stamper chased after her. He ran until his chest was on fire, yelling for her to stop. He thought of Julie Spreniker, abducted from her home, beaten, thrown off a bridge. When he was close enough, he threw himself at the passenger, tackling her to the ground.

She fought against him, wriggling beneath him in the snowy road, but he got the cuffs on her.

Panting hard, he flipped her over.

They did look alike. Of that, there was no question.

* * *

Each in their own interview rooms, neither of the Grahams was talking. Like Dumain had predicted, they wanted their lawyer. The thing was, the lawyer had to drive up from New York City — the snowy roads would keep him busy for a while — so Stamper had time.

He went into the room with Katelyn first. Despite the accident, she was unharmed, medically cleared.

"I told you," she said, "I have nothing to say."

"Why was your car at the Black River Chasm bridge?"

She didn't answer.

He stayed just inside the door, leaning against the wall, arms folded. "Your husband was worried about you. When I spoke to him yesterday, he told me you'd needed to get away. You left, came up here, but he hadn't heard from you. Was that because something happened?"

Stamper sat down across from her, scraping the chair legs. "Talk to me, help yourself out here. Did someone take your car? Did you leave it at the bridge and forget? I mean, what happened?"

She just stared, defiant.

"Okay, fine." Stamper shifted gears. "I know about Keith Rossi."

Her expression twitched with recognition. But a second later, she was stone-faced again.

"I know his family. I actually was involved in a case against his father. Years ago, that was. So we knew about the cabin in the woods. He probably didn't tell you that part, though, did he? That his father was once wanted by the FBI, as part of a RICO case?"

Waiting, he took a deep breath, let it out slowly. The small interview room at Dumain's headquarters smelled like sweat and mildew.

"You know how I know about Keith, though? We have him on video. Leaving Julie Spreniker and Colton Rossi's home. Chasing them. With a gun."

He let that sink in, before adding, "And we have you on video, too, coming out of the same home, not three minutes later."

She finally broke. "If you had something like that, you'd be charging me."

He found the video on his phone from Shane Robbie's ring cam, played it for her. He watched her expression as she viewed it. She was good, he thought. She stayed perfectly neutral, not giving anything away, but at the same time was rapt with attention. When it was over, she leaned back. "I'm not sure I understand why you're showing me some woman, hours from here in a situation that has nothing to do with me."

"You don't think that's uncanny? How alike you look? I mean, you could be twins."

Katelyn only stared a moment, then the corner of her mouth twitched in a grin. "I see. You want me to admit that's me. All of this shit you're talking — no evidence, just coincidence — you want me to confess to some crime, just because I look like this person. You're not very good at your job, are you?"

He tapped the phone screen. "There's no way this is Julie Spreniker. My partner and I timed it out. She couldn't have run back around the house and changed her clothes, come back out in three minutes. It's impossible."

"If you say so. Still doesn't mean it's me."

"Fair enough." He scrolled through the video until he had what he wanted. "Keith, though — Keith just looks like Keith. No mystery there who he is. What I'm wondering is how long do you think it'll take until he cuts a deal with us? Because there he is, on camera, with the gun that killed Colton Rossi, his own brother. He's your trigger man, isn't he? And he's the guy that drove up here in your car. Unsurprisingly, your prints are all over it. But there are none from Julie Spreniker."

She stayed quiet for a while, but he could see her thinking. Something had shifted. "Someone took my car, yeah."

"Is that right?" Setting aside the phone, he took his notebook out and clicked a pen. "Did you see what they looked like? When was this? Where were you when it happened?"

"I didn't see them."

"But where were you?"

"I got out of the car. I had to . . . I had to go to the bathroom. And then someone jacked it. That's it. That's all I know."

"How did you get home?"

"I hitchhiked."

He watched her a moment, unspeaking, just letting the moment breathe. She was definitely tough.

"Ms. Graham, listen — it's just a matter of time. Either Keith dimes you out or you tell me, right now, what your deal was with him. Because otherwise, you're getting charged with murder. This whole scheme to avoid an embezzlement conviction and some couple of years spent in white collar prison where you play tennis and talk about your feelings, that's all gone. Murder is state prison, decades of your life. Out of the frying pan, into the fire."

"I'm sorry, I told you — I don't know anything about it."

He clicked the pen a few times. "How did you do it, anyway?"

"I didn't do anything. Someone stole my car. That's all I know."

"You gained his trust somehow. Colton's. You had to get him on board. Did you sleep with him? I know he got around a little bit . . . I met someone who told me she slept with him, too."

Katelyn didn't respond.

"I bet that was your way in. But then you had to promise him something. More than money. Excitement. Danger. Maybe yourself. That he'd get you in the end."

"I don't know anything about Colton fucking Rossi, okay? The only reason I'm not going to say anything else until my lawyer gets here? I was in a car accident. My husband and I were going into town and all of a sudden we were being chased. He lost control of the vehicle, and we had an accident. Honestly, when my lawyer arrives, I'm going to ask him to file a lawsuit against the County Sheriff, and against you personally."

Stamper let that settle for a moment. Her threat meant he was getting somewhere.

"You spent a lot of time working on this, huh?"

She looked away from him into a corner.

"You probably think you're smarter than you are, though. Being born rich can have that effect, I reckon. But here's the thing." He leaned forward, blinking at her with his best Paul Newman eyes. "I don't think disappearing, avoiding trial, avoiding a conviction, was really your goal. I mean, maybe. If it worked, great. But in your heart, it was the attention. You and Colton Rossi. A match made in narcissist heaven."

She had met his gaze again around 'born rich' and stayed eye-locked with him.

"I want a fucking lawyer, like I said ten times already," she said. "And you know what I think of you and your

281

pretty-boy antics? You're just some guy who couldn't pull off whatever he really wanted in life and became a shit cop instead."

* * *

Stamper took a drink of water from the fountain in the hallway, trying to wash away the bile from interviewing Katelyn Graham. Then he entered the second interview room and sat down across from Trevor Graham.

"I told you we'd talk today."

"You're wasting your time."

He was a little more banged up than she was, but not too bad. Just a white bandage over his eye, where it had split. A scrape on his jaw. Lucky, the both of them.

"I think I understand something now," Stamper said. "I'm pretty sure Kate seduced Colton Rossi — gave him a fake name. Fed him some bullshit story. Slept with him. That helped sustain this whole thing." He waited a second before saying, "But was that her idea? Did it just happen? Or was it your idea? Because I know some guys like that sort of thing . . ."

"Fuck off."

"I'm sure there was money involved. But the guy wasn't the murdering kind, I don't think. No, she seduced him. And she lied to him about how it would all wind up. She promised him money, maybe she promised she'd leave you, be with him down the line."

Trevor's face was darkening. A dangerous flush was creeping up his neck.

"But let's go back a bit. She had to get to him in the first place, somehow. Had to approach him."

Trevor's jaw twitched. He was avoiding Stamper's gaze.

"And you needed a place to go out in the sticks. You needed to plant fake messages to support the domestic-trouble narrative. You needed help, basically. Is that when you reached out to Keith?"

Trevor's eyes came back. "This has nothing to do with me, or my wife. You're targeting us. And we're gonna sue your fucking ass."

"She said that, too. And I bet it's partly true. You set all of this up, but you didn't do the actual killing. You or Katie. I'm betting that was Keith Rossi. Both Colton, and the attempt on Julie." Stamper leaned in. "Maybe you're tough, but how do you think you're going to do in prison? There won't be any Charlie to solve your problems for you up at Dannemora. So you should start thinking it through."

Trevor looked at him fully now, eyes blazing. "Don't threaten me. You don't know anything about me."

"The kidnapping of Julie and Colton, crossing state lines — that's federal. You're going to have to face that. But right here, right now, you and me, we make a deal. Tell me how much you paid Keith Rossi. Or rather, how much Katie did. Because it's her money, right? Whatever she siphoned off from her family's business she hid away before any assets were frozen. She's got enough to make investments, to start over, to keep living the life you're accustomed to. Fifty million? More? You've got nothing without her. But that's good for you — it all falls on her. It's all her dime. Right, Trevor? Talk to me . . ."

* * *

When Cuthbert finally got there, Stamper was running on fumes. Despite all his threats, neither of the Grahams was talking.

"They're just not going to say anything," he complained to Cuthbert. "They're going to take their chances."

She stood leaning against the countertop in the little kitchen at Dumain's HQ. After thinking a moment, she said, "Let me try."

When she told him, he said, "Aim for the father. He's got the soft spot for Katie."

* * *

"Listen to me," Cuthbert said when Evelyn and Phillip Cade arrived. Notified by Charlie, they'd turned around on their way back to New York, and now the two of them crowded in facing Cuthbert, with Dumain and Stamper hovering at the edges. "Drop the lawsuit."

Evelyn started out of the room, Phillip right behind her.

Cuthbert cut them off, blocking the doorway. "Tell Katie you'll take care of her here. Legal defense, everything. And that she'll get a clean slate with you and the family, the business."

Evelyn studied her. "Why?"

"What we want is the murder of Colton Rossi. We'll make sure they get charged with it, in the first degree — your daughter and your son-in-law."

Evelyn held her gaze, searching for the bluff.

"Or," Cuthbert continued, "right now, she tells us the truth."

No one spoke for half a minute.

"What if she paid him?" Phillip Cade asked from beside his wife. The Cades stood in that peculiar way of theirs, close but never touching.

"That's solicitation of murder," Cuthbert answered. "She'd get twenty years mandatory. But if she pulled the trigger, she could get life. It's your choice."

* * *

When the lawyer finally arrived, the Caledonia County Sheriff's Office had already charged and booked the Grahams. In her mugshot, Katelyn Graham at last had tears in her eyes.

After talking with her father, she'd confessed to hiring Keith Rossi for a million dollars. Half up front, half still due. What was more, she'd admitted that Keith Rossi and Trevor Graham had known each other in seminary school. For two years, junior high, they'd had the same nun for a homeroom teacher.

"It was all Keith's idea." Katelyn had sobbed convincingly throughout her statement. "He wanted money. He said

284

he would take care of the whole thing. We went along at first, but he was crazy . . . I didn't think he would actually go through with it . . ."

Yeah, yeah, Stamper thought.

There was no chance Rossi would try to approach them for the rest of the money — Julie Spreniker's survival was national news. And Rossi's number was disconnected, his apartment in Rochester cleaned out. The FBI were looking for him, but Stamper didn't hold out hope.

The guy was ex-military, highly motivated to stay hidden.

CHAPTER FIFTY-FOUR

The day after she returned home, Stamper visited Julie Spreniker to ask her some questions. He fought through the reporters to get inside and signed in with the officer at her door.

Her memory was still coming back, she said, a little at a time. They had cut her, she remembered now. Sliced the back of her scalp to get her blood all over the shed. He was still trying to get a look at her medical records, so he didn't know for sure. But she offered to show him.

"Here," she said, lifting her hair.

He peered through the follicles and thought maybe he saw a small cut, mostly healed. The kind of cut you might make with a jack knife. Or a fruit knife. With so many other lacerations from her time in the river, it was hard to tell.

She took him through the house, showed him where things had happened, explained how the woman — she called her "Monique" — went downstairs, as if to leave, and then the men came in. When she talked about Colton, she welled up. Her face was still covered in more of the cuts and bruises. Hard to even tell what she'd looked like before.

"How's everything with your dad?" he asked.

"Good. We've been talking some."

"Good."

There was more, maybe. There would always be more, but he could see she was tired, and her father and brother soon shooed him off.

The door closed, leaving her battered face lingering in his mind.

He hurried past the shouting reporters down the street to his car. Maybe some things just worked out. Like Cuthbert said. Some things in this crazy, fucked up world actually turned out okay.

Maybe.

Maybe he could believe that.

Of course, life, as Julie Spreniker knew it, was completely over. For a few more weeks, anyway, the media would hound her. She needed to grieve, yet she'd become a celebrity.

And her fiancé was dead.

He just couldn't imagine.

"I mean, who comes back from that?" he said, starting up the engine. Hardly anyone. Maybe because she was a therapist, she stood a fighting chance. He supposed she had a good support group. She had people like Annette Peters, at least.

He checked the side mirror and, seeing only hungry reporters, pulled out into the street. He noticed another car also pull out into the road, but then he was taking the bend, driving the same route the van had driven that fateful morning one week ago.

Not home invaders, now that Julie's memory was returning. Not robbers, nor people to whom Colton owed money. Not people who worked for his father, either — but an heiress to a pharmaceutical fortune and her husband, both of them headed to trial for embezzling millions from their rich family and looking for a way out.

But Julie had survived.

Her years of swimming had saved her. After careening nearly a mile down river, knocked about by icy rapids and jagged rocks, she'd managed to crawl ashore, find her way to a camper and then to a truck stop where she flagged down a ride.

A story of pure grit and determination, the media were calling it. An absolute miracle. Woman, hero.

Maybe that was the look in her eye. Maybe, at the end of the day, she was only human, and knowing that she was now the darling of the moment thrilled her a little. He could hardly blame her. Perhaps she deserved it, too. After all she'd been through, shit, give her an appearance on *Oprah*, for God's sake. Why not? Get her a book deal. Let her tell her story.

In the meantime, Katelyn Graham had all but disappeared. She wasn't even glimpsed entering or leaving a courthouse. Her family was doing a good job of shielding her. It was Trevor who was vocal, acting indignant, claiming police harassment, thumbing his nose at the deal Stamper and Cuthbert had made. The whole thing was ludicrous, Trevor said. He didn't know Julie, had never met her — and of course there was no such scheme to body-swap her for Katelyn. This Spreniker woman was obviously off her meds, attention-seeking, prone to wild confabulation.

She'd taken a drive to a bridge, Trevor said, and tried to kill herself. When it didn't work, she made up a wild story.

"There is no evidence whatsoever that I was ever at some cabin in the Southern Adirondacks," he told the TV cameras, "or that Katie was."

And he was right — there wasn't. It had been a tough scene to process, but so far there was nothing in the van or at the cabin to link them to the scene.

Bullshit rich people. Stamper would get to the bottom of it. He'd show up in court for as long as it took, keep cooperating with the prosecutorial team. He'd make sure those two got what was coming to them, even if it wasn't capital murder. The world needed to know they were guilty of some of the most twisted and sadistic shit he'd ever encountered in his career.

And maybe he'd make a name for himself, too, enough that he could stop chasing this vainglorious goal in life, to be seen and noticed. *Just give me one.* That was all he needed.

One big win and he would rush right home and make a baby with his beautiful wife. Because it was time to grow up. It was come to commit to—

The car behind him was coming up fast, flashing its lights.

He had left Herkimer behind — two turns and a single traffic light — and was now on the stretch between it and the next town, not much around but forest. What the hell did this guy want?

Ah, whatever.

He slowed and pulled over to the shoulder a bit, mindful there could be a ditch under all that snow.

Instead of going around him, though, the vehicle behind also slowed. Stamper rolled the window down and made a waving gesture. "Come on, just go, man. The heck is wrong with this guy?"

Agitated, he considered getting back up to speed, but it seemed like the wrong choice. The motorist didn't want to go around. He wanted Stamper to pull over. Fine.

He brought the vehicle to a stop. Keeping his eyes on the side mirror, he checked his weapon. The driver had his blinker on, left the car running. Stamper wasn't just going to sit here and let the guy come on him.

He opened the door and the driver opened his door, too.

Stamper then stood and the driver stood.

It was dark. The headlights made it a little hard to see, but there was enough light to get a look at his face.

Keith Rossi.

Stupid, Stamper thought. *Shit, shit — stupid.* He pulled his piece, but it was too late.

He felt the impact of the round in his chest before hearing the sound, before even seeing the gun.

The next thing he knew, he was on the ground, trying to get up. His one hand felt around where he thought he'd been shot and came away with blood on his fingertips.

Keith Rossi loomed over him and bent to pick up Stamper's firearm. He handed it to the guy who appeared next to him. Stamper recognized him. It had been years, but Dale Rossi looked about the same.

The two men stared down at him.

"I thought he'd be bigger," Keith said. "He doesn't even look like a cop."

Dale Rossi nodded.

Stamper tried to speak, but the bullet had pierced a lung, and all that came out was a dry wheeze.

Keith raised the gun, pointed it at Stamper's face, and fired.

CHAPTER FIFTY-FIVE

One year later

He woke up feeling like his breath was caught, then inhaled deeply, breaking the spell. He was alive. He'd left Julie Spreniker's house that day and driven back to the barracks without incident. It was just a recurring dream.

Cara stood beside the bed with a mug of coffee and his phone. She set the coffee down and held the phone out. "It's your partner."

Stamper sat up and took the phone, thanking Cara. She gave him a concerned look as she walked out of the bedroom.

"Hello?"

"Hey," Cuthbert said. "You sleeping?"

"I'm up." He half-consciously touched his chest, his arm, just to assure himself he was real. Not shot.

"They got him."

The words brought him fully back. He didn't need to ask who Cuthbert meant.

"Dead for six months," she said. "Found in Nevada, outside of Las Vegas. Him and his father. And get this — gunshot wounds to the head, execution-style."

Neither of them had to say it, but both were thinking it: Falzone. Or, if not the crime family from Utica, then some other criminal organization the Rossis had gotten mixed up in. Guys like them seemed to always wind up dead, having outlived their usefulness or gotten greedy. But in this case, it was probably the unwanted attention of the FBI. Whoever Keith and his father were using for protection had tired of the game.

"Thanks, Lindsay," he said.

She sighed. "Yeah." Then, "Enjoying your day off?"

"I am," he lied.

They chatted another minute, then he hung up, showered, worked out, and he and Cara went for a walk. She asked him about it, but he was more interested in hearing about her, what she had going on.

"Like you don't know," she said, gripping the baby stroller. "Same as any other day: take care of *mi pollo*. Maybe I'll do some shopping this afternoon."

Mi pollo, named Eloise, after Stamper's mother, looked up from her swaddling blankets, and started to cry.

Stamper turned to Cara, her nose tipped red in the cold, a fur-lined hood framing her pretty face, and he laughed, and she laughed, their breath rising together in the air.

CHAPTER FIFTY-SIX

One of the best things about PT was the swimming. It had been so long, she'd forgotten the sense of freedom, almost like flying, of being in the water.

She had scars. Nightmares that came and went. Keith Rossi, Colton, trading faces. Always in the cabin — a place she had never gone back to since.

And, of course, "Monique."

Julie pushed off the wall of the pool, knifing through the water, breaking the surface, and thought.

Katelyn Graham. Her doppelganger. The woman who'd tried to use her as a body double to escape her own life. She was infamous now. Famous, too — she had a fan club. The usual whackos who liked killers and wanted to get to know them. Sentenced to thirty-three years in prison, just two weeks earlier. Trevor Graham got twenty-five years.

A movie about it all was coming out in just a couple more months on a streaming service — crazy how fast these things happened.

Julie worked her overhand strokes until she reached the far end of the pool and then flipped under the water and started back the other direction. It was amazing how it all came back. She'd do a few more laps and then call it a day. It wasn't even really physical therapy anymore. It was the old competitive muscles.

But gone was the performance anxiety she'd once had about swimming. Her father wasn't wrong. When her mother first got sick, it had provided an excuse to release the pressure. It wasn't the hard work, it wasn't even a fear of failure. It was this sense that her life was no longer her own.

And maybe it hadn't been. Maybe it never would be. Maybe none of our lives were our own. Maybe we belonged to something bigger. To everyone else we ever made a connection with. She didn't know. But she had plenty of time to find out; she didn't plan on going anywhere anytime soon.

She was Miracle Julie. She was the woman who survived the impossible. In the weeks and months of recovery that followed, Julie had allowed people in: reporters and authors and movie producers. She would tell them the story, over and over again, about what happened that morning on the bridge. They would ask how far a drop it was to the river below — far. A hundred and twenty feet. They would ask how cold was the water — cold. Forty degrees Fahrenheit. They would ask what she did, how she'd survived. They wanted to understand how it was possible so they could get the story right.

She didn't know, really, so they drew their own conclusions. She'd been a champion swimmer in high school. She'd been a fearless teenaged cliff jumper in the rugged Adirondacks where she'd grown up.

It could have been down to these things; who knew.

Finishing her last lap, Julie hauled herself out of the pool. Voices echoed — children, other adults, splashing water. She liked coming to the Y. She liked seeing kids get exercise in the pool, older people keeping limber, working out the kinks.

In the locker room, she showered and changed. She'd come here straight from work at the clinic but brought clothes with her for the evening. She was going to go out with Annette, get a bite to eat.

After she dressed, she fixed her hair. Eyes on the mirror, she still wasn't used to the scars on her face, the worst of the tears from the river rocks. Her nose had been broken, too; now it turned slightly to the side. Still had that bifid tip.

Someone else was in the locker room, some squeal of a child's laughter, a slam of a metal locker, the patter of feet, and then they were gone.

Julie put her hands on the sink and leaned towards the mirror, staring into her eyes.

"You're Julie Spreniker," she whispered. "That's who you are."

She blinked, and the feeling came, the sense of inhabiting someone else's body. Which one was she? The twin who'd survived, or the one who'd been absorbed, somehow back, reincarnated and taking over?

Julie Spreniker, she thought again. *Julie. Fucking. Spreniker.* Only daughter of Arlene and Tom. Sister to Jack.

She picked up her things, packed her bag, threw it over her shoulder and headed out of the locker room, feeling, maybe for the first time in twenty years, that she was capable of anything.

That she wasn't scared.

She was ready.

THE END

ACKNOWLEDGMENTS

Book ideas can come from strange places. I read about a woman who allegedly murdered her lookalike to fake her own death and didn't think about it again until I had another idea for a couple abducted in the middle of a break-up. The two ideas became one story.

Thanks to my long-time collaborator on all things police procedural, Trooper Kristy Wilson, who also happens to be my cousin, and one of the Buzzells to whom this book is dedicated.

Thank you to my early readers (we say "beta" in the biz), Michelle Green, Veronika Jordan, Steve Hardy, John Ramirez, and the indomitable Bob Sirrine. I give the book to you at a crucial stage when it's barely able to stand on its legs, and it's only with the benefit of your insights, critical thinking, and keen eye for typos that I dare submit it for publication. This book is your book.

Thanks as ever to everyone at Joffe Books, to my agent, Tom Cull, and to my family — even the dog, our ten-pound Cavapoo who is, at this moment, upstairs barking at some passerby on the street, keeping us all safe so that I can work.

THE JOFFE BOOKS STORY

We began in 2014 when Jasper agreed to publish his mum's much-rejected romance novel and it became a bestseller.

Since then we've grown into the largest independent publisher in the UK. We're extremely proud to publish some of the very best writers in the world, including Joy Ellis, Faith Martin, Caro Ramsay, Helen Forrester, Simon Brett and Robert Goddard. Everyone at Joffe Books loves reading and we never forget that it all begins with the magic of an author telling a story.

We are proud to publish talented first-time authors, as well as established writers whose books we love introducing to a new generation of readers.

We won Trade Publisher of the Year at the Independent Publishing Awards in 2023. We have been shortlisted for Independent Publisher of the Year at the British Book Awards for the last four years, and were shortlisted for the Diversity and Inclusivity Award at the 2022 Independent Publishing Awards. In 2023 we were shortlisted for Publisher of the Year at the RNA Industry Awards.

We built this company with your help, and we love to hear from you, so please email us about absolutely anything bookish at feedback@joffebooks.com

If you want to receive free books every Friday and hear about all our new releases, join our mailing list: www.joffebooks.com/contact

And when you tell your friends about us, just remember: it's pronounced Joffe as in coffee or toffee!